2   15⁰⁰

D0615610

JOIE D'AMOUR

Also available

PLAISIR D'AMOUR

JOIE D'AMOUR

AN EROTIC MEMOIR
——— OF PARIS IN THE 1920s ———

ANNE-MARIE VILLEFRANCHE

Carroll & Graf Publishers, inc.
New York

Copyright © 1983 by Jane Purcell

All rights reserved including the right of reproduction in any
form or by any means.

First Carroll & Graf edition 1984.

Carroll & Graf Publishers, Inc.
260 Fifth Avenue
New York, N.Y. 10001

Library of Congress Cataloging in Publication Data

Villefranche, Anne-Marie, 1899–1980.
  Joie d'amour.

  Text in English.
  1. Erotic stories, French—Translations into English. 2. Erotic stories,
English—Translations from French. I. Title.
PQ2643.I4494J6 1984   843′.912   84-12179
ISBN: 0-88184-098-X

Manufactured in the United States of America

PARIS IN THE 1920s

The interest which greeted publication of a small selection of Anne-Marie Villefranche's stories under the title of Plaisir D'Amour has encouraged me to persevere with the translation of another selection. As before, these candid tales of her friends are by turns tender, comical and outrageous, depending on the reader's own attitudes towards sexual encounters between men and women.

There is no need to repeat here how these stories were written or how they became my property after the author's death, since that was set out in the preface to Plaisir D'Amour. What may be of interest to those few who read prefaces is to learn of the large number of letters I received after the publication of that little volume, from people who still remember Paris as it was between the two Wars. The majority of my correspondents were amused by Anne-Marie's stories, but a few professed to be offended by such intimate revelations. Plus ça change, plus c'est la même chose, as the French say: the more things change, the more they stay the same.

For any clumsiness of translation in the present volume I can do no more than offer my apologies. The spirit of the French language is unlike that of English and the author's style is all her own, sometimes breathless, sometimes reflective, sometimes humorous. I hope that I have done it some measure of justice.

Anne-Marie's stories were written to amuse herself. If this new selection gives as much pleasure to readers as the first, it may be that eventually she will be accorded the esteem she merits as an observer of the follies and caprices of her friends.

Jane Purcell
London 1983

GINETTE ON THE METRO

For Michel Brissard to travel on the Metro was an unusual occurrence. Not that he had any strong antagonism towards it – indeed, he supposed it to be a most useful means of conveyance for the many who needed to travel about Paris quickly and cheaply to reach their place of work or to return to their homes in the evening. For himself he prefered something more suitable, more convenient, more comfortable and more exclusive.

Yet one spring day he found himself, for reasons which are of no consequence to what took place, standing in a crowded carriage of a Metro train down below street level. He was thankful that his station was the one after the next. Little did he imagine that he was about to embark upon a curious adventure – an adventure which would involve two things of great importance to him – a pretty girl and money.

The train rattled to a halt on the track between two stations, evoking a chorus of dismayed groans from the passengers. After it had been at a standstill for a minute or two Michel addressed himself to a young woman standing next to him – one might almost say pressed against him by the crush of home-going passengers.

'Excuse me, Mademoiselle – do you think that we shall be here for long?'

She looked over her shoulder at him and smiled.

'A few minutes, perhaps, who knows? It is not unusual, Monsieur.'

Until that moment Michel had paid no great attention to her since her back had been presented to him, so that his view of her had been only of her hat and coat. She wriggled herself round to face him and he saw a pretty face with high-arching eyebrows and a little pointed chin. Her eyes were large and lustrous, their colour a dark velvety brown. In short, she made a deep impression on

1

him with no more than a glance. He put her age at about twenty-five or six – ten years younger than himself.

'Are you in a hurry, Monsieur?' she asked, 'an urgent appointment, perhaps?'

Her smile of amusement indicated what sort of appointment he might be hurrying to – an hour or so with a charming woman friend to enjoy the pleasures of love before going home to dinner with his wife and family. Michel smiled back and removed his hat as he answered her.

'No, it's not that – just the inconvenience of being stranded here.'

'Obviously you are not very familiar with the ways of the Metro,' she said. 'How far are you going?'

'The stop after the next, if we ever get there. And you, Mademoiselle?'

'Alexandre Dumas,' she informed him.

To Michel that seemed almost as remote as Indochina. It was somewhere out in the east of Paris, out beyond the Place de la Bastille. Yet the young woman on her way to so outlandish a place was dressed pleasantly enough in a green woollen frock and a three-quarter length jacket. Department stores clothes, he noted, but chosen with an eye to style. Her shoes were good of their kind, so far as he could make out in the crowd.

'A long way,' he said sympathetically, 'at this rate it will take hours.'

She shrugged.

'No one is waiting for me,' she said.

To a man of Michel's temperament the words were virtually an invitation.

'If I may make a suggestion,' he said 'let us get off this miserable train at the next stop and have a drink together. You are in need of some refreshment to fortify you for your long journey.'

She studied him carefully – his face, his expression, his dark and waved hair, his expensive suit and silk shirt, his tasteful neck-tie, the gold wedding ring on the hand with which he was holding on to the overhead strap. All this

2

took no more than three seconds and Michel was aware that she was making an assessment of his standing in life.

'Thank you, Monsieur,' she said, smiling at him in the most charming way, 'I would like that.'

Eventually the train clattered into the next station, they got off together and walked side by side up the steps to the street, Michel's hand placed courteously under her elbow to assist her. He took her into a cafe nearby, ignoring the pavement terrace and leading her inside in case anyone he knew might pass by and see him with her.

Her name, he learned, was Ginette Royer and she worked as a sales assistant in a big store in central Paris. She was unmarried and lived alone. Her father had been killed in the War and her mother lived with a sister near Orleans. By then she and Michel were on first-name terms, naturally, and both understood what was going to take place after they left the cafe. After all, this was the most natural thing in the world and far from the first time for either of them.

'If you will excuse me for a moment,' said Michel, glancing at his watch, 'I must make a telephone call. After that I shall escort you home, if you will permit me.'

He made his call and his arrangements, explaining most convincingly that urgent business would prevent him from being home for dinner that evening – the usual convenient little lies which husbands make use of on these occasions. That done, and with a clear conscience, he paid the bill and found a taxi. No more standing on the Metro for Michel that night!

During the time the taxi was travelling through the evening traffic along the rue de Saint Antoine he put an arm about Ginette's waist and kissed her. She responded warmly to his advances and after another lengthy kiss he went so far as to stroke her breasts lightly through her woollen frock.

'Michel,' she murmured, 'you are an impatient man.'

'And you, chérie?'

'You have guessed it – I am an impatient woman.'

'Then we shall get on well together.'

3

By the time the taxi reached the Avenue Alexandre Dumas Michel's hand was up her skirt, stroking her bare thigh above her stocking-top. The touch of her skin aroused him enormously, it was so smooth and soft. He slid his hand higher up her thigh towards her warm sanctuary.

'That's what I want,' he said, kissing her neck.

'You shall have it,' she answered, turning her head so that her mouth could find his and cling in another long kiss.

Once off the Avenue, the taxi threaded its way through narrow streets and stopped at the address Ginette had given the driver. In his mood of exhilaration Michel added a more than generous tip to the fare and was rewarded by an insolent wink from the driver. In this high state of arousal the stairs up to Ginette's apartment seemed endless – flight after flight – yet with a pause on each landing for him to hug Ginette to him and kiss her, his hands on her bottom to press her close to him.

But at last they were there. She opened the door and led him into a sparsely furnished yet very clean and neat room – her sitting-room, dining-room, bed-room and kitchen all in one. Michel would have pulled her to him again to resume his kissing but she slipped from his grasp to pull off her hat and coat and drop them on a chair as she went across to the divan bed. She had her dress off in a moment, then her knickers, and sat on the side of the bed wearing only shoes, stockings, and a pale green chemise, her arms stretched out towards Michel. He moved towards her, his breath rasping in his throat. As he reached the bed she let herself fall backwards, so that she was half-lying on it, her feet still on the floor. She pulled her chemise up round her waist and spread her knees to expose herself.

'That's what you said you wanted,' she gasped, 'it is yours to take.'

Michel stared round-eyed at her parted thighs and the brown-haired nest between them, enraptured by the pouting lips at the entrance to her shrine, yet amazed at the eagerness with which she had made herself available. For

4

a moment he wondered whether he had been picked up by a professional, but commonsense told him that, if she were that, she would have asked for money first. And confronted by an offer so tempting as that spread before him – a warm and fleshy place in which to satisfy his desire – what man could turn away? Certainly not Michel. He shed his jacket and tie and was fumbling at his trousers as he fell to his knees on the thin carpet beside the bed. His fixture was hard and strong and sank into her easily. At that moment he expected no more surprises from Ginette, only the vigorous climb together to an apex of delight. Yet once again she amazed him. Before he had attained the full length of his forward thrust she gasped and shook in a manner that warned him that she was about to reach the culmination of her pleasure! He pressed on, her reaction grew stronger until, at the moment his hardness was fully inserted, she reached an abrupt climax of passion. Her clenched fists beat against his back and her loins jerked furiously upwards against him – so furiously that he was compelled to seize her by the shoulders and hold on tightly until her violent shuddering ran its course and ceased.

'Oh, that was good,' she exclaimed, 'thank you, Michel.'

'You have been without a man for a long time,' Michel observed, smiling at her pink-flushed face.

'Far too long. I am so glad that I met you this evening.'

'And so am I. Do you want to rest a little?'

'No, no – I am ready for you. Do it to me, please.'

No further encouragement was necessary. In truth, it was remarkable that he had been able to contain himself for so long after entering her, but his astonishment at her instant response had temporarily suspended his actions. But now, her hot body under him and her moist flesh clasping his male part like a soft glove, he gave full rein to his natural ardour.

It must have been that Ginette's unexpectedly fast response had aroused him more than he realised. Or perhaps it was her little cries of pleasure as he burrowed

5

between her legs. Whatever the cause – or combination of causes – the act of love was briefer than usual for him. Though not the outcome – his vital essence rushed from him a flood of voluptuous sensation.

'There,' said Ginette, stroking his face, 'now you have caught up with me.'

'But this is terrible,' said Michel, 'you did not share the pleasure with me.'

'It was too soon after the first time. But it doesn't matter – I am content.'

'But of course it matters. I am mortified!'

'We were not synchronised either the first time or the second time, that's all,' she said with a smile.

'Synchronised – what a strange word to use,' said Michel, 'yet it is apt.'

He eased himself away from her and planted a light kiss on her little patch of brown fur before attending to his underwear and trousers. Ginette closed her legs and sat up on the bed so that the pale green chemise slid down her body to cover her belly.

'I hope that you will dine with me,' said Michel. 'Is there a good restaurant anywhere near here?'

'There's a place within walking distance which serves good food. At least, I think it's good, but to you it may not seem so.'

The restaurant was a quarter of an hour's walk away on the Avenue Alexandre Dumas. It proved to be small, but the food was acceptable, though simple. The wine was drinkable. Michel enjoyed his dinner less for the fare than for the company of Ginette. For the outing she put on her new frock, tidied her hair and face to make herself as pretty as possible, and kept him amused by stories of the peculiar ways of customers in the store where she worked. He wondered whether, just possibly, one of the customers at whose mannerisms he was laughing might be his own wife, her demanding manner in shops being a longstanding cause for irritation with him.

After the meal they strolled back under the street-lamps to her apartment. They sat together on the bed and kissed

6

and Michel began to undress her. The entire scene had been played so swiftly before that there had been little opportunity to admire her body – or even to see it properly – apart from the exciting little entrance between her thighs. Matters were less urgent now. Michel stripped her completely naked and touched her all over – her small round breasts, flat belly, the soft cheeks of her bottom – he enjoyed every morsel of her to the utmost.

'Off with your clothes too,' she said as he nuzzled her breasts for the hundredth time, 'let me see you.'

Then it was her turn to get to know his body. She ran her finger-tips over his broad and hairy chest and found words of admiration for all of him, above all for his upstanding part, though with as much modesty as becomes a woman naked with her lover. In this respect, of course, women are at a certain disadvantage, for while it is accepted that a man will praise the entire delicious body of his mistress, for a woman to appear too enthusiastic about the fifteen centimetres of a man's body which bring her the greatest pleasure may awake in his mind a suspicion that she has been familiar with more of those invaluable parts than he considers fitting in one on whom he is bestowing his intimate affections. For as all the world knows, the standards set by society for men are not those set for women.

Such considerations apart, Ginette's careful approval of the strength and appearance of his cherished organ won Michel's heart. Matters proceeded between them in the most natural and pleasurable way, to the moment when he rolled her onto her back and was poised to make his grand entrance.

'This time we shall be *synchronised*, I hope,' he said, smiling.

'This time, yes,' she answered, spreading her legs for him.

So it proved. There was no premature crisis on her part as he slid into place. What occurred was well-managed and afforded them both equal delight, if intensity of delight can be compared. The climax of passion was

7

perfectly timed – Ginette shuddered in ecstasy and drummed her heels against his bottom at the instant he discharged his spasms of gratification into her.

In the weeks that followed, Michel regarded his chance meeting with Ginette on the Metro as a most fortunate event. Unlike the other woman who had played an important role in his adventures away from his wife, Ginette had no extensive social life and was always available when the mood took him. She did not ask, much less insist, on being taken to chic restaurants where he might be recognised – she was content with the small and unknown establishments he took her to. She did not expect expensive presents from him – on the contrary, she expressed touching gratitude for whatever small gift he brought. From his point of view it was an ideal liaison and Ginette was a perfect mistress, always pleased to see him, always good-humoured, always ready to make love and totally undemanding. This affaire of the heart had an idyllic quality which Michel had never before encountered.

Perhaps that itself should have cast a faint shadow of doubt on his new-found happiness. Or at the very least, it should perhaps have occasioned the raising of an imaginary eyebrow in his mind. Yet the longer he knew Ginette and the better he got to know her, the more he esteemed her. But neither women nor men are perfect, for this is a very imperfect world in which we live, however Mother Church may try to explain that inconvenient fact. The relations between men and women are, of necessity, never perfect – and almost never uncomplicated. While Michel was getting to know Ginette, she was getting to know him, and this knowledge she intended to use to her advantage. And why not? He was a rich and clever man, one of the Brissard family, beholden to no one. She was a poor young woman, likely to remain poor all her life unless she did something to change her fortunes. That she proposed to do, for she was ambitious, besides being pretty.

She revealed her ambition to Michel cleverly, not all at once, but bit by bit over several weeks, over meals and in the intervals while they were resting between love-making. In this way he accepted it as the most natural thing possible. He was himself imbued with the entrepreneurial spirit of his family and he recognised and respected this quality in others – especially when it appeared that a share of the profits might fall into his hand.

'A fashion boutique, Ginette? No doubt there is money to be made from such a venture, as you say. My wife spends a fortune on clothes. So do all her friends. But this is a business I know nothing about.'

'But I do,' she said, 'my job for the last five years has been observing women's taste and selling them clothes in the store. Now I'd like to do it for myself.'

On another occasion, as they lay relaxed together on her bed, her head on his chest, she took the matter further.

'You remember we talked about opening a fashion boutique – well, I've found the right premises to let.'

'Really?' he said lazily, 'where?'

'In the rue Cambon.'

Michel blinked. That was in the most fashionable part of Paris, running between the Boulevard de la Madeleine and the rue de Rivoli. The rent of a shop there was likely to be exorbitant. And to stock a boutique with clothes that would be interesting to the women who shopped in that district would be very expensive. He said so.

'Not nearly as expensive as you think,' she answered, 'I know where to buy everything at very good prices – I have made a point of this. In the fashion business one buys cheap and sells very dear.'

Eventually they reached the point where they talked money. The sum she named was very much less than he had expected, well within his means if he were to dispose of some other investments that, as Ginette explained it, produced a much lower level of profit than her projected venture. In the end she persuaded him. He put up the money, she left her job and opened her boutique on the rue Cambon.

From the very beginning it was successful. The first time he visited it he was delighted by the taste and variety displayed in the choice of its wares – frilly silk blouses, pencil-slim skirts, beautiful stockings, delicious under-wear – a profusion of women's apparel to send a man's imagination racing and his heart to beat a little faster. Sales were brisk and it was obvious to Michel after only a month that Ginette had found her metier and that he had made a very good investment. Whenever he had the time during the day he strolled round to the rue Cambon for the double pleasure of observing money being made for him and of fondling Ginette in her small office at the back of the boutique. This had become important , for now that she was running a business she had much less time and was not so readily available as she had been in the past. However, she was always delighted to see him and, even when busy, she would leave the customers in the care of the two assistants she had engaged, so that she could retire into the office with him for half an hour.

There was a morning in July when he found himself at liberty for an hour before a lunch appointment. He made his way to Ginette's boutique, noted with satisfaction that there were three or four ladies of fashion examining expen-sive items, said 'Good-day' to the assistants as he passed through and into the office. It was a tiny office with hardly room for an Empire-style table against one wall to serve as a desk, and two small chairs. But within this confined space a scene was being played which struck Michel dumb with astonishment. Ginette was standing at the desk, her hands flat on it so that she was bent forward at the waist in a manner to thrust her rump out to the rear. Her pleated silk skirt of lime green was hitched up her back to expose the plump cheeks of her bottom, innocent of any covering of underwear. Behind her, standing between her widely parted feet and clasping her tightly by the waist, was a man in a beautiful grey suit. That is to say, he was partly in his beautiful grey suit, for his trousers were down around his ankles and his jacket had slipped from his shoulders and hung halfway down his back from the vigour of his exertions! And those exertions – a fast plunging of his hips – were proof enough, if any proof were needed, that his male part was deeply embedded in Ginette.

Michel stared with bulging eyes at the pair of them, still oblivious of his presence, for they were sideways on to him and very much involved just then with their own emotions. Ginette's eyes were closed and on her face was an expression of exquisite pleasure. The man's eyes were open but they saw nothing, for at that very instant his final thrusts caused him to convulse in climatic passion.

Michel spoke acidly:

'Good-day Ginette. I regret to interrupt your *business meeting* but perhaps you will be so good as to explain to me what is going on.'

Two startled faces turned towards him.

'Who the devil are you?' the other man demanded angrily, 'Get out!'

'Michel,' said Ginette, recovering from her surprise, 'I did not expect you until after lunch.'

'Obviously!'

'But it was time that the two of you met,' she continued with a sang-froid which amazed him, 'Monsieur Michel Brissard – Monsieur Armand Budin.'

To introduce a lover who had discovered her in an act of infidelity to a lover still embedded in her warm body – and her own spasms of delight not long past – this required such remarkable self-composure on the part of Ginette that the two men were at first astounded and then amused.

Michel held out his hand and grinned.

'Monsieur Budin, it is an honour to make your acquaintance,' he said with heavy irony.

Armand took the offered hand awkwardly, being still pressed firmly against Ginette's bare backside.

'If you will excuse me for a moment, Monsieur Brissard,' he said.

'But of course,' and Michel turned his back politely while the two lovers at the desk disengaged themselves. When he turned again, Ginette was sitting on one of the small chairs, her skirt just covering her knees. Armand

11

was leaning elegantly against the wall, perfectly decent again and lighting a cigarette.

'I know your face,' Michel said, 'where have we met?'

'We have never met formally before, to the best of my recollection – if you regard this occasion as a formal one,' said Armand, smiling, 'but I am a friend of your sister Jeanne.'

'Of course! I remember you now. But what are you doing here? I was under the impression that I had an understanding with Mademoiselle Royer.'

'I had the same impression,' said Armand, 'I am a partner in her business.'

'But so am I!'

The two men glared at each other for a moment and then laughed as the implications became clear to them.

'It would seem,' said Armand, 'that our little Ginette has a more highly developed sense of commerce than either of us suspected.'

Michel seated himself on the other chair and looked at Ginette thoughtfully.

'Tell me, my dear,' he said, 'are there any other partners we don't know about?'

'Only one other,' she answered calmly, 'Monsieur Falaise.'

'And who is he?'

'He is the director of the department store where I used to work – a most charming man – and enormously useful in advising me on establishing and running the boutique. As you are aware, we are making very good profits and some of this is due to his advice and experience.'

'So we are a partnership of four?' Armand asked, 'Does Monsieur Falaise also drop in from time to time to . . . discuss business matters with you, Ginette?'

'Of course, though not as often as either of you. He is much older, you understand.'

'There is one other matter which Monsieur Budin and I ought to know about,' said Michel, 'is it your intention to offer any more partnerships in the business?'

'No,' Ginette said with great sincerity, 'I find that three

12

partners are enough for me in a venture of this kind. Of course, if either of you desires to withdraw from the arrangement now that you are in possession of the full facts, I am sure that it would be no particular problem to find someone to buy out your interest.'

'Not I,' said Armand at once, 'the boutique is an excellent investment. And besides, I enjoy our little business discussions.'

'I am very pleased,' said Ginette. 'How about you, Michel?'

'I am in complete agreement with Monsieur Budin. There is no question of withdrawing from the arrangement. However, it seems to me necessary that we should reach a more businesslike agreement as to when we each call to discuss our interests with you, dear Ginette. To prevent any embarrassment in future, you understand.'

Armand nodded his approval of the suggestion.

'It is difficult to know which is the more inconvenient,' he said, 'to be interrupted in conversation with Mademoiselle Royer and perhaps to lose the thread of one's discourse, or to interrupt by chance a conversation between her and another and be a reluctant witness to another's private concerns.'

'For myself the inconvenience is equally unfortunate both ways,' said Ginette. 'How shall we arrange matters? Alternate days or mornings and afternoons?'

'I propose mornings and afternoons alternating weekly,' said Michel.

Armand was looking a trifle puzzled.

'Not so fast,' he objected, 'let me be certain that I have understood what it is that you are suggesting.'

'Of course,' said Michel. 'This week, for instance, you make your visits here in the mornings and I make mine in the afternoons. Next week I have the mornings and you have the afternoons. Then the next week we change back, and so on. Does this suit you?'

'An excellent proposal, very convenient and admitting of no misunderstandings. Ah – but what about our other partner, Monsieur Falaise. We must not overlook him in our arrangements.'

'As to that,' said Ginette, 'he is an extremely busy man and is only able to call here on Mondays. So if that is satisfactory to you both, neither of you visits me on Mondays – but of course you have Saturdays, when the boutique is open for business all day.'

'That seems reasonable to me,' said Michel.

'And to me,' Armand agreed, 'but what about the evenings – how do we arrange that?'

'I must have my evenings free,' Ginette said quickly, 'to be with my fiancé. Otherwise he would only see me on Sundays.'

Michel and Armand looked at each other over her head, their eyes wide with surprise. Michel recovered his voice first.

'Your fiancé – how full of surprises you are, Ginette. Have you been engaged to be married for long?'

'Since just before the boutique was opened.'

Armand shrugged and smiled broadly.

'Yes, you must have your evenings free to be with your fiancé. It would be unthinkable to keep a young woman apart from the man she loves and intends to marry. I am sure you agree with me, Monsieur Brissard.'

'Unquestionably. But if I may be permitted a question on behalf of both of us – is it possible that he may wish to become a partner in the business?'

'No, not in the business,' Ginette assured them both, 'he has no talent for commerce. He is a teacher at the lycée.'

Then all seems to be settled,' said Michel.

'Excellent, then I will take my leave,' said Armand, bowing slightly. 'To be quite certain that I have it right – it's the mornings that are mine this week, yes?'

'Yes,' said Ginette as he kissed her hand. 'I shall expect you tomorrow morning. Au revoir, dear Armand.'

When he had gone Michel sat down again on one of the chairs and looked pensively at Ginettel

'This has been a day of surprises,' he said, 'not entirely pleasant, I fear.'

Ginette raised her eyebrows at that.

'Really? Do you feel that I have in some way deceived you, Michel? Tell me truthfully what is in your mind – let us dispose of this matter fully.'

'By chance I have learned things in the last half-hour which I feel that I should have been told before.'

'Let us be practical, my friend – you would probably have refused to participate in my business plans if I had disclosed certain other interests.'

'That is possible.'

'And that would have been to your disadvantage.'

'Perhaps you would explain that to me.'

'Does it need explaining, Michel? You are a partner in a very promising business venture. The money you have invested will produce good profits, year after year. That must please you.'

'In that matter I am content.'

'That there are others concerned in this business – well, I doubt very much if you would have been willing to subscribe the whole of the money. One-third was a reasonable sum for you.'

'I have already told you that I have no complaint about the business aspect of our arrangements.'

'Then it is as I thought – you are troubled by the more personal aspect. But dear Michel, where is the problem? You and I have been intimate friends for months now. As far as I am concerned we shall continue to be so.'

'How can you say that? Two other men have the same privileges as I have. I say nothing of your fiancé, since that is another matter altogether.'

'But what has changed? Whenever you want me, I am yours, just as before.'

Michel's experience with the many women who had played important parts in his life, and his experience with his wife, had long ago led him to the inescapable conclusion that it was futile to argue against feminine logic. A sensible man proceeded differently.

'I came here today because I have not seen you for two

days and I wanted you,' he said. 'What did I find? I found you in the intimate embraces of another man.'

'That was most unfortunate,' Ginette said at once, 'I shall never forgive myself. But can you forgive me, Michel?'

'I am heart-broken,' he said, 'you in the arms of a stranger!'

'Not entirely a stranger, as it proved. At least, not a stranger to your sister. And you recognised him.'

'That has nothing to do with it,' said Michel, feeling that he was on uncertain ground.

'Of course not. But let us be frank with each other. You and I have given each other a great deal of pleasure. For my part I would like that arrangement to continue. As for the others – well, you are not my fiancé. He perhaps has a right to complain, except that he knows nothing of my personal friendships and never will. Even now you know everything, do you not still love me a little, Michel?'

She looked so charming as she held out her arms towards him that his heart was touched. He rose to his feet and embraced her, holding her slender young body close to him as he kissed her.

'Ah,' she said between kisses, 'something hard and strong in your trousers is pressing itself against me. Am I forgiven, then?'

'Of course,' he breathed, 'I am on fire for you, Ginette.'

She knew better than to propose an encore of what he had observed taking place between her and Armand. She moved back a short step or two, pulled her slim pleated skirt up around her waist and seated herself on the short side of the table-desk. Michel's glance travelled in admiration slowly up her shapely legs in their fine silk stockings to where her garters held them above her knees, then on up the smooth white flesh of her thighs to the brown-fleeced treasure between them.

'Adorable,' he said.

'Then come to me.'

He stood between her knees, his hands fondling her breasts through her thin silk blouse while she occupied

16

herself with unbuttoning his trousers to extract his stiff part and handle it in a most friendly manner.

'Dear Ginette, your touch is unmistakable,' he said softly.

'And so is yours,' she sighed as his finger-tips caressed her nipples.

Their touching of each other's bodies continued in the most natural way in the world, to signs of contentment and little gasps of pleasure, until the imperious throbbing of the fleshy protruberance in her hands advised them both that the moment was fast arriving for a closer embrace. Ginette released the cherished part she held and used her pretty fingers to open for him the soft lips between her legs, showing him her moistly-pink interior and her little bud of passion. Then as Michel steered his prow into it, she lay back on the neat stacks of invoices and delivery notes and paid bills which covered her desk and brought up her knees to grip him by the hips as he leaned over her and plunged within.

She had been well prepared by her earlier encounter with Armand. The way had been made smooth and slippery by the exertions and emissions of love. The sensations imparted to Michel by the clasp of her supple sheath of warm flesh caused him to utter a long sigh of delight. And Ginette, her earlier pleasure having been cut short by the appearance of Michel almost at the very moment when Armand was lifting her to the heights of passion, she too sighed in deep delight to feel within herself that sturdy male baton. Almost at once Michel was intensifying their mutual pleasure by means of long and slow thrusts.

'Oh yes,' she murmured, 'that's marvellous!'

His hands were on her breasts, squeezing them through the thin silk in rhythm with the swing of his loins. Ginette's head rolled from side to side on the desk-top, her face pink with emotion. She was content – a difficult situation which could have turned into angry drama between the two men had been so well managed that no better outcome could be imagined. And as proof of that,

17

here was Michel bestowing on her with great eagerness the pleasure she most enjoyed in life!

As every lover knows, it is ordained that such transports of joy cannot be long sustained. Michel's slow probing transformed itself all too soon into a series of short and fast jabs and these brought about an ecstatic convulsion in Ginette and an outburst of hot passion from Michel, to their mingled gasps and sighs.

'You were magnificent, Michel,' she said at last.

'And you are adorable, chérie,' he answered, smiling at her as he withdrew from her satisfied body.

Ginette sat up and got off the desk to adjust her creased skirt and blouse.

'I must change these clothes,' she said, 'it would never do for customers to see me crumpled from the tender embrace of love.'

'Yes, it would be a poor advertisement for your boutique,' he agreed.

'Then you must leave. I shall see you tomorrow, I hope.'

'You may rely on it,' and he kissed her hand and left her to repair the damage.

As he passed through the boutique he noted that one of the assistants was dealing with a customer and the other was carefully folding a delicious little garment to return it to its box – a pair of camiknickers in ice-blue silk with broad lace bands at the legs and bodice. Michel paused to smile at her.

'A charming little fantasy to grace a beautiful woman,' he said.

'You like it, Monsieur Brissard?' she asked, holding it up so that he could appreciate it fully.

Naturally she knew his name. Ginette had instructed her assistants most carefully so that they would recognise her three wealthy backers when they visited the boutique.

'I am sure that it would look very chic on you,' he said, a wealth of implication in his tone.

As her sales assistants Ginette had engaged two very slim girls of about eighteen. Both were this day dressed in the same modish skirt and blouse which Ginette herself was wearing and which she was now changing in the privacy of her tiny office – evidently this must be a style which the boutique was promoting. The girl Michel was talking to had a *gamine* look about her which Michel found provocative. Her dark brown hair was cut very short, her little nose was slightly turned-up and her eyes were bold.

'Do you think so, Monsieur?' she asked, giving him a tiny impertinent grin, 'it is not really my colour.'

'What is your colour, Mademoiselle . . .'

'Gaby.'

'Well then, Gaby, which colour suits you best?'

'We have this chemise-culotte in damson-red also, and that is utterly beautiful.'

'Especially if you were to wear it,' he suggested.

'There is little chance of that, Monsieur – it costs as much as I earn in a month.'

'Perhaps something could be arranged.'

She smiled and shrugged slightly – just enough to make her pointed little breasts move excitingly against the thin material of her blouse.

'Would you care to see it?' she asked.

'By all means.'

When she held the garment up in front of her by its shoulder-strings Michel could hardly repress a sigh of admiration. The silk was so fine that it was almost transparent and the rich colour against bare skin would be incredibly provocative. The top was cut so low that, held against Gaby's body, he observed that her breasts would be scarcely covered at all if she were to wear it.

'It is charming,' he said, 'it would suit you admirably.'

The pink tip of her tongue showed for a moment between her lips.

'A marvellous gift,' she said, 'one which no woman could refuse.'

'Wrap it for me,' he answered, reaching for his money, 'you know Fouquet's on the Champs Élysées, about ten minutes walk from here?'

'I know where it is.'

'If you were to meet me there soon after five this evening for a drink, I will have this beautiful little gift with me. We could discuss going on to a suitably private place where you might be disposed to let me see the effect of this damson-red creation against your skin.'

Gaby hesitated for a second before replying.

'If Mademoiselle Royer were to find out,' she said, 'it would be most unfortunate – she would dismiss me instantly.'

'Have no fear of that,' he assured her, 'I shall be very discreet.'

'Then until later, Monsieur Brissard,' she said, handing him the neat little package.'

Michel left the boutique well pleased with himself. He adored Ginette, of course, and he anticipated years of profitable and pleasurable partnership with her. But he felt that she owed him something more in return for her lack of frankness over the business arrangements and the personal arrangements. He intended to repay himself, without her knowledge, by making full use of her staff, starting with Gaby that evening.

A LESSON FOR BERNARD

As all the world knows, male pride is usually based on possessions, such is the illogicality of men. Possessions of wealth, of a superb house, of a country estate, of a fast automobile, of a beautiful wife or mistress – the list could be extended without end. For some men it lies in possession of a fine physique, inherited, one need hardly say, from their parents. Or even a portion of themselves, for it is well known that some men are excessively proud of the part of themselves which is at its largest during the encounters of love.

Bernard Gaillard was such a man. He was of no more than average height and had averagely handsome features. His station in life was assured and might yet become distinguished. He was thirty years old, unmarried, had many friends and an active social life. None of which explained a certain air of pride about him, which impressed most of those who knew him, an aura of self-assurance no one could miss.

The cause of his pride lay between his thighs. This particular possession set him above the average, a fact known to a large circle of married and unmarried women. A whisper had been set in motion years before by Marie Gauquin, his mistress at that time. In discussing Bernard with a woman friend she had referred casually to his physical attributes. The word had been passed on from woman friend to woman friend until it became a topic of almost open discussion among the women of the social circle in which he moved. This worked greatly to his advantage – after all, women have a highly developed sense of curiosity. There were many who would not have considered him more than an acquaintance or a friend of their husband's, who could not resist the urge to find out for themselves whether all they had heard about Bernard was true, or merely exaggerated gossip.

In consequence, Bernard never lacked for female companionship and was never tempted into marriage. His affairs of the heart were usually of no more than a few months duration, but their termination had never prevented the continuation of the friendship between him and the woman concerned. The truth was that when their curiosity had been amply satisfied, women found him more entertaining as a guest at their dinner-table or receptions than as a lover.

It was at a large party at the home of Maurice and Marie-Thérèse Brissard that Bernard first met Madame Lebrun. The contrast between her shiny black hair and her pale ivory complexion was the first thing about her to catch his eye, then he found himself drawn by her vivacious manner. She was standing near the grand piano in the Brissards' salon, a glass in her hand, two or three male admirers about her, when he was introduced by Marie-Thérèse.

Her lustruous eyes, so dark-brown as to be almost black, blinked once when Marie-Thérèse spoke his name. Bernard kissed Madame Lebrun's free hand and smiled at her. He knew the significance of that blink – he had observed it many times in the past. It meant that his name was not unknown to her and that she had been made aware by some friend of his endowment. He joined in the conversation and as more and more of Madame Lebrun's attention centred itself upon him, the other men about her took the hint and moved away to find other companions to talk to.

'Have you known the Brissards long?' Bernard asked.

'No, we met only recently when my husband became involved in some business venture with Maurice.'

Bernard glanced around the salon for faces he did not know.

'Is that your husband over there talking to Jeanne Verney?'

'Oh no, he has a dreadful cold and dare not come out tonight. Do you know a friend of mine, Marie Derval?'

That was the information Bernard had been fishing for.

22

Marie and he had been lovers for five months the previous year. Without question it was she who had passed on to Madame Lebrun the secret – or perhaps one should say semi-secret. To judge by her manner, Madame Lebrun's dormant curiosity was fully awakened now that she was face to face with the possessor of so fortunate an attribute.

For his part, Bernard found Madame Lebrun very desirable, since his affections were not engaged elsewhere at that moment. Under her elegant black frock her body was lithe and graceful. He put her in her late twenties, though the diamonds round her neck were worth a fortune. That was to be expected – the Brissards were not likely to involve themselves in financial ventures with men who had not already demonstrated their ability to make money. Madame's jewellery testified that Monsieur Lebrun had that ability.

When a man's imagination is truly captured by a woman, his whole manner reveals it. He stands a little straighter and taller, speaks with more than his usual confidence, his gestures become more animated and his conversation more lively, even if he is speaking of nothing more than social trivialities. He is hardly aware of the others in the room – if you ask him the next morning who was at the party, he will not remember speaking to his closest friends. All his attention is concentrated on one person – he sees no one else – but he sees her in extraordinary detail. Everything about her is totally fascinating! The sheen of her hair, how delightful! The shape of her face, the colour of her eyes, how perfect! Her clothes and jewels – chic beyond belief! The soft skin of her bare arms, her slender wrists and long fingers – marvellously elegant! Her perfume – sensuous and modest at the same time!

His desire conjures up visions in his mind of the loveliness concealed by the clothes that suit her so well. She has small soft breasts, of course, just the right size to fill his hands if only he were permitted! And naturally, her hips are narrow, her buttocks taut and pert, the skin of her thighs as smooth and pale as alabaster! And between them, inside her delicate silk underwear – a treasure to make a man's mind reel in delight at the mere thought of it!

All this the would-be lover discerns, which is to say that Bernard discerned, through thousands of francs worth of expensive clothes – or if not discerned, at least imagined.

And she – Simone Lebrun – the object of his ardent imagining, knew exactly what was in his mind, because women always know, and his every gesture proclaimed it as clearly as any words. She knew that she had made a conquest, if one may employ the normal, banal expression. She was amused and flattered. Like all women, even while preening herself before him, she was considering whether her conquest was worthy of further encouragement or whether it would be more sensible to disengage herself gracefully from the conversation and move away. This question of where the balance of advantage lies is usually decided by women in a very short space of time.

Bernard smiled at her again – not a polite smile but one that hinted at much more – that he was interested in her, that he knew she might be interested in him, that he would welcome her interest with every fibre of his being – and so on, for the routine is known to all. Simone understood his smile, glanced down for a moment as if in modesty – or in thought – then met his gaze fully and smiled back in a manner that indicated that she was as eager to proceed as he was.

When the party dispersed, it was unthinkable that Madame Lebrun should make her way home unescorted. As one of the few unaccompanied men present, it was only courteous for Bernard to escort her. She told him that she lived quite close to the Brissards, close enough to walk, she insisted, rather than bother with taxis.

It was a pleasant enough evening for a stroll – pleasant enough for October, that is. The early evening rain had stopped at last and the pavements glistened under the soft golden lights of the stree-lamps. The breeze was very cool, but Simone was fully protected from it by a magnificent full-length fur coat.

24

Not far from the Brissards' home she slipped her arm familiarly into his and walked close enough to him for his hip to press into the luxurious fur that enswathed her.

'That look you gave me!' she said, 'I almost dropped my glass.'

'A glance of admiration,' said Bernard, 'a heart-felt tribute to your beauty.'

'It was more than that and you know it,' she said, speaking quickly and with evident emotion, 'it was as if you were kissing my breasts!'

Her lack of restraint pleased Bernard. The preliminaries required by Simone would be brief, the conquest certain.

'It was inevitable,' he said, 'we looked at each other and knew in an instant that we were meant to be lovers. To deny this would be like denying that there is a moon in the sky.'

'Perhaps. But if my husband had been present and seen that look, he would have killed you.'

'Then he must never know. This formidable secret of the emotions you and I feel for each other must remain ours alone, my dear Simone.'

'I confess to you,' she said as they turned into the street on which she lived, 'my legs are trembling. I feel as if I have been struck by lightning.'

'We have both been struck by the same lightning-flash,' Bernard told her. 'Come home with me now – your breasts need to be kissed and I need to kiss them.'

'That's impossible. Léon is waiting for me. He will not sleep until I am home.'

She stopped outside a modern apartment building and unlocked the street door with a key from her tiny evening bag.

'I must kiss your lips at the very least,' said Bernard.

'Then come in off the street.'

Inside the wrought-iron and glass street door they were in a small courtyard, surrounded by the six-storey apartment building. At that late hour of the evening many

25

windows were dark and the rest obscured by drawn curtains. All was quiet.

Bernard drew Simone close in against the wall and kissed her ardently.

'When, when, when?' he murmured.

'Very soon, I promise.'

'Tomorrow?'

'Perhaps.'

'Even tomorrow is too long,' he said, his hands groping in the dark until he had her fur coat open and could take her by the waist to press her to him. His celebrated part was at full stretch, its entire length against her belly through his clothes and hers.

'I must know!' she sighed as his hands caressed her breasts through her frock.

'What?'

By way of answer she unbuttoned his dark double-breasted overcoat. Her hand slid down between the waist-band of his trousers and his shirt, seeking a route for itself. Baffled at first by the complications of his clothes, she resumed her assault avidly until she had his shirt-front up out of his trousers and could force her hand down inside his underpants until she touched the object of her curiosity. Her hot palm enclosed the swollen head, her long fingers stretched down the hard stem.

'You are thoroughly excited,' she whispered, ' and, my God, how dramatic the result!'

'Now do you believe how desperately I want you?'

'I see that I shall have to be very careful in future about letting you kiss me,' she teased, 'anything could happen if you are so susceptible.'

As she spoke her awkwardly placed hand was gently massaging what she held and Bernard, shaken by tremors of delight, was attempting to stroke her nipples through her clothes.

'It is you,' he sighed, 'there is something about you that threw me into a frenzy even before I kissed you . . . I shall die if you say no to me . . .'

'My poor Bernard,' she said, 'tonight I must say no to

you because there is no way I can say yes. But tomorrow afternoon, perhaps . . .'

'Yes, I implore you. You cannot be in any doubt of the strength of my passion for you.'

'No doubt whatsoever,' she whispered, 'and getting stronger all the time! Heavens, I shan't be able to sleep or rest until I have seen this with my own eyes!'

'Tomorrow for sure – at three – say yes!' Bernard implored her, half-delirious with the pleasure suffusing his body from the jerky caress of her hand.

'Such strength!' she exclaimed incredulously, 'I do believe that in another instant you will make a protestation of your passion.'

Her free hand whipped the silk handkerchief from his breast pocket and pushed it down the front of his trousers as his legs shook and his hands gripped her tightly by the waist.

'Simone!' he gasped, the evidence of his desire pouring into the ready handkerchief.

'Magnificent!' she crooned to herself. 'Oh, magnificent!'

At last Bernard sighed contentedly and was still. She removed the handkerchief from its guard-post and stuffed it into his overcoat pocket.

'I must kiss you,' he murmured.

'One moment,' and she tucked his shirt-front down his trousers before letting him take her in his arms and press his lips to hers fervently.

'You have given me a foretaste of Paradise,' he said.

'Then tomorrow we will enter the gates and enjoy the full joys,' she said, 'but for now I must leave you, my dear. My husband is waiting. Au revoir.'

'Until tomorrow.'

She patted his cheek and walked away across the courtyard.

With what joyous anticipation Bernard prepared for Simone's first visit to his apartment can scarcely be imagined. His two servants, a middle-aged married couple

27

well accustomed to his ways, grinned and winked at each other behind his back as he paced about giving them instructions. They knew well that a new woman in his life meant a good many afternoon and evenings off for them while he entertained in his bedroom.

'Put the best sheets on the bed, make sure that there is a full bottle of Eau de Cologne in the bathroom, fresh flowers in the sitting-room, all the furniture to be dusted, polished and shining, check the stock of champagne' he reeled off the list of preparations which his servants knew as well as he did (if the truth were told, even better than he did).

'Well!' said the maid to the valet after he had gone out, 'I've never seen him this excited before. It must be someone special he's met. Do you think he's fallen for this one?'

'Hope not,' said the valet, 'working for a married couple is a lot more hard work than working for a bachelor.'

'We don't have to worry about that,' the maid said scornfully, 'he only goes for married women.'

'Not always – there was Madame Vosges the summer before last. The tall woman who wore pearls all the time – you remember.'

'Oh, her – that was Madame Toussaint. What makes you think she wasn't married?'

'Because she often used to stay all night here and sometimes he stayed overnight at her place.'

'She was separated from her husband, but she wasn't divorced.'

'She was the one you used to complain about leaving lipstick on his underpants.'

'No, that was the one after her – Madame Benet. Madame Toussaint broke one of her necklaces in bed with him. I was on my knees half the morning looking for loose pearls.'

'If you kept any you didn't tell me about it.'

'Not a chance! Rich women know exactly how many pearls or stones there are on every piece of jewellery they own.'

'A pity. Still, it's interesting, what you said, about him being so steamed up over the new one, whoever she may be. I wish some rich and beautiful woman would lie on her back and wave her legs in the air for me.'

'Just let me catch you!' the maid said tartly, 'rich or poor, you'll soon regret it. Now get on with your work, he wants us out of here straight after lunch.'

Simone arrived a little after the appointed time, as was her natural right as a woman. She was well wrapped against the inclement autumn weather in a superb astrakhan coat, with a toque of the same fur on her head. To enhance her appearance she wore on her wrist, outside her fine black glove, a bracelet of golden yellow topaz stones.

The greetings were warm, and as swift as good manners permitted. Bernard kissed both of her gloved hands and helped her out of her coat. Simone took off her hat and expensive gloves and embraced him. They held each other close and kissed with passion. Less than three minutes from the time she entered the apartment she was in Bernard's bedroom. He assisted her to undress, murmuring words of heart-felt praise as her slender body was progressively revealed to him, then flung back the impressive Gobelins tapestry bedcover so that she could slip between the sheets.

She lay propped on one elbow, a tender smile on her face and one pretty breast exposed, waiting for him to join her in bed.

After so much anticipation, after so much fervour, there at last she lay! What man's heart would not beat like a drum sounding the charge at such a moment! Alas, the chagrin of love pierces more keenly in such idyllic circumstances, when all seems perfect and yet there is something concealed which is less than perfect. In the next quarter of an hour Bernard was to learn that Simone's approach to love was not his! Romantic that he was, his concept of love-making was traditional, even stereotyped, one might say. He desired above all else to lie in close embrace with her, to feel her warm body beneath him, her arms about his neck and her mouth seeking his while he plunged and plunged again in the motion that would launch them both into climactic rapture.

Stripped of his clothes, he posed with one knee on the bed, fully aware of the effect which the sight of his proud staff of flesh had on the hearts of women. Simone stared at it, her dark eyes gleamed and her lips were trembling as she whispered, 'Stupendous!'

She took it in both hands and planted a kiss of homage on its tip. Matters were progressing extremely well, thought Bernard, easing himself into bed beside her. His arms reached out to clasp her to him, but she twisted in the bed until her head was at the level of his loins and her hands were gliding up and down the impressive length of his hard pride.

'I never imagined . . .' she murmured, 'not even after last night. Oh, Bernard, this is magnificent beyond words!'

He let her have her way, flattered by her reaction and her almost incoherent words of admiration – above all by the look of rapt attention on her face as she stared at what she was caressing so expertly.

'Take care,' he murmured after a time, 'you are giving me such sensations of delight that things might go too far.'

'I want to give you the most marvellous sensations you have ever experienced, Bernard. It would be a pity to hide it away inside me before I have expressed my admiration fully.'

'Yes, yes . . . but if it were inside you it would also give you such sensations of pleasure as you have never known.'

'Later,' she breathed, 'ah, it's bigger than ever – look at the size of it now!'

Bernard stared through half-closed eyes at his mighty part and what her delicate hands were doing to it.

'It's time,' he gasped, 'I must put it in you now!'

'It jumps and throbs in my hands!' she exclaimed, 'like a trapped animal struggling to be free!'

'Simone!'

'Yes, a strong and fierce animal that I have caught.'

30

By then, of course, nature was taking its appointed course and it was too late for Bernard to make protestations. He moaned and twitched, lost in ecstasy.

'Oh, what a fountain!' Simone cried aloud joyfully, her busy hand manipulating him, 'again, again, again!'

To Bernard the rapture seemed to last forever, wave after wave of bliss rolling through his shaking body, until at last her hands were still. He stared at her face, aglow with pleasure, her eyes intent on his impressive part in open admiration.

'I must confess that I do not understand why you did that,' he said when he was capable of coherent speech.

'But why not?'

'It is not the usual way in which lovers pleasure each other.'

'Perhaps not, but why must we follow the usual way? After all, to observe so magnificent a fellow as yours performing the entire cycle of love is a sight not to be missed. Do you object? Has it never been done to you by a woman before?'

'That's not the point, Simone. Certainly I have no objection – but that was not what I expected from you.'

'How can I know what you expect of me – and does it follow that we shall only do what *you* expect? Have you not considered what I may expect from you?'

'That is my only desire,' he said, taking her into his arms while he wondered where this conversation was leading him.

'What is?'

'To give you pleasure by demonstrating my passion for you.'

'Good, you succeeded very well. Your passion gave me extraordinary pleasure.'

'I can understand that you . . . how shall I put it . . . that you feel a certain admiration for me . . .'

'Yes,' she sighed, hugging him close, 'I have never seen one that size before – I am lost in admiration!'

'Then we must put it to its proper use. That will give you even greater pleasure than what you just did to it.'

'Impossible,' she said, 'there cannot be any pleasure greater than that I have just experienced.'

'You mean that only by playing with me you achieved a climax?'

'Yes, of course.'

Bernard was bewildered by what he heard.

'The mere sight and touch did that for you?' he asked, wondering if he and she were talking about the same experience.

'Yes!'

'I find that extraordinary,' he said.

'Do you? Perhaps your experience of women has been limited to those dutiful ones who lie passively on their backs.'

'By no means.'

'Then you have encountered something which for you is new and different – are you not grateful?'

'But of course,' he replied, stroking her breasts, 'you are beautiful and very exciting, Simone.'

His hands strayed down her body and between her thighs. The touch told him that she had been aroused to the full – confirmation, if it were needed, of what she had said.

'Let us now do it my way,' he whispered amorously, 'I promise to give you such pleasure that the memory of what has gone before will be as nothing.'

'I doubt it,' she said, 'but I see that you won't believe me until you make the attempt.'

At a measured pace Bernard went through his customary repertoire of kissing, touching, fondling, stroking, until the moment arrived for him to assume his normal position above her. Simone smiled and placed herself on her knees and elbows, her black-haired head down on the pillow and her bottom up in the air.

Yet another caprice, Bernard said to himself, an astonishing one perhaps, but Simone was proving herself to be altogether an astonishing person. He stationed himself behind her on his knees, the better to observe the charms offered so generously to him.

32

His heart skipped a beat and a tiny moan of sheer delight escaped his lips at the sight of her bottom. The cheeks were so perfectly rounded, the skin so deliciously silky. And there below, between her well-parted thighs, a tender mound covered with black fur as fine as astrakhan! In an instant Bernard presented the head of his beloved appliance to the pink cleft marking the entrance to Simone's secret boudoir and eased himself into it. He need not have feared – no constriction impeded him. On the contrary, he was accepted and contained as comfortably as if he were of no more than average dimensions.

Simone's head was turned to look at him over her shoulder.

'Are you happy now that you've got what you wanted?' she asked.

'You are divine,' he murmured, 'I adore you.'

She said no more as he rocked to and fro, his hands grasping her tightly by the haunches to steady her. In short, he did what any man does when he is lodged in a woman, until an involuntary cry of triumph announced that he had reached the peak of physical sensation and was presenting her with his bodily tribute.

As soon as his spasms had ended Simone pulled away and rolled slowly over sideways to stretch out her legs. Bernard sank back onto his heels and regarded her in confusion.

'That pleased you?' she asked.

'Never mind that – it obviously did not please you.'

'I did try to warn you.'

'You gave me your body and nothing else!'

'But my impression was that it was my body you wanted, Bernard. What else did you expect?'

'Lovers give their hearts along with their bodies. You gave me only your flesh.'

'I gave you pleasure. Is that not enough?'

'Not nearly enough.'

She slid round on the bed so that she could reach between his thighs and take hold of the limp part dangling there.

'The pleasure seems to have been sufficient, to judge by the condition of *this*,' she said, 'I do not understand what is troubling you. Should I have gasped out *I love you* at your critical moment?'

'You are laughing at me.'

'No, I am trying to ascertain why an experience which produced the desired result for you was apparently unsatisfactory.'

'Because it was entirely physical and had no element of emotion in it.'

'Ah, you require every woman who goes to bed with you to be in love with you – is that it?'

'Not in love, that would be absurd. But unless there is a mutual affection the true pleasure is absent.'

'But I do feel affection for you, Bernard, a great affection – otherwise I would not be here with you now, naked in bed.'

'I am confused,' he confessed.

'Evidently. I think you are mixing up love and pleasure.'

'But if there is no love at all, only pleasure, then all that remains is the satisfaction of a physical need.'

'And what is wrong with that?' Simone asked. 'This fellow here in my hand is big enough to have the most urgent needs to satisfy.'

'You are confusing me further.'

'Surely we want as much love as is necessary to enhance our pleasure, not to invade and confuse our hearts?'

Her fondling was causing strength to flood back into his deflated part.

'My God – how superb!' she exclaimed, 'how can you sit there fretting yourself about nonsense while this giant is rearing up again like a flag-pole?'

'Simone! I forbid you to do that until we have discussed this matter and reached an understanding of each other.'

'Don't be silly,' she replied, her hand caressing his elongated shaft, 'first things first – we can talk all you like after I have given this fellow what he is sitting up and begging for.'

About a month after he first met Simone, Bernard invited his friend Jean-Albert Faguet to dinner in his apartment. The food was well-chosen and lovingly prepared, the wines were very fine. Faguet, a man devoted to good living, fell to with a hearty appetite.

'So what do you want my advice about?' he asked when they reached the *caneton à l'orange*.

'Why do you think I want your advice?'

'My dear Bernard, why else would we be dining here like a pair of old bachelors? If this were a social occasion we would be in a good restaurant with a couple of pretty women. What's the problem – you've made your mistress pregnant and you want me to relieve her of her guilty burden? That's no trouble – send her along to my clinic. Twenty per cent discount for an old friend like you. Thirty per cent if you pay me cash.'

'That's not it at all,' said Bernard, 'it's a much more complicated and delicate matter.'

'Really? You'd better tell me about it.'

As they ate Bernard described the strange course of his month-long *affaire* with Simone. Naturally he did not mention her name, for that would have been the height of indiscretion. Jean-Albert Faguet listened in mounting amusement and finally broke into loud laughter, much to Bernard's embarrassment.

'Forgive me, Bernard,' he said, dabbing his eyes with his table napkin, 'A thousand pardons! I can see that this is not comical from your point of view. Have you told me everything?'

'I believe so.'

'Then let me see if I have followed you properly. You have a new mistress, beautiful and elegant, as you have said. In your lovemaking her pleasure is in handling you, not in sexual connection. Correct?'

'Yes.'

35

'She does not deny you her body, so long as you comply with her desires at other times.'

'But she does not participate, Jean-Albert. She lets me have my way when I insist, as if she were a cocotte I was paying for her services.'

'So you tell me.'

'What shall I do?'

'Find yourself another mistress, of course.'

'But I want *her*.'

'Ah, I see – you love her.'

'Love her?' said Bernard in surprise, 'I've never given it a thought. But now that you raise the question, I suppose I must love her in some strange way. That first time I saw her at – never mind where – there was an odd and magnificent sensation in my heart. I thought it was desire, yet now I recall it, perhaps it was something more.'

'Then the case is altered.'

'Oh, this is infuriating!' said Bernard. 'Do you think that I am making a fool of myself?'

'Without question.'

'What do you suggest?'

'I am puzzled as to why you should seek my advice, Bernard. My experience of love is no more extensive than that of any man of my age.'

'But your experience of women is prodigious.'

'As to that,' said Jean-Albert, helping himself to more wine, 'it is perfectly true that in the course of a month's work I have the honour of putting my fingers between the thighs of more women than you can hope to in a lifetime. I am better informed about what women have under their skirts than any doctor in Paris.'

'Exactly!'

'I venture to say,' Jean-Albert continued, 'that if my patients visited me wearing masks, I know them so intimately that simply by raising their clothes I could identify each of them by name. Could you do as much with all the women you have made love to?'

'But this is mere boasting,' Bernard objected.

'You think so? Let me assure you, since it seems that

you have been most unobservant, that these tender parts you love and which provide my living are infinitely variable. I approach my work in a truly scientific and professional spirit. I observe, I note, I compare, I remember.'

'The fur varies from blonde to black,' said Bernard, 'and the texture from silky to bristly. That much is true.'

'Any fool knows that after he has been with two or three women. In reality there are many more variable factors and each woman presents a different combination of these factors. I assert without fear of contradiction that no two women in Paris are identical in this important respect.'

'Be more specific, if you please.'

Jean-Albert rolled his eyes upwards in mock-despair.

'What sort of lover are you?' he demanded. 'Are you so unaware of the individual charms of your mistresses? To cite an obvious example, in some women the insides of the thighs touch all the way up to the top, whereas in others there is a gap between the thighs at the top. In the first type, all but the hair is more or less concealed until she opens her legs for you. In the second type the soft lips remain visible even when she is standing upright. Which type is the lady we are discussing?'

'Now that you have directed my attention to the question,' said Bernard thoughtfully, 'she is of the second type you described.'

'At least you have noticed that much about her. We may proceed then to the size of the Mount of Venus itself. In some women it is markedly protruberant and fleshy, in others it does not exist at all. Between these extremes there are innumerable graduations.'

'Jean-Albert . . .'

'We may consider the shape and size of those fascinating outer lips, ranging from luscious to elegant, naturally pouting or delicately closed until aroused. Nor must we overlook the . . .'

'Jean-Albert!' Bernard interrupted, 'your disquisition on the appearance of the female apparatus of love can be

37

postponed until a more appropriate time. My problem is urgent. Without regard to the lusciousness or elegance of the object of my desire, how am I to persuade its alluring owner to let me make regular use of it?'

'But that is a matter of the heart, not of the anatomy.'

'I know that. I am asking for your advice.'

'Why me? My knowledge of women is confined to the expanse between navel and groin. About that I know everything. As to what goes on in their hearts, I know as little as you.'

'I cannot believe this. The two areas are closely connected.'

'So much I have observed. But I am far from understanding the nature of the connection.'

'But if you fail me what am I to do?'

'Either say *Adieu* to her or accept her as she is, what else? Women have their reasons, whether they understand them or not, for the multiplicity of ways in which they seek pleasure. Oh, the stories I could tell you! But the point is this, my friend – these reasons are her own business and no one else's. The person who has captivated you lives her life in her own way, not yours. If she is satisfied by what she does, it is not for you to object.'

'I am sure that if I can hit on the right method I can assist her to fulfil herself in love.'

'Good God, what arrogance! You are not her doctor, her confessor or her husband. If you wish to be her playmate, then you must play her game. If her game does not please you, find another playmate. There, that's all I intend to say on the subject.'

'But . . .'

'Not another word!'

Bernard shrugged, deeply disappointed.

'Do not behave as if you were playing in a tragedy,' Jean-Albert reproached him, 'life is given to us to enjoy – good food, good wine, pretty women. We are enjoying two of these gifts of God at this moment. After dinner I propose that we enjoy the third.'

'What is it you have in mind?'

'Though you are of the wrong sex to be a patient of mine, for the sake of our friendship I am prescribing a course of treatment for you. There will be no fee.'

'I am listening, doctor.'

'A short time ago I had the good fortune to make the acquaintance of a young woman who appears nightly on the stage at the Moulin Rouge. She is amazingly pretty and only nineteen years old.'

'I congratulate you.'

'I suggest that we conclude this excellent dinner you have provided with a glass or two of cognac and make our way to the Moulin Rouge to arrive at the moment when this dear friend of mine has concluded her performance for the evening and is ready to be entertained. A little light supper, a bottle of champagne – and so on.'

'Jean-Albert – this is true friendship – to offer me your little friend to cheer me up,' said Bernard, his eyes moist with tears of affection.

'Are you mad? Offer her to you? Certainly not!'

'What then?'

'I have no doubt that Mademoiselle Gaby will bring along one of her friends from the dancing troupe to be your companion. There – what do you say?'

'You are a good friend. I will follow the course of treatment you prescribe.'

The outing planned by Jean-Albert was uncomplicated and entirely pleasing. Gaby did indeed have a friend in the chorus line willing to complete the party, a fluffy-haired and pert-nosed blonde of nineteen or twenty who called herself Mademoiselle Lulu.

After the sumptuous dinner they had enjoyed, Bernard and Jean-Albert ate sparingly in the restaurant with the two girls, though Gaby and Lulu proved to have voracious appetites which belied their slenderness. It was a most convivial supper, Jean-Albert footing the bill. Afloat on half a dozen bottles of champagne, they decided to make a whole night of it and eventually found themselves in the rue de Lappe, drinking cognac in a cheap establishment where they danced to the music of an accordion. Around three in the morning they had progressed to Les Halles, where amid the noise and bustle of the market what seemed to be enough food for the whole of Paris for a week was being bought and sold. In a tiny restaurant in the nearby rue Coquillière they ate onion soup with grated cheese on top and rubbed elbows with market porters bracing themselves with a tot of spirits.

In due course they found taxis and parted, Jean-Albert with Gaby, Bernard with Lulu, she to offer what recompense she could for her supper, he to complete his therapy. That too was uncomplicated. Mademoiselle Lulu stripped naked the instant she was in Bernard's bedroom and slid between the sheets.

His evening clothes scattered across the floor, Bernard joined her. They kissed and fondled each other for a few moments and she murmured,

'Don't keep me waiting, chéri!'

She had a dancer's body, slim and yet muscular. Bernard would have preferred to have paid it more attention. Now that Jean-Albert had planted in his mind certain lines of enquiry about the interesting area between women's thighs, there was much that he desired to examine and classify. But Lulu was impatient.

'My God!' she exclaimed as he inserted himself, 'What have you got there – a truncheon?'

'Something worthy of you,' said Bernard, not over-pleased by her reaction, 'do not be alarmed, I know how to use it to please you.'

'Do it slowly then, or you'll maim me for life!'

He proceeded with care and eventually made her cry out in rapture. Even so, when he finally delivered his compliment, she uttered a sigh of relief.

'Was that good?' he asked, lying beside her again.

But she was already asleep.

When Bernard woke it was after midday and Mademoiselle Lulu was gone from the bed. He rang for his maid, but it was the valet who came into the room and drew the curtains.

'Pierre, I brought a young woman home with me last night. What happened to her?'

'She left about ten, Monsieur. She said not to wake you.'

'Did you give her breakfast before she left?'

'I served her myself in the kitchen.'

'In the kitchen!'

'It was her own suggestion,' said Pierre, picking up the clothes strewn across the carpet, 'and it seemed appropriate. Would you like your coffee now?'

'Yes, just coffee.'

Bernard sat up in bed, realised that he was naked and got into pyjamas before the maid brought in his coffee. She had a most disapproving expression on her face, but said nothing.

My domestic staff believe that I behaved foolishly in bringing that dancer home last night, he thought, yet Jean-Albert thought it was a good idea. In retrospect, what do I think about it myself? She had an attractive body, but she did not encourage more than the minimum use of it. Well, after all, she had been dancing on the stage all evening and then we were eating and drinking until nearly dawn. Without doubt she was tired. She offered me what she had as quickly as possible so that she could go to sleep. An honest enough creature in her way, but hardly what I am used to.

For Jean-Albert that sort of adventure may be satisfactory, he thought, but he is looking for light relief and quick thrills after the heavy emotional burden of comforting some of his most important patients, who probably find him irresistible after he has had his fingers between their legs in the line of duty. For me that sort of thing is unsuitable. I need an intelligent, educated and charming woman as an intimate friend. I shall telephone Simone and try again with her.

She accepted his invitation readily enough and came to his apartment. But then she sat in his drawing-room and said that she wanted to discuss matters with him.

'I am amazed,' said Bernard, 'when you were here

41

before and I wanted to talk to you about my feelings you completely diverted me. You can't have forgotten what you did.'

'We were in bed then,' she said, smilingly at him, 'that is no place for discussion.'

'I see. What do you want to talk about now that we are not in bed?'

'My impression on that occasion was that you were dissatisfied with me in some way. That is an impossible position for a woman to find herself in. Let us be clear about each other, Bernard, so that we do not involve ourselves in stupid and futile arguments, if we are to continue meeting.'

'That is in doubt, is it?'

'You know it is.'

'On what does it depend?'

'On a sincere exchange of views. What is it that you want from me? Tell me that and I will respond by telling you what I want from you. Then we can each decide whether there is any sensible basis on which to continue meeting each other. Or if our aims are incompatible, we can say *Goodbye* now and go our different ways.'

She looked so desirable, sitting on a chair with her legs crossed at the knees and a few centimetres of silk-clad thigh showing where her skirt had ridden up that Bernard was almost at a loss for words to answer her.

'With you it seems to be a question of logic and not of the emotions,' he said. 'Well then, I want to be your lover, Simone.'

'That is not very precise, my friend. Try again. Do you want me to love you or do you want me to give you pleasure?'

'Cannot the two go together?' he asked in astonishment.

'You are a most conventional person. Do you never examine your own motives? Is there no moment when you are totally frank with yourself?'

'I gave up going to the confessional years ago. You are suggesting that I should be my own priest and hear my own sins – is that it?'

42

'Perhaps,' she said, smiling at his manner of expressing himself.

'But to what end?'

'In order to give yourself absolution, perhaps, and cease to be either guilty or confused about your own life and desires.'

'I feel no guilt, I assure you. I live my life without harming anyone. What more is there?'

'Yet you are not honest about your feelings. You deceive yourself.'

'About what?'

'At this moment, about me and about what it is that you want from me.'

'Does it seem like that to you, Simone, tell me honestly.'

She smiled and stroked her knee with her finger-tips.

'You have answered your own question,' she said.

'You are telling me that it is clear in your mind what you want from me,' he countered.

'Certainly. What I want from you is pleasure, Bernard. What I do not want from you is love. I have that from my husband. I have no wish to complicate my life by attempting to love two men or be loved by two men.'

'That's frank enough! And so what you offer me is pleasure, that and no more?'

'Exactly so.'

Bernard breathed out heavily while he thought about her proposition. She watched him in amusement and waited.

'You are an extraordinary woman,' he said.

'Look at it this way – you and I are negotiating in the hope of reaching an arrangement satisfactory to both of us, not an arrangement which favours one at the expense of the other. To me it appears simple.'

'So be it,' said Bernard, 'the contract is that we each provide the other with pleasure and no more. Do you want it signed and sealed.'

'You may take me to bed,' she answered, 'we will seal the contract there.'

* * *

43

For months they persevered with each other after that day. They had reached a compromise and both made an effort to make it work. Simone had her way with him and he had his way with her alternately. Each tried to enter into the spirit of the other's pleasure and in this they succeeded to an extent which surprised them both. Bernard gradually lost his feeling of being cheated when Simone took hold of his proud implement and put it through its paces so that she could closely observe the final outcome. By reconciling himself to her desire he was able to take great pleasure in the extremely skilful way in which she handled him. For her part, Simone by stages lost her impatience with him when he inserted his fleshy stamen into her and slid to and fro. She took no pleasure from the process but it was her side of the bargain and she kept it faithfully.

Bernard came to know a good deal about her in time – her parents and background, her devotion to her six year old son, named Léon after his father. About her husband he learned little and asked less, though he was introduced to him at a reception soon after the New Year. Monsieur Lebrun was a short and heavily-built man who wore a white carnation in the lapel of his expensive suit. His manner with Bernard was somewhat unfriendly and he gave him a stare which made Bernard wonder for one atrocious moment whether Lebrun suspected anything.

Simone laughed at his fears the next time she came to visit him. Her marital relations with her husband were a subject of occasional speculation to Bernard, but it would have been unforgivably impolite to ask her. Had Lebrun lost all interest in her, perhaps, except as the mother of his son and organiser of his household? Or was his desire for her still active? Did he insist that she lay on her back for him, which might go some way towards explaining why she preferred other ways of pleasure with Bernard?

There was a particular Thursday in April when Bernard was expecting Simone to visit him after a parting of almost a week. He was in a very good humour that day and decided to give her a little surprise. After his servants had

44

left the apartment with instructions to return between six and seven o'clock, Bernard went into his bedroom and took off all his clothes. The afternoon was to be one of mutual pleasure – very well, it would start that way. He would encourage Simone to gratify herself in her individual manner and then claim his own satisfaction from her.

She was due at three. Ten minutes before the hour Bernard was seated naked on a chair in his entrance hall. He stroked his impressive part with warm affection, his thoughts intent on the anticipated delights of Simone's beautiful body. The truth was that he no longer found anything untoward in the position she favoured when it was his turn to enjoy her – head down on the pillow and pale-skinned bottom up in the air. There was much to recommend it, he had found. For one thing it facilitated his admission into her tender entrance and made it possible for him to plunge as deeply as he wished without causing her discomfort. And for another thing, it gave him the joy of caressing her belly and breasts throughout the act of love.

He sat enthralled by a delicious fantasy – Simone would enter the apartment to find him naked and ready for her. At once she would fall to her knees in admiration and, still wearing her hat and coat, would take his magnificence between her gloved hands and kiss it fondly. Then, all else forgotten, she would stroke it to a superb discharge of passion! And to save her clothes from being splashed, at the critical moment she would open her pretty lips and take the shiny red tip into her mouth!

After that he would lead her into the bedroom, undress her slowly and have his fill of her. Twice at least – perhaps more – for she knew how to keep him aroused. Ah, what pleasures lay ahead in the next hour or two!

Hastily Bernard took his hand away from his trembling part and switched his thoughts away from Simone. He had been so lost in his reverie that he had almost gone too far. Another few moments and he might well have scattered his compliments before Simone was there to appreciate

45

them! He was aflame! He prayed that she would not be late. Every second now seemed to him like an hour – a lost hour that could be an hour of delight.

The bell rang at last. With almost unbearable joy in his heart he went to open the door, his proud appurtenance waving about in front of him. He flung the door wide, a welcoming smile on his face as he exclaimed:

'Simone, chérie – see what I have for you!'

Simone's husband, in a black homburg hat and a dark overcoat, stood facing him. There was an expression of deep anger on his face. The anger turned to shock and then, as Lebrun's gaze travelled down Bernard's naked body to the mighty baton sticking out from between his thighs, to black hatred.

THE ITALIAN COUSIN

On the other side of the Alps, as all the world knows, the Italian sun ripens women into early bloom and then into luxurious physical maturity. For this best of all reasons the four Brissard brothers were greatly interested when their mother informed them that a cousin of theirs from Italy was shortly to visit Paris with her husband. Naturally, they had heard of this cousin before – she was a daughter of one of their mother's sisters, Aunt Marie, who had married a wealthy Italian about thirty years before. Only their parents had made the journey to Rome the year after the War ended to see Aunt Marie's daughter married in sumptuous style to the Marchese di Monferrato by no less a dignitary than a Cardinal. The Cardinal was, of course, the brother of the Marchese, since the Monferrato family maintained the tradition of putting one son into the Church in each generation, leaving to the first son the management of the estates, so that in this time-honoured way the family retained a hold on both spiritual and temporal influence.

The first introduction of the Monferratos to Paris society was at a reception arranged at the home of the Brissard parents. The four brothers were there – Maurice, Michel, Charles, all with their wives, and Gérard, the youngest and as yet unmarried son, their sisters Jeanne and Octavie – Jeanne with her husband Guy Verney and Octavie, widowed tragically early by the war, alas alone. Then there were the brothers and sisters of Monsieur and Madame Brissard senior, with their spouses, their sons and daughters and their spouses – in all, over forty members of the family assembled in the salon of the Brissard home to make the acquaintance of their noble Italian relations.

Teresa di Monferrato, it must be said plainly, was not beautiful, as had been expected. She was marvellously

47

well-groomed, expensively dressed, spoke French well with only a slight accent – but . . . what subleties, what worlds of implication are carried by that little word *but*! She was a little too short and certainly a little too plump for her lack of height – a result perhaps of over-indulgence in Italian cuisine. Her complexion was a little too olive, her expressive mouth a little too wide – a stern critic could endlessly catalogue her tiny shortcomings. Perhaps they can best be summarised by saying that there was no visible trace of French descent to be discerned in her – and when one has said that of a person, all has been said!

The contrast between her and the Brissard wives present was very marked. Her raven-black hair was longer than their fashionable bobs. Her bosom was fuller than was considered chic. Her frock was *haute couture*, but by no means Parisian *haute couture*, for it relied less on purity of line for effect and more on the dramatic. To the women present she appeared somewhat unstylish.

That being the case, after close inspection and discussion between themselves, the Brissard wives exhibited every sign of affection towards Teresa. They arranged to take her on shopping expeditions, recommended their own hairdressers, shoemakers, glovemakers, dressmakers and other suppliers of luxurious goods and services so essential to the woman of fashion. This affection for Teresa was based, very naturally, on a certain feeling of superiority on their part. Their cousin may have married into the Italian aristocracy but, when all was said, she was not a Parisian and therefore lacked style. From that it necessarily followed that she represented no possible threat to themselves and she could safely be patronised, shown around and befriended.

Such are the vagaries of human nature – and the important differences between the mental processes of men and women – that in the matter of Teresa di Monferrato the views of the Brissard men were diametrically opposed to those of their women. As men of the world they kept these views to themselves, there being no reason to become involved in any kind of disagreement with their wives over the visitor. Yet the plain fact of the matter was that there emanated from the charming Marchesa subtle waves of sensuous magnetism that drew to her the interest of every man at the reception, as unerringly as a flower draws to itself bees by means of its colour and scent – bees eager to enjoy the delicate nectar in the secret recesses of the blossom. This magnetism could be discerned – by men, that is – in the way she gestured with her hands as she talked, the way she sat, above all in the manner in which the cheeks of her generous bottom rolled under her frock when she walked. In short, all four of the Brissard brothers judged their Italian cousin very desirable and each secretly determined that he should enjoy her most intimate favours during her stay in Paris.

But how was this to be arranged? In the evenings the Monferratos entertained lavishly in the grand house rented for their stay on the Avenue Carnot. They gave receptions and dinners, were invited to other people's receptions and dinners, they attended the Opera frequently, they dined out in those restaurants which had established a reputation with gourmets – Androuet's, Lapérouse, Maison Prunier, Joseph's on the rue Pierre Charron off the Champs Élysées. They visited the well-known places of entertainment which every visitor to Paris knows of – the Moulin Rouge, the Folies Bergère and the rest of them. In all, a strenuous round of social activities. During the daytime the Marchese himself, Rinaldo, was off to see other amusements of Paris, generally accompanied by one of the Brissards, their father assigning them in turn to the task of being Rinaldo's guide and companion. He, this plump nobleman of fifty, wanted to see everything, from the Tomb of the Emperor Napoleon to the Flea Market at St Ouen!

Rinaldo was not the problem. As for Teresa herself, every morning seemed to be devoted to another shopping excursion with one of the Brissard women. That left the afternoons, yet her Italian dedication to the siesta appeared to be total. For more than a week the brothers, each acting independently and in secrecy from the others, tried to pierce this apparently impregnable barrier of lack of time.

It was Charles who won this extraordinary race – Charles who combined in his person the stylish masculinity of his father with the gentle grace of his mother and who was, by common consent, the best-looking of the four handsome men. By diligent bribery of Teresa's personal maid he gained her mistress's ear – and in due course certain other and more interesting parts of her pampered body.

On the appointed afternoon the maid, whose name was Caterina, admitted Charles surreptitiously by the servants' entrance of the grand house. She was a plump woman of fifty who wore ankle-length black and spoke hardly any French at all. But her eyes, as shiny as the black buttons on her clothes, saw everything and understood everything – especially the power of banknotes of large denominations. She led Charles up back-stairs to the door of Teresa's boudoir, tapped gently and nodded to him to go in.

The room was charming – not too large to inhibit expressions of close affection, not too small to make such expressions seem furtive. The floor was richly carpeted, the long windows hung with curtains of emerald-green tussore silk. The door beyond, which evidently led into the Marchesa's bedroom, was discreetly closed, as one would expect. In this elegant boudoir, reclining on a chaise longue, was Teresa, Marchesa di Monferrato. In preparation for her customary siesta – or so she would have said if anyone had been discourteous enough to ask her – she had removed her fashionable clothes and was wrapped in a flimsy peignoir of dark orange silk. Charles advanced to her side and bowed to kiss her hand, his heart joyful at the sight of how very lightly she was clad – for her peignoir was so loosely and negligently tied that her round breasts were exposed almost to her nipples.

'Dear Charles,' she said, 'it is kind of you to call on me.'

He responded gallantly that it was kind of her to receive

50

him and, so as to lose no moment of this precious meeting, launched forth at once upon an account of his devotion to her, his enslavement to her charms and the many nonsensical things that men feel obliged to say at such moments. Teresa listened to him with a smile of interest and pleasure until, greatly encouraged, he went down on one knee by her chaise longue to kiss her bare foot in token of his homage. She had a fine little foot, high-arched, the toe-nails beautifully manicured and tinted pale pink. As he raised it carefully in his hand, a few centimetres only, the better to press his lips to it, the smooth silk of Teresa's peignoir slipped from her legs and she lay open to his gaze of admiration to mid-thigh.

Immediately Charles pressed his advantage, as what man in his position would not! From her foot his lips moved upwards to her knee and then, as he trembled in anticipation, he moved higher and kissed her delicately on the silky smooth inside of her thighs.

'I have heard about French gallantry,' she sighed, 'but I have never experienced it. Oh Charles, is this how Frenchmen make love?'

'It is how I make love,' he said, kissing her thighs again.

He turned back the silk folds of her wrap to reveal a thick bush of jet black hair at the join of her legs.

'How adorable!' he murmured, running his fingers through it as if combing it for her.

He unknotted her belt-tie and opened the peignoir fully, feasting his eyes on the comfortable embonpoint of her belly and then the enchanting domes of her breasts. He covered them lightly with his palms and squeezed gently.

'This familiarity between cousins,' she said, her lustrous dark eyes on him, 'Is it usual in Paris?'

'Between you and me it is a necessity,' he answered, 'you must feel that yourself or you would not have agreed to receive me here.'

'A necessity, I agree,' she sighed pleasurably and, as he bent over her to kiss her firm nipples, her hand touched the front of his trousers and opened the buttons one by

51

one. She groped under his shirt until she could take hold of his stiffness and fondle it with vigour.

Lips still busy with her breasts, his own hand passed slowly down her warm belly to the dark thicket below. He parted the soft petals of flesh and found that she was quite ready for him. In the emotions of their encounter, Teresa began to lose her grasp of the French language and lapsed into her native Italian.

'*Ah, che bello!*' she exclaimed as his finger-tips brushed over her tiny bud of passion.

The words were sufficiently like French for Charles to understand that it was an expression of pleasure. He continued his tender manipulation for some moments until she tugged his upright part out into the open and stared at it in affectionate anticipation.

'*Mettimelo dentro!*' she implored him.

Charles kissed her breasts again, not knowing what her words might mean. She repeated what she had said, this time more insistently.

Her splendid legs parted wide as she spoke and she pulled his projection towards her in a manner that left no room for doubt. Charles shrugged off his jacket and obligingly spread himself over her on the chaise longue and sank the object of her desire deep into the welcoming furrow between her thighs.

'*Adesso . . . prendimi! Sfondami tutta!*' she exclaimed joyfully.

The words meant nothing to Charles, but what need is there of words in any language, when a man and a woman have joined their bodies together in the most intimate and exciting way possible? Teresa's movements, her sighs, the tight grip of her hands on his shoulders – these told Charles all that it was necessary for him to know at that moment. The lady was enjoying his close attentions as much as he was enjoying paying his tender respects to her. If the whole truth were told, to judge by the enthusiasm with which her splayed legs were grasping him and her hot loins lifting rhythmically to meet his thrusts, her enjoyment was perhaps even greater than his!

'Teresa . . . I adore you!' he murmured as the delicious sensations coursing through him became ever stronger and more irresistible.

'*Piu forte, caro!*'

The bucking of her body told him that she was urging him to increase the intensity of his attack. He lunged and plunged and revelled in sensation.

'*Sto venendo!*' she shrieked, bouncing up and down on the chaise longue so furiously that Charles was compelled to cling tightly to her as he approached his climatic moment.

'*Dio!*' she moaned as he poured out his silvery treasure into her tender purse, '*Dio!*'

There were tears of ecstasy on her face, something Charles had never seen before. He kissed them away and stroked her hair until she was calm again.

'There is much for me to learn in Paris,' she said, smiling at him.

'It will be my pleasure to teach you,' he replied, easing himself away from her.

After a while he was able to sit in a relaxed manner on the chair facing her, his trousers decently fastened, to tell her of his endless admiration and devotion to her. Teresa, her peignoir modestly rearranged to conceal all, stretched out a languid arm from where she half-reclined on the chaise longue and rang a little silver bell. Almost at once the black-garbed maid entered the room with a huge silver tray.

'Will you take a little refreshment?' Teresa asked. 'Coffee? Lemonade? Or something stronger?'

'Coffee,' said Charles, thinking to himself that the timing of the maid's entrance signified that she must understand very well the space of time her mistress required for the completion of a passionate episode and could be punctually at the door, her tray prepared, waiting for the tinkle of the little bell. Yet since Teresa seemed to find nothing remarkable in that, he concluded that the Italian way with servants was perhaps more familiar than was ordinarily the custom in France.

He sipped his coffee and chatted politely to Teresa as if this were no more than a social visit. But the respite was brief – as soon as the maid was gone, Teresa set aside her cup and stretched out her arms towards Charles. The loose sleeves of her dark orange wrap fell back, showing him her fine wrists and slender forearms.

Charles perched on the edge of the chaise longue and took her in his arms to kiss her. Through the thin silk the warmth of her flesh enchanted him, his hands glided appreciatively over her shoulders, down her back, along her sides – and returned inevitably to her breasts. For a while he contented himself with caressing her firm nipples through the silk, and this she obviously found extremely arousing, for her palm was laid on his thigh and stroked upwards. Afire with emotion, Charles opened the loose top of her peignoir to gaze fondly on her domed breasts in wordless admiration before pressing his lips to their delicate skin.

Teresa's preference in love-making, he discovered that afternoon, was not for long-drawn-out encounters of tender passion leading to an overwhelming discharge, but for a series of short and forceful episodes, with little periods of rest and refreshment in between. This he attributed to her Italian temperament – the fiery spontaneity which impelled her to urge him on with staccato expressions the moment he was lodged in her beautiful body and which forced such uninhibited shrieks of delight from her lips in her ecstatic crisis.

He gave her three proofs of his devotion that afternoon before she suggested that it was time that he left so that she could make herself presentable before her husband returned. The suggestion appeared to be a sensible one. Charles adjusted his clothes and kissed her hand in farewell.

'When may I see you again?' he asked.

'Very soon, I hope, dear Charles.'

'Tomorrow?'

She smiled at that.

'Tomorrow I cannot. Let me think . . . Friday. Yes, Caterina will arrange everything.'

Before he had time to protest that he could never survive for three whole days without her company, she tinkled the little bell and at once the maid came into the boudoir.

'Au revoir,' she said sweetly.

She had pulled her peignoir loosely over herself to cover her thighs and most intimate parts – though one delicious little red-brown nipple was peeping above the orange silk. Even so, the slight dishevelment of her hair, her faintly flushed face and the contentment of her attitude as she half-lay on the chaise longue spoke eloquently of what games she had been playing, and since she made no effort whatsoever to disguise any of this from her maid, Charles wondered if the faithful Caterina had been listening outside the door throughout!

'Au revoir, Teresa,' he answered, bowing slightly.

Charles had reason to congratulate himself in secret on his achievement. It was the first time he had made love to an Italian woman and the experience had been very rewarding. It was also the first time he had made love to a Marchesa and that conferred a certain prestige on their encounter, he thought. It was not the first time he had made love to a cousin – Marie-Véronique had that honour, the wife of a nephew of his mother. On the other hand, Marie-Véronique was only a cousin by marriage, so perhaps one ought not to count that. It could be said that Teresa represented a triple success!

But, all unknown to Charles, his brother Maurice was pursuing the same quarry. By temperament Maurice was more forthright and more formidable than Charles, there being more of their father in him. For Maurice there was no question of slipping into a house by the servants' door and climbing back-stairs. That would be an impossible affront to his dignity! When the Marchesa was at last persuaded to meet him in private, he escorted her to a small furnished apartment he maintained in the rue Lafitte. He had acquired this useful pied-à-terre some time before so as to have a suitable place in which to entertain ladies in comfort and privacy. Its existence was unsuspected, needless to say, not only by his wife but even by his brothers.

One result of Teresa's innumerable shopping trips around Paris was that she looked incredibly chic that day in a winter coat of black vicuna with huge astrakhan cuffs that swept back almost to her elbows and a broad trim of the same fur round the hem – the creation of a master of haute couture! With it she wore a little black cloche hat with a diamond spray pinned to the side. Even as he congratulated her on her appearance, Maurice thought to himself that the visit to Paris was costing Rinaldo di Monferrato an amazing amount of money. His estates must surely be far more productive than one had imagined! But of that Maurice knew nothing – all discussions of matters of business had been confined to close discussion between Rinaldo and Brissard senior.

As soon as the apartment door was closed and secured behind her, Teresa threw herself into Maurice's waiting arms and kissed him hotly.

'Dear Maurice,' she breathed, 'Show me the bedroom. I cannot stay with you for very long.'

Maurice discarded his hat and overcoat and led her to where she wanted to be.

'But how charming!' she exclaimed, glancing round the room, which was elegantly furnished in the modern style, 'this is where you bring your mistresses – this pretty little room?'

'My dearest Teresa,' he replied, helping her off with her beautiful coat, 'there are no mistresses. This is all for you.'

He lied, naturally, as a man must on these occasions. Teresa knew that he lied and accepted it, as a woman must in these circumstances. She smiled and took off her hat and shook out her jet-black hair. Then with a gesture that delighted him, she kicked off her expensive black lizard-skin shoes, sending them sailing across the room towards the broad and low bed.

'Help me off with my frock, Maurice.'

'Perhaps you should have brought your maid,' he said,

feeling for the fastenings down the side of her tight-fitting peacock blue creation from Patou.

He was joking, but she took him seriously.

'I almost did – but then I thought that her presence might embarrass you. But I am sure we don't need her – you must have long experience of assisting women to undress.'

The frock came off over her head to reveal her standing in a crêpe-de-chine slip which terminated well above her knees and was trimmed at top and bottom with ecru lace on which were set tiny pink rosebuds. At this point she twined her bare arms around his neck and pressed against him while she kissed him, the warmth of her soft belly through his clothes causing his male part to stiffen itself against what would shortly be required of it. When she released him Maurice shed his jacket and waistcoat hurriedly, and by now the carpet was strewn with discarded garments.

'You are very beautiful,' he said.

'But you haven't seen me yet, Maurice, only my clothes,' and she took the hem of her slip in both hands and pulled it over her head.

'More beautiful than I imagined,' he continued.

She sat on the side of the bed and smiled at him affectionately, wearing only stockings and the smallest silk knickers he had ever seen on a woman, cut to cover only her most secret delight and fully exposing her belly and thighs to the groin.

'An Italian style?' he asked, 'It is very charming.'

'Will you take off my stockings or should I have brought my maid?' she asked.

'I shall take them off with pleasure, dear Teresa.'

She posed voluptuously for him, half-reclining on the soft bed on her elbows, one stockinged foot up on the edge of the bed to raise her knee high, the other leg outstretched. *Such* legs she had, Maurice observed with approval – and with the experience of a man who had been privileged to see, and to caress, the legs of a very considerable number of pretty women. Such legs! From

57

her well-rounded thighs down to her knees, her perfectly-shaped calves and her slender ankles surely a subject for a painter! Except that Maurice would not trust any painter to observe Teresa in a state of near nakedness without being quite sure that the man was securely tethered to the wall and unable to throw himself at her feet and swear eternal devotion in return for the honour of kissing her foot!

Teresa's garters were the same shade of peacock blue as her frock and delicately frilled with fine lace. He removed her silk stockings with finesse and left the garters on, for the pleasure of seeing the contrast with the smooth olive skin of her bare thighs. Naturally, from his vantage point at her feet the sumptuousness of Teresa's body was overwhelming. Those magnificently full round breasts – so tantalisingly close and so generously offered for his delight! Even Maurice's ready tongue was at a loss to find words that had sufficient emotional force to describe them or to praise them. It would have required a poet in the highest order of talent to find a phrase that would do justice to those enchantingly firm-pointed playthings! To say nothing of the satin-skinned expanse of her belly, displayed so freely – the felicities of language necessary to convey its attractions would be beyond the capabilities of even the Académie Française in plenary session! And there below, at the join of one upraised thigh and one outstretched thigh, a little triangle of peacock blue silk which covered but did not quite conceal her most secret treasure. The thin material was stretched in a delicious outward curve that hinted at a plump mound – and through the translucence of the silk there was faintly visible the dark shadow of her jet-black fleece.

Between almost inarticulate murmurs of admiration Maurice kissed along the warm inside of her raised thigh until he reached her groin and the silk-covered bulge that aroused him – all unaware that his brother Charles' lips had followed this same golden route only the day before.

'Ah, Maurice,' she whispered, 'how marvellous is this moment!'

In a state of high exhilaration he pulled off the remaining tiny garment that protected her modesty and rained kisses on the gently pouting lips he had unveiled.

'*Madonna mia!*' Teresa sighed, her legs opening wider.

Exquisite though the moment was for them both, there was still more of her ripe body to be adored. Maurice took hold of her hips and rolled her over on the bed until she was face down and the elegant rotundities of her bottom were in plain view. He ran his hands over the silk-skinned cheeks, enraptured by their supple fleshiness. He squeezed them, he kissed them – he bent over her to bite them gently, causing Teresa to utter little cries of pleasure.

It continued, this most enjoyable lovers' game, until Maurice was impelled to tear off his clothes and get onto the bed with her to seek even more exciting forms of play. He kissed his adorable cousin from the tip of her straight Roman nose to the tips of her beautifully-tended toes, missing out nothing in between – curves, plains, protruberances, hollows, smooth parts, fleecy parts – not one enravishing centimetre was left unkissed. By then the hot-blooded Teresa had temporarily forgotten her French in the tremors of pleasure he was provoking and, his stiff part a willing captive in her hand, she was murmuring '*Oh, si . . . ancora . . . di piu!*'

Maurice threw a leg over hers and rolled into position on her belly, the upstanding tips of her breasts pressing against his dark-haired chest. Teresa's hands were between their thighs before his could get there, to open her portal wide for his entrance. In an instant Maurice was deeply embedded, Teresa exclaimed '*Meravigliosa!*' and crossed her ankles over the small of his back to pull him tightly into her. The only question at that moment left to be answered was which of the two of them, he or she, would reach the apex of passion first, for they were both thrusting furiously against each other. In the event it proved to be Maurice, but an instant later Teresa shrieked in ecstasy as she felt him discharge his rapture within her.

After that they rested for a while and exchanged endearments over a glass or two of champagne from

Maurice's well-chosen supply in the apartment. All too soon for him Teresa enquired what the time was and explained that she had to go home to prepare for dinner that evening with Michel and his wife.

'So soon?' said Maurice, 'must you really go so soon, dearest Teresa?'

She relented and said that she could stay another quarter of an hour, but no more. Maurice was not a man to let time slip past and opportunities to run to waste. His hand insinuated itself between her legs to seek and caress her dew-soaked rosebud and at once she was ready for a repetition of their earlier delights. This time he turned her over on her front, three soft pillows under her belly, so that he could lie on the voluptuous cheeks of her bottom and feel them bounce under him as he pierced her from behind with his sturdy probe and brought on a second ecstatic crisis in her and himself.

'Tomorrow?' he asked when they were dressing to leave.

'No . . . that's not possible . . . Wednesday. I shall come here at three.'

Maurice bowed to kiss her gloved hand.

'I shall be here waiting for you,' he promised.

The visit to Paris of the Marchese and Marchesa di Monferrato lasted for more than three months – the whole of the fashionable autumn season. Towards the end of December they returned to Italy, the end of their stay marked by a magnificent reception in their grand house, at which flunkeys in green and gold livery served chilled champagne and a string quartet played music which was lost in the high-spirited chatter of the hundred guests present. A day later the Monferratos took their departure by train, accompanied by four servants and a mountain of baggage.

In the autumn of the following year Aristide Brissard entertained his four sons to lunch at his favourite restaurant. From the tenor of the of the invitation they surmised that he had news of importance to communicate to them – perhaps, they speculated, he intended to retire from active participation in the daily affairs of the family business and hand over to Maurice. If that were so, then it was understood that Maurice would appoint Michel as deputy head, thus giving more scope in turn to Charles. The prospect was an interesting one, Only Gérard, still intent on his studies at the University, would remain unaffected by such an announcement and so, though he was present at the lunch, he was the least concerned and probably the one who enjoyed his lunch most.

In the event, Aristide's news was to affect Gérard also, for the old man had not the least intention of handing over responsibility – at least, not of the financial type.

'My dear sons,' he said at the end of the meal when a fine cognac was being served, ' I have something to tell you which will give you occasion for rejoicing. Your mother has received a letter from her sister Marie to inform her that the Marchesa di Monferrato has been delivered of a son, an heir to the title and estates. Will you join with me in drinking to the health and prosperity of the child, his mother and our good friend Rinaldo.'

Glasses were raised in salutation, even while silent calculations counted back the months and established the uncomfortable fact that Teresa must have conceived during her stay in Paris with her husband. On the other hand, the fact that she was with her husband gave some reassurance.

'But how solemn your faces are!' said Aristide, 'even you, Gérard, our family joker! Is anything wrong?'

'No, no,' a chorus of voices answered from around the table.

'Rinaldo is naturally delighted to have at last a son to carry on the name of Monferrato,' said Aristide, 'as you know, he is very much older than Teresa. There is also the consideration that before his marriage his life was one of extreme devotion to the pleasures of love. He indulged himself with a formidable number of women, from princesses to peasants, not to mention women of a certain profession – of the highest sort, you understand. But there were fears that the well had run dry, if I may express myself plainly. The extended stay here was obviously most fortunate in its outcome.'

'Ah, Paris – city of love and pleasure!' Gérard commented with hidden irony and Maurice shook his head at him warningly to shut him up.

'A fortunate outcome indeed,' said Charles carefully.

'My opinion exactly,' said Maurice.

'I am perfectly aware,' said Aristide, 'that your cousin Teresa is a very desirable woman. And being far more Italian than French, it may be that her blood is hotter than is seemly in a married woman.'

'Really, Papa – how can you suggest any such thing!' said Maurice.

'I am also aware,' Aristide continued, ignoring him, 'that during her visit to Paris last year her intimate friendship was bestowed upon – well, let us say that her husband's privilege was extended to . . . someone not her husband. No, do not trouble to deny it, I am not a fool.'

'Of course not, Papa,' said Gérard, the only one of them grinning.

'We are men of the world,' said Aristide, 'I have educated my sons to conduct themselves with courtesy and discretion in matters of the heart. Even you, Gérard, I hope.'

'I hope that I have not disappointed you, Papa.'

'Not in the least. I am proud of all my sons.'

'There is something I must tell you,' said Charles. 'Naturally it would have remained a secret forever, but after the news you have given us, I feel it is my duty to advise you that I am the father of Teresa's child. I confess this with pride.'

'You?' Maurice exclaimed, 'impossible! It is I!'

Gérard howled with laughter, drawing attention to himself from all parts of the restaurant.

'What is ridiculous in that?' Maurice demanded angrily, 'do you think I am unacceptable as a lover to a woman of charm and rank?'

'No, not that, Maurice,' Gérard said, struggling to control his mirth, 'but the fact is that I too was honoured in the same way by the lady. That makes three of us – so how about you, Michel – were the same privileges bestowed upon you?'

'Yes, by God!' Michel said, red-faced. 'It seems to me that our Italian cousin distributed her favours very liberally.'

'The little devil!' said Maurice, 'she was hot-blooded to an extent I for one did not envisage. Yet perhaps the signs were there all the time – her enthusiasm and her desire for more and more embraces.'

'The warmth of those embraces!' said Michel, 'how inspiring, no matter how often repeated.'

'How delightful she was, even in her most eager moments,' Charles said reminiscently.

'And that magnificent backside!' said Gérard.

'Enough!' Aristide said in reproof, 'we are speaking of a lady who is distantly related to our family. Let us choose our words with decorum, if you please.'

'Tell me one thing,' said Maurice, his agile mind working, 'was the purpose of the visit to Paris for Teresa to become pregnant?'

Aristide tapped the side of his nose with one finger.

'No indiscreet questions. Be content, all of you. While you were paying your respects to your cousin I was able to make certain arrangements with her husband in regard to part of his extensive holdings, and this will not only increase his income substantially – it will also return a handsome profit to us for many years to come. In all, the visit to Paris may be counted a success, for everyone has benefited from it in various ways. There is to be no more discussion of it, do you understand?'

'The secret is safe with us,' Maurice answered him on behalf of them all.

'That I do not doubt. It is, after all, a proud secret – that one of you is the father of the next Marchese di Monferrato.'

MONIQUE AND GÉRARD DISCUSS ART

The official attitude, had there been such a thing, of the Brissard family towards Monique Chabrol was one of formal disapproval and regret that a woman of her background should live her life in an uncompromisingly bohemian style. It was fortunate that she was not a blood-relation, for that would have made matters even more serious. It was bad enough that she was a Mont-Royal, a family allied to the Brissards by marriage.

Monique lived alone in Paris and painted. Sometimes her paintings were hung in the important exhibitions and on such occasions the Brissards would make a point of going there – partly to see what new scandal she was perpetrating and yet partly, it must be said, to demonstrate family support for her, even though they disapproved. Undeniably Monique had talent. Thankfully she painted in the traditional manner, not the slap and daub rubbish produced by the modernists. But, and here lay the problem, the subjects she chose seemed to the discreet Brissards unsuitable for public exhibition. Monique's interest in sexuality, it had to be admitted, was a little too open. What was done in private was a man or woman's own concern, that was understood, however strange or improbable the paths they followed to their pleasure. But a painting in a gallery was a public statement of private matters, and that they could not approve. At least she had the good sense to change her name to Chabrol.

A portrait had been commissioned from her some years ago of the head of the family, Aristide Brissard, and even that was a cause of some annoyance. It depicted him in classical portrait style, wearing a formal dark suit, wing-collar and cravat, his features caught to the life. Yet in some way that was hard to put precisely into words, Monique had managed to convey a lurking twinkle in the eyes that did not exactly conform to the image of a serious-minded and distinguished man of business and devoted father of seven children. It was more the twinkle of a man who would not hesitate, away from his home and family, to slip his hand down the top of a young woman's frock. If the truth were told, Aristide himself was secretly pleased with the picture, but as his dear wife was not, he held his peace about it.

Aristide's four sons firmly supported the official line of disapproval of Monique and all her doings, family loyalty being bred into them. Privately they found Monique amusing and interesting and called upon her from time to time for a glass of wine and some spritely conversation. Needless to say, the wives were not informed of this. The youngest son, Gérard, still a student at twenty-three, had no wife to concern himself about and was the most frequent caller of them at Monique's apartment. He had the additional interest of a great liking for art and music and, perhaps most important of all, he admired the way in which she set the pattern of her own life and refused to fit into anyone else's pattern.

Naturally, as an admirer of the surrealist painters, he deplored the fact that she persisted in painting in what he regarded as an outmoded style. Her men and women were always anatomically correct – a trifle no modernist would bother himself with – and she put them in recognisable settings – rooms, parks, riverbanks – copied from nature. For this he chided her sternly and she retorted in the same vein, describing his contemporary heroes as purveyors of the grotesque and unintelligible. In short, Gérard and Monique had a good-natured affection for each other.

He was in her sitting-room one evening, a glass of good Beaujolais in his hand, taking her to task for faults he discerned in a new painting of hers which hung on the wall.

'As a piece of work it must have taken you Heaven knows how long to complete,' he said, 'and what is the result – a pastiche of a well-known picture by Ingres, painted eighty years ago. As such it has no aesthetic purpose.'

'I painted it as a joke,' said Monique, 'you take it too seriously.'

'Then explain the joke to me, if you can.'

'Why don't you look at it more closely.'

Gérard got up and walked across the room to study the picture close up. It showed a low sumptuous divan covered in turquoise damask, on which lay a naked and beautiful woman. Her arms were behind her head on the cushion and her body was half-turned towards the viewer to afford him the sight of her young breasts and smooth belly. Behind her on the floor sat cross-legged a young man in Turkish costume – baggy orange trousers, an emerald green tunic and a bright red fez, playing a curiously shaped musical intrument something like a slender guitar.

'It is copied from Ingres' *Harem woman and slave*,' said Gérard, 'and yet there is something different about it. Of course – you have made the slave with the guitar a man instead of the original woman! And good God – you have given him the features of my brother Charles! What does this mean?'

'Do you notice anything else?' Monique asked.

Gérard scrutinised the colourfully-dressed slave closely and grinned broadly as he discovered, pressing outwards against the baggy trousers, the unmistakable shape of an erect penis.

'This picture hints at events of which I know nothing,' he said, returning to his seat, 'Charles and a Turkish slave – what can it signify? Tell me, dear Monique, before I explode with curiosity.'

'Ah, Gérard,' she teased him, 'I cannot reveal to you a secret concerning another. If Charles has not told you of this adventure, then I certainly will not.'

'Charles and a naked slave woman – surely this is impossible. He has never said a word to me about this. It must be connected with his visits to Istanbul. Did he tell you, Monique?'

'I will answer no more questions.'

'But who is the woman? – she is delightful.'

'I said no more questions. You either like my picture or you don't – to me it is a matter of indifference.'

'I like it more now that I understand a little of what it is about. For you it seems that art copies life.'

'Not always. Sometimes life copies art.'

'How?'

'To explain that to you would take forever and you are an impatient young man, Gérard. Perhaps the time has come for a demonstration of what I mean. If you dare, that is.'

'If I dare? Of course I dare! You would be astonished at some of the things I have dared.'

'Student pranks,' said Monique condescendingly.

'You insult me,' Gérard exclaimed. 'Try me! What is your proposal?'

'A small experiment, no more than that, to ascertain the relative merits of my old-fashioned style, as you call it, and the modern style you admire.'

'Go on then – how?'

'I will arrange two little experiments here in my home. Afterwards we will discuss which had the greatest effect on you.'

'I am ready for anything. I must warn you before we start that you will never change my views.'

'Perhaps. We shall see. Let us say tomorrow at eight in the evening. One thing – I must have your word that you will engage yourself fully in the spirit of the experiment and not attempt to change the course of things, however bizarre they may seem to you. Is that agreed?'

'Agreed.'

In this way it came about that promptly at eight the next evening, intrigued by the prospect of adventure, Gérard presented himself at Monique's apartment in Auteuil on the western edge of Paris. He had been instructed by telephone that morning to dress in a dark jacket and grey trousers, though the purpose of the mode was beyond him. Monique opened the door to reveal herself wearing a long-sleeved Persian-style caftan of red and gold.

'An Arabian Nights party? Then what am I – the European traveller?' he asked in amusement.

67

'Certainly not,' she answered, offering her cheek to be kissed, 'I have arranged an evening that is to be essentially French, though perhaps not typically so.'

While he was puzzling over that she led him into her sitting-room, where two other guests were sipping champagne and conversing with each other.

'Mademoiselle Marchand, allow me to present my cousin, Monsieur Brissard,' she introduced him formally.

Mademoiselle Marchand was in her early twenties. The expression of her classical features was calm and dignified as she held out her hand for Gérard to kiss. Her red-brown hair was worn long, not cut short and waved in the modern style, and it was drawn back from a central parting to an arrangement at the nape of her neck. She was sitting straight-backed in her chair, her legs crossed elegantly. Apart from her grey suede evening shoes she was completely naked. As Gérard bowed to kiss her hand and murmur *Enchanté, Mademoiselle* it required a most determined effort of will to prevent himself from staring at her alluring bare breasts.

The other guest, a man in his thirties, rose to his feet to bow and shake hands as Monique introduced him as Monsieur Creux. Like Gérard, he was wearing a dark jacket and grey trousers.

Gérard sat on the sofa by Monique and was handed a glass of chilled champagne.

'Monsieur Brissard has some claim to being a poet,' Monique announced to the company, 'unfortunately he has fallen under the malign influence of the anarchists who describe themselves as Surrealists, whatever that may mean.'

'Opinions differ on these matters,' said Gérard stiffly, 'and you, Monsieur Creux, are you also a painter like my distinguished cousin?'

'I have that honour,' Creux replied, 'evidently you are not acquainted with my work.'

'To my regret, no. Have you exhibited recently?'

However much Gérard tried to stop himself from staring at Mademoiselle Marchand, it was becoming almost impossible to ignore her rounded breasts and the tuft of red-brown hair showing above her crossed thighs. Especially when she spoke to him.

'I had the pleasure of posing for one of the pictures which Monsieur Creux exhibited in last year's Salon,' she said.

'If only I had seen it!' he said, 'I could never have fogotten so beautiful a woman.'

She accepted the compliment with a graceful inclination of her head.

'The time has come for our picnic in the woods,' said Monique. 'Come with me, Mademoiselle, while the gentlemen finish the bottle before they join us.'

To observe Mademoiselle Marchand rise and follow Monique out of the room was an enchanting experience. The rounded cheeks of her bottom swayed in a motion that was the purest poetry. Gérard's male part, already stiff inside his clothes, trembled with excitement.

'Mademoiselle Marchand is a friend of yours?' he asked as Creux poured out the last of the wine.

'A friend? Perhaps. A model from time to time. I have known her for some years. She has a good body for painting, very well-proportioned. Had you noticed?'

'A little fuller of bosom and rear than is considered chic,' said Gérard, attempting to be nonchalant.

'Chic!' exclaimed Creux contemptuously, 'that word has no place in the vocabulary of an artist. It is a word for dressmakers and magazine writers. Finish your wine and let's go.'

'But where are we going?'

'To a picnic, of course, you know that.'

'At this time of day?'

In effect, they went into Monique's studio. All the clutter of her work had been removed and she had procured ten or twelve shrubs and small trees in tubs, arranged round a central clearing. A large green rug covered the open space and on it sat the naked Mademoiselle Marchand unpacking food from a wicker basket. Monique had shed her caftan and wore only a thin linen chemise that came halfway down her strong thighs and did little to conceal her big breasts and width of hip. She was busy pulling the cork from a wine bottle.

'But of course!' said Gérard as he and Creux seated themselves beside the women, 'I have it now! This is Manet's *Dejeuner sur l'Herbe* brought to life!'

'I told you that we are to have an essentially French party,' said Monique.

'In spite of your admiration for the modernists,' said Mademoiselle Marchand, 'it appears that you are acquainted with the work of our great French painters of the past.'

'Naturally, Mademoiselle,'

In the circumstances it seemed oddly appropriate to him that they should address each other formally.

'And is Monsieur Manet's celebrated picture one of which you approve?'

'I have been told that it caused a certain amount of unease when it was first shown. People asked themselves by what extraordinary train of events did two fully dressed men find themselves at a picnic in the woods with two unclad women. What was to happen next, they speculated. The picture was judged scandalous by polite society.'

'Perhaps we shall find out what happened next,' said Monique, 'we have recreated to what extent we can the setting and the characters. Let us hope that the spirit of what the artist intended may inspire us.'

'The experiment has a certain interest,' said Creux, raising his glass, 'Manet, dear departed master, in whatever heaven you now pursue your work, I salute you!'

'To the illustrious past,' Gérard joined in the toast generously.

'My role is only to take off my clothes and stand or sit or lie while artists paint pictures with me in them,' said Mademoiselle Marchand, 'yet it seems to me that the untalented daubers who now pass for artists have in their blind arrogance kicked away all the support of the past and wish to pretend that they and they alone have just invented art. Is that not so?'

While he was answering her, Gérard could not avoid

observing that Creux had pressed Monique onto her back, pushed her chemise up to expose her generous belly and filled her naval with wine from his glass. Gérard's words trailed off as Creux leaned over Monique to lap up the wine with the tip of his tongue. That pleasant task completed, he hitched the chemise higher and with finger-tips dipped in wine set himself to tickle Monique's nipples.

Gérard was stretched out on the green rug on his side, one knee up to relieve and disguise the urgent pressure of his penis inside his trousers. Mademoiselle Marchand sat facing him, one leg tucked under her and the other extended gracefully, the whole of her beautiful body from breasts to furry groins presented to him. Her face was serene as she contemplated what Creux was doing to Monique.

'Are you lovers, you and Madame Chabrol?' she asked.

'Why no – our pleasure together has been solely that of conversation,' Gérard answered, a little surprised by the question.

'Your preference is perhaps for the fashionable women one sees window-shopping in the rue de la Paix?' she continued, 'flat-chested, no more behind than a boy and hair cut as short as a convict's?'

In truth Gérard was beginning to ask himself, as he watched Creux handle Monique, why he had never taken the opportunity on a visit to her apartment to make advances to her. Those full and fleshy breasts Creux was rolling in his hands – the sensation of fondling them must be marvellously sensual! As Creux moved back to push up Monique's knees and transfer his attentions to the capti-vating area between her thighs, Gérard was overwhelmed by the sight of the neat strip of hair that covered her plump mound. He sighed loudly as Creux stroked it for a moment or two before splitting it with his thumbs and inserting two fingers.

'Monique is beautiful,' said Gérard thoughtfully, 'I wonder that I never noticed it before.'

'You lack the artist's eye,' said Mademoiselle Marchand simply.

71

She reached out casually to unbutton Gérard's trousers and take out his straining erection.

'Now you have seen her through Monsieur Creux's eyes,' she added, fingering him gently, 'therefore you have become aware of her beaty – as this indicates.'

'To be truthful,' he said, 'I have been in this condition since the moment I saw you. Without in any way detracting from Monique, my salutation is for you rather than for her.'

'I find that difficult to believe,' Mademoiselle Marchand retorted, her hand moving pleasurably up and down his stiff part, 'you have scarcely looked at me – your eyes have been entirely for Madame Chabrol.'

'As to that, I did not wish to embarrass you by staring directly at your loveliness.'

'How could you embarrass me? I make my living by posing nude for art classes and painters who can afford to pay me. It does not embarrass me in the least to have men stare at my body.'

Creux opened his trousers and mounted Monique, his distended part positioned to drive into her.

'But these artists and students see you perhaps as a subject for their work,' said Gérard, fascinated by the penetration of his cousin by Creux, 'they do not regard you with the eye of a lover?'

'As to lovers, I am not without experience of them.'

Gérard reached out a trembling hand to caress Mademoiselle Marchand's superb breasts and their delicious pink tips.

'Then you must recognise the desire in my glance,' he murmured, 'you must feel the fire in my touch.'

'There is something in what you say,' she replied calmly, 'if indeed this that I have in my hand is displaying its strength for me and not for Madame Chabrol.'

'It is, I assure you!'

'Then courtesy demands that I should respond. Lie on your back, Monsieur Brissard.'

He did so and in an instant she was kneeling astride him, one hand steering his boisterous part in the direction

72

he ardently wished it to go and the fingers of her other hand opening wide the soft entrance to her dearest sanctum.

'There,' she said as she impaled herself on his rigid projection, 'is that what you want?'

'Ah, chérie – that is most agreeable!'

'Really!' she said, a little offended, 'we have only recently been introduced, Monsieur Brissard. Endearments such as chérie are over-familiar and in poor taste.'

'I beg your pardon, Mademoiselle Marchand,' he gasped as her slithering up and down his shaft sent shivers of delight through him, 'I must mend my manners.'

'Most certainly you must, if we are to continue our conversation.'

'I would not have it interrupted for all the world, believe me.'

'Heavens!' she exclaimed, her attention distracted from his lapse of manners, 'Look at Monsieur Creux!'

Gérard turned his head on the rug and saw Creux's grey-trousered bottom thumping up and down like a great steam-engine piston. Beneath him Monique was uttering little squeals of pleasure and urging him on by thumping him with her heels.

'Such transports!' said Mademoiselle Marchand as she carried on bouncing gently up and down on Gérard, 'How exhilarating! Would you like me to do the same?'

'I would be most obliged,' he gasped, almost at the limit of his endurance.

At that she set to with a will, her breasts jerking up and down in the most luscious way to the rhythm of her movements.

'Oh!' she said in a tone of surprise.

'What is it?'

'I'm about to . . . no, it is too soon . . .'

From Gérard's right came the long-drawn 'Ah' of Monique attaining her climactic release under Creux's pounding. Mademoiselle Marchand's mouth opened wide in a silent echo of that cry and her hot loins thrust at Gérard in a sudden flurry of movement. Ecstasy coursed

73

through him as he fountained his appreciation into her wildly shaking body.

After a while they sat and talked normally again, the two men fully dressed, Monique with her shift down to conceal the contours of her voluptuous body, Mademoiselle Marchand stark naked and utterly composed. They drank more wine, they sampled the food – excellent slices of cold roast duck, crusty fresh bread and good Camembert cheese.

'Are the possibilities of Manet's picture becoming apparent to you?' Monique asked Gérard.

'I already see it in a new light.'

'Then it seems we are making progress. Do you suppose that Manet would have approved of the manner in which we interpreted his intentions just now?'

'I feel certain that he would have approved of an intention which has formed in my mind.'

'Which is?'

For answer he put his hand on Monique's bare thigh and slid it upwards to the hem which just concealed her most secret citadel – a citadel which had been stormed by Monsieur Creux only a quarter of an hour before. His finger-tips touched the fleece on her warm mound.

'Until this evening I had not appreciated the bounties of your body,' he told her, aware that Creux and Mademoiselle Marchand were listening and watching. A curious situation, yet he could do no more than trace to its end the pattern that had been set – the soft and moist lips under his fingers made any other course of action impossible. He moved closer to her to remove her chemise, but she prevented him.

'That is out of the scope of the original picture,' she said, 'Manet painted two men fully dressed, one woman naked and one in a chemise. It would be unthinkable to change his concept.'

Gérard pulled her down to lie facing him and put his hands up inside the loose chemise to play with her abundant breasts.

'Perhaps you should have chosen another picture as our model – one in which all the figures are without clothes.'

'Perhaps, but I like this one. There is a touch of perversity about it which gives a certain thrill.'

Between his fingers the tips of her breasts were very firm. His hand moved down to massage the satin-smooth skin of her belly for some considerable time before at last seeking the wet entrance between her legs.

'You are ready for me,' he whispered.

'I am ready more often than you or any other man will be,' she said, smiling at him.

'We shall see about that,' he anwered, his pride stung.

He rolled her onto her back and her legs parted wide as he got on top of her. She undid his trousers for him and in an instant he slid deep into her pliant opening with a single push.

'Slowly, dear Gérard,' she murmured, 'do not exhaust yourself too quickly in an attempt to demonstrate your virility. Mademoiselle Marchand's little gratification was proof enough of that. Delight us both, but conserve your strength, for we are only at the beginning of the possibilities of the masterpiece we are exploring together.'

He took her advice and probed in a stately motion which set up enravishing tremors of pleasure in her and him alike. He noted that Creux had set Mademoiselle Marchand on her hands and knees and was behind her, thrusting his taut stem into her with what appeared to be his customary vigour.

'No, no,' Monique sighed, 'slow down, Gérard, do not imitate him. He will be done for after that, but you must last a long time yet. Mademoiselle Marchand will want you again, and so shall I.'

Gérard slowed his pace, to the extreme delectation of his cousin. But when he observed Mademoiselle Marchand shaking in violent ecstasy as Monsieur Creux discharged into her, the sight was too much for him. Gérard cried out in joy as he delivered his copious compliment to Monique, while she sobbed and bit into the shoulder of his jacket.

It was as she said. Creux took no more interest in the proceedings after that. He settled comfortably on his

75

back, his eyes closed, and dozed off, the picture of respectability in his dark jacket neatly buttoned and his grey trousers. Gérard poured more wine for the two women and for himself and resumed the conversation on art.

'Now that you have opened my eyes to the possibilities of paintings,' he said, 'the scope seems boundless. There are thousands of famous paintings one could live through.'

'For example?' said Mademoiselle Marchand, self-composed and formal again after her energetic interlude with Creux.

'Well, a picture I have always liked very much is Boucher's portrait of Louise O'Murphy – that delicious fifteen-year-old girl face-down and naked on a chaise-longue to show off her pretty bottom for King Louis.'

'There is no man in the picture,' said Monique, 'and the rules of the game preclude any additional persons. If we stage that, the young lady would have to pleasure herself with her fingers. I can arrange that for you with an enchanting girl who poses for me sometimes.'

'No, that would be too frustrating, just to watch,' Gérard admitted, 'I know – Fragonard's woman on a swing! There is a man in that – lying on the grass to look up her petticoats as she swings up into the air.'

'That might be interesting,' said Mademoiselle Marchand, 'yet I wonder how one makes love on a swing? A way could be devised, I am sure.'

'Or Poussin's *Bacchanal*,' Gérard suggested, 'half a dozen men and women enjoying a naked romp round a statue of the god Pan. What do you think, Monique?'

'It has possibilities. Any others?'

'Do you know a woodland picture by Wateau which shows five or six women sitting under trees and a man of distinction strolling past to admire them?'

'You flatter yourself,' said Monique, 'five or six women! Two will be more than enough for you.'

'I am certain of it,' Mademoiselle Marchand agreed with a little sigh.

Her long fingers had worked their way into his trousers as they were talking and she teased his limp penis.

'Do you not find it significant that all the artists you have named are from the glorious heritage of the past?' Monique asked, 'not one dadaist, cubist, futurist or surrealist among them. Why is this?'

Mademoiselle Marchand's delicate stroking was having its intended effect on Gérard. His sleeping adjunct awoke, stirred itself and began to stretch.

'I cannot deny what you say,' he answered Monique, 'the images that came into my mind were all of pictures I have seen in the Louvre Museum and other galleries.'

The hand clasping his treasured possession was now sliding briskly up and down it, rousing wild emotions in him. His own hand found its way between Mademoiselle Marchand's naked thighs so that his fingers could feel for her tender bud of passion and caress it.

'Do you not agree that Mademoiselle Marchand has the perfect face and body for an artist's model?' Monique enquired, observing their amorous progress. 'Her features are the classical type one sees on ancient Greek statues. She has very well-shaped breasts, with nipples pointing forwards and upwards, not outwards as one sees on so many women – my own, for instance, point slightly outwards, though, thank God, not downwards! Her thighs and legs are marvellously proportioned and her bottom is exactly the right size to balance the swell of her breasts. Her skin is a joy to paint – it is so smooth and unblemished that it has a certain sheen when the light reflects from it. It is no wonder that she in in such demand.'

Mademoiselle Marchand had never in all her life been in greater demand than she was by Gérard at that very moment. He scrambled to his knees between her spread legs, his extension pulsating visibly as he aimed for his target. She brought her knees up to her breasts to aid his ingress and he paused, entranced by the vivid contrast between her widely-split pink notch and the serenity of her beautiful face. But the pause was only of an instant's duration – the image was one to savour in recollection later on, when his urgent passions had been slaked.

She gasped pleasurably as he struck home, rocking on her back to his fierce thrusting. Moment by moment as he plunged deeply within her, the composure of her face was annihilated, to be replaced by an expression of uncontrolled rapture. At the very last she was uttering little staccato screams of delight, which blended into a long wailing climax when Gérard's passion erupted into her.

'Your stamina is admirable, dear cousin,' Monique said when Gérard and Mademoiselle Marchand were lying side by side on the green rug, recovering their breath.

'Thank you,' he answered politely, 'I am impressed by your deep understanding of art, as demonstrated here this evening.'

'My understanding of art? Is that all.'

'By no means,' he said, sitting up, 'pour me another glass of wine and let us continue our discussion. There is much that I want to say to you, Monique.'

'Much? That is surely an exaggeration.'

'To you,' he said, raising the glass she handed him.

Like Monsieur Creux, Mademoiselle Marchand had dozed off, he on his back and snoring lightly, she curled up on her side with one arm under her head as a pillow.

'We are the survivors, you and I,' said Gérard, 'did you expect that?'

'I thought it possible. I am familiar with Monsieur Creux's capabilities. As for Mademoiselle Marchand, she has had a tiring day posing for a life-class and your most recent efforts evidently fatigued her unduly.'

'She participated with great enthusiasm that time.'

'And why not? You are a vigorous young man and you gave her good reason to participate fully.'

She is, as you said, a delightful creature,' Gérard said, eyeing the sleeping Mademoiselle Marchand's long thighs and supple bottom.

'Do you want her as your mistress? It can be arranged and she will not be too expensive for you. Her tastes are simple.'

78

'I am grateful for the offer, Monique, but the encumbrance of a regular mistress is not for me. What I would like is something quite different, but also within your power to arrange.'

'Tell me what it is you want.'

'The privilege of visiting you.'

'But you have that already,' she said, pretending not to understand him.

'Visits of love, not social visits.'

Monique was lying on her side facing him, propped on one elbow. She smiled enigmatically at his words and stroked one of her breasts thoughtfully through her chemise.

'A man as handsome and enterprising as you can find all the young girls he wants,' she said, 'I am fifteen years older than you. Outside the scope of our experiment in art-appreciation, why would you seek pleasure from me? Mademoiselle Marchand would be more suitable in every way.'

'She is adorable, of course, but I have made love to scores of women like her.'

'Then are you suggesting that there was something out of the ordinary about out little entracte a while ago?'

'How can I explain it except by telling you that it was an experience I would like to repeat.'

'You shall – as soon as you are able,' she answered.

Her hand moved down to her thigh and Gérard's dormant interest began to rise again as he watched her caress herself lightly.

'Let me do that for you,' he offered.

'Certainly,' and she raised one knee to permit his hand free access.

'You are handling my most precious *objet d'art*,' Monique murmured. 'One which gives me unfailing delight, day by day, sometimes many times each day. Yet to you it can seem nothing more than that which you find between any woman's legs, indistinguishable except for the shade of the hair from the scores you have fondled.'

Gérards fingers played delicately within the pink and

79

moist folds of flesh and over the rose-bud just beginning to flower into crimson passion.

'I understand your meaning well, Monique. To me also the fifteen centimetres of flesh between my legs is a marvellous object, the source of all pleasure and inspiration. Yet to a woman it must seem no more than another ordinary stiff thing to put inside her.'

'Perhaps you do understand,' Monique sighed, her plump belly heaving with exquisite emotion under his careful manipulation.

'We are discussing the difference between subjective and objective perception of the same data,' he said gravely.

'Is that what we're doing? To me it feels far more interesting than that.'

'Is is a very interesting topic for discussion for it leads to the question of whether subjective and objective perceptions can be reconciled satisfactorily.'

'Does it?' she panted. 'The Sorbonne is turning you into a philosopher, Gérard, but a most satisfactory one – Oh!'

Her breasts shuddered under her chemise and she pressed herself hard against his fingers as she reached the culmination of her desire and dissolved into quaking gratification.

'We understand the value of each other's prime possession,' he said, 'you can hardly refuse me the right to visit you from time to time to attempt a reconciliation of our assessments of each other.'

Monique rolled slowly over onto her back and pulled her chemise up above her breasts.

'We shall see about that later,' she whispered, 'for the present, why not put your jewel into my jewel-box so that we can compare sensations?'

'With the greatest of pleasure,' he said, climbing aboard her.

Gérard's second lesson in art-appreciation took place a few days later at three in the afternoon. This time he was given no instructions on how to dress and when Monique opened the door to him he noted that she was wearing a not very new peasant-style blouse with a draw-string neckline and a loose skirt of shiny black. She led him straight into her studio.

'This is Denise,' she said, gesturing towards the girl lying on an old red blanket on the studio floor, 'Denise, this is Gérard, a sort of cousin of mine.'

Denise was thirteen or fourteen years of age, Gérard judged. She was totally naked and her body was too thin, her breasts only just starting to grow and only the wispiest of floss showing between her thighs. She was on her side with one knee up to expose herself and beside her lay a battered and stringless Spanish guitar, evidently a prop.

'You are working?' Gérard asked after greeting Denise politely.

'Yes, would you care to inspect my work?' Monique replied.

On the easel was a large sheet of white paper on which she had been making a water-colour picture of the girl. With surprise Gérard saw that it was in the modern style – the body of Denise was distorted and her skin colour was depicted as pale green. The guitar, oddly misshapen, appeared in dark blue.

'Very good,' Gérard said, 'you really can do it when you try, Monique.'

'I find it excessively boring, but it is in a good cause.'

'What cause?'

'The furtherance of your education in art, of course. Denise, it is time for a rest. Join us for coffee.'

Monique's studio was one large room of her apartment. The side nearest the window was where she worked and the other side, in contrast, was furnished for her comfort when she gave herself and her model a break. A sofa and a pair of chairs were grouped round a small table on which a spirit lamp kept a large pot of coffee permanently hot.

Monique sat on the sofa and poured coffee. The girl, wrapped in a thin and almost shabby pink kimono which

81

was part of Monique's clutter of equipment, seated herself next to her. Gérard took one of the chairs and smiled at the young girl.

'Do you pose often for Madame Chabrol?' he asked.

'Yes, sometimes,' she said, almost shyly, glancing towards Monique for support.

'What is the picture you are working on to be called?' Gérard asked.

'If it were a sensible study,' said Monique, 'it would have a sensible title such as *Young girl with guitar*. But in this modern style it must have a title as absurd as the picture itself. Do you have any suggestions?'

'I will put my mind to the problem before I leave. It is a truism, of course, that the shape of a guitar echoes, in its double curves, the shape of a woman's body. But you have chosen so young a model that the truism does not apply. I wonder what was in your mind?'

'Perhaps you will find out. More coffee?'

'Thank you, no. Do you play the guitar, Denise?'

'No, it is only for the picture.'

'I shall teach you how to play,' said Monique, her dark eyes lighting up.

'Oh Madame – will you really?'

'Certainly. You shall have your first lesson now while Monsieur Gérard is here. He may be able to assist.'

'But it has no strings,' Gérard objected.

'No matter. There is much theory to be taught before we reach the practical part.'

What strange fancy had entered Monique's head? her cousin wondered. He had good reason to know that her imagination was both fertile and vivid.

'The first thing you must understand, Denise,' she said, 'is the importance of delicacy of touch. To obtain the best results you must treat the instrument as the living creature it is and handle it with love and respect.'

'Yes, Madame,' the girl said dutifully.

'There is only one certain way in which to impress this upon you. I shall demonstrate it, using you as my guitar.'

'But how can you do that, Madame?'

'You will see. Lie across my lap on your back,' and Monique spread her legs under her loose skirt to provide a broad base for the girl.

'Like this?' Denise asked, taking up the position suggested, the pink kimono held tightly around her.'

'Exactly. Now, I support your head with my left hand, as I would hold the neck of the guitar. Do you follow me so far?'

'Yes, Madame.'

'Good. Put your arms straight down by your sides – guitars do not have arms. That's it.'

Gérard watched in fascination as Monique parted the untied kimono to reveal Denise's flat little belly and over-prominent hip-bones.

'With my other hand I play across the strings,' said Monique, trailing her finger-tips across the girl's belly. 'Do you feel how very delicately I play?'

'Oh, yes!'

'Later on, as the music progresses, my touch will become firmer and eventually, at the very end of the piece, we shall reach a crescendo. But for now the fingering is extremely gentle.'

Her hand was sweeping lightly across the tops of the girl's thighs in a butterfly caress.

'Musicians call this mode of playing *pianissimo*,' she continued, smiling at Gérard over the exposed body of the girl in a manner that could only be described as conspiratorial, 'is that not so, Gérard?'

'I believe that is so,' he replied, keeping his voice calm even though his male part was at full stretch inside his clothes.

'It is an Italian word which means *very, very softly*,' said Monique, 'you must remember that, Denise.'

Her fingers had strayed to the small mound between the girl's legs and were stroking the tender lips under their thin covering of light-brown fluff.

'Oh, Madame,' Denise gasped, 'what is this music called?'

'It is a piece by a modern French composer,' Monique

answered with a faintly malicious smile, 'its title is *Pavane for a dead Princess.*'

'Maurice Ravel,' said Gérard, his mind still functioning in spite of the strong emotions aroused in him by the scene he was witnessing, for Monique was stroking lightly upwards along the soft lips of Denise's small inlet, to part them.

'She must have been beautiful, this princess, to have such music,' Denise murmured, her thin thighs trembling.

'The music becomes a little stronger now,' said Monique, her finger-tips fluttering within the girl, 'do you feel the change?'

'Yes! Oh, Madame!'

What emotions were coursing through Gérard at that moment as he observed the proceedings in growing discomfort of body and agitation of mind! Denise was three or four years too young and undeveloped to be sexually attactive to him, but to see her used in this way by Monique as an object of sexuality was unbelievably arousing in its perversity. Especially now that Monique's strumming of her living instrument was eliciting moans of pleasure like chords of music! Denise was squirming on her player's lap, her thin legs shaking wildly, the pink slit between her thighs open and wet – and Monique was staring defiantly at Gérard, daring him to relieve his passion by forcing his way into that tender aperture.

'No!' he gasped, his face flushed red with emotion, 'she is too young.'

'So much the worse for you,' said Monique, 'you must endure your suffering then until I am prepared to assist you.'

Denise squealed in rapture and collapsed limply across Monique's lap.

'Good,' said Monique, 'you have learned your first lesson well, Denise. Sit on the sofa now and rest for a little while.'

The expression in her eyes as she stared at Gérard was unfathomable.

'A few days ago I gave you a lesson in art-appreciation,'

she said, 'today I am giving music lessons, it seems, and it is time to move on from the beginners to the more advanced players. Are you as much interested in music as in painting and literature, Gérard?'

'My interest is intense,' he assured her and she chuckled.

'I have no doubt of that,' she commented and rose from her place on the sofa to seat herself cross-legged between his widely-parted feet on the rug.

'A guitar lesson?' she suggested, reaching for his trouser buttons, 'I think not.'

'My own strong preference is for a duet,' he said as she brought his hard-straining part into the light of day.

'That may be, but I am the teacher here and it is for you to obey me unless you wish to discontinue the lesson. How proudly it stands, Gérard! Tell me what has put you in this condition – surely not the sight of the girl's body?'

'Not her but what you did to her,' he answered, watching her fingers glide lightly up and down his pride.

'Naturally. Perhaps if we become very close friends I may allow you to observe me do it to myself. Would that interest you?'

'Dear Monique – what is of supreme interest to me at present is to make love to you, as we did the other evening.

'Is that so? But have you never strayed from the beaten path to explore any of the amusing byways of love? You boasted to me not so very long ago that you had dared many extraordinary feats.'

'I must confess that they were all adventures along what you are pleased to call the beaten path,' he murmured as she continued to manipulate him most pleasantly.

'How strange – and you a devoted follower of the bizarre imaginings of the surrealists! You seemed to me to be very comfortable in the nineteenth century setting of Manet's picnic, which is surprising, in view of your artistic beliefs. Admit it, at heart you are a traditionalist.'

'But that is entirely another matter,' he objected, 'you are confusing art with the pleasure of love.'

'You find them easy to separate and distinguish, then?'

With her free hand Monique plucked at the bow holding the draw-string of her peasant blouse, then pulled the blouse itself right off her shoulders and down below her full and dark-nippled breasts.

'Ah,' Gérard exclaimed in appreciation, but she was just too far away for him to touch them.

Monique turned her head to speak to the girl curled up on the sofa watching the proceedings.

'Denise, bring me the guitar.'

Obediently Denise fetched it from the other side of the studio and stood by the side of Monique. She had not bothered to tie the belt of her borrowed pink kimono and the delicious little mound between her thighs was clearly visible to Gérard. For her part, Denise stared unashamedly at his upright and twitching device in Monique's hand.

'This is your second lesson, Denise,' said Monique, 'watch closely and you will learn the action of a man's musical instrument.'

'Yes, Madame,' the girl answered.

Monique's fingers played crescendo until Gérard's body started to tremble in incipient deliverance. At once she seized the stringless old Spanish guitar from Denise and pushed it between his thighs so that his leaping part entered the round hole in the instrument's belly, into which he poured his sudden passionate outburst.

'You understand now the purpose of the male instrument?' Monique enquired of Denise.

Gérard stared down in amazement at the guitar between his legs – this fragile wooden instrument which had received his offering.

'What is the name of the music this time?' Denise asked with a knowing smile.

'It is another very modern piece – by Schoenberg, I think, though I am not an expert in these matters,' Monique answered with a broad smile, 'it is called *Sonata for flute and guitar*.'

DR FAGUET AMUSES HIMSELF

According to Jean-Albert Faguet it was during his service as a surgeon in an Army hospital during the War that he made a great decision about his future. On his return to Paris he put this decision into effect and became a happy and fulfilled man – in addition to being a fairly wealthy one. Not all of his friends believed this story, partly because he told it in a frivolous manner and partly because he was a frivolous person. Or if not entirely frivolous, he was at least a constant pleasure-seeker and his most important interests were known to be women and the theatre.

These interests he succeeded in combining very cleverly with his profession by specialising in the intimate problems of women and making himself well-known to female members of the theatrical world. In less than ten years from the end of the War he was recognised as an outstanding and sympathetic practitioner. His patients were not merely the wives of well-to-do men but, by deliberate choice on his part, a great many actresses, singers, dancers and show-girls. Some of these entertainers were considerably better-off than their salaries suggested and some of them only pretended to be so. Nevertheless, they were all content to pay Jean-Albert's higher than average fees, such was the confidence he inspired.

It is not hard to discern the reasons for this. The greatest asset of any young woman, it goes without saying, is her appearance. If a kindly Providence – and her parents – have endowed her with a beautiful face and an elegant body, then the gift is one of inestimable worth in a world where men, to an unneccessary extent, are in possession of wealth and influence. Why this unequal state of affairs exists, and whether it should continue to exist in the twentieth century, is a question for philosphers and theologians to answer, but as a fact it is undeniable.

Clever women may deplore it and argue against it, but until the world changes, beautiful young women have an obvious advantage over their plain sisters.

That there are successful actresses of no great beauty is true enough, as anyone who has observed Madeleine Lambert or Edmée Favart on the stage will acknowledge. Even so, the vast majority of young women seeking an independent career as entertainers are provocatively pretty.

To any woman, the most important part of her body – the part to which men are drawn as a compass needle is to the North – is the intimate area between her thighs. All the rest – hair, face, bosom, legs – are signposts, as it were, to steer men, or at least one chosen man, in the direction of the eventual goal. Needless to say, the importance of this area to a stage entertainer cannot be stated too highly, for it is an essential part of her success, if she is to achieve any success in her career.

To cast no aspersions on the many talented women who at present grace the stages of the places of entertainment and drama, one may take as example a name from the classical French theatre of a century ago – the illustrious Rachel herself! As all the world knows, she found her way onto the boards of the Théâtre Français before she was twenty years old only because she had attracted the interest and aroused the passions of Louis Véron, a man more than twice her own age. From him she progressed to the even older and very much richer Baron Hartmann. While it may be said that Véron admired Rachel's acting talents equally with her slender body, the interests of the Baron lay entirely in the secret shrine of passion between her legs and, for the sake of that, he backed her acting career with his money.

Jean-Albert Faguet, doctor of medicine and specialist in the intimate problems of women, numbered among his patients a great many of the pretty young women who may be seen on stage at the Casino de Paris, the Folies Bergère – and even such establishments as the Théâtre Daunou and the Théâtre de la Madeleine, where the performers keep all their clothes on and declaim lines of dialogue written by a dramatist!

Nothing has changed in a hundred years, except perhaps that France has become a Republic instead of an Empire. And from the example of Madame Rachel it may readily be understood that the most intimate parts of actresses and entertainers require constant supervision. The young women who consulted Jean-Albert made very frequent use of their most precious asset in the furtherance of their careers and, at times, a little carelessness could produce unfortunate results. Jean-Albert was known to be highly expert in correcting such undesirable errors.

A favourite patient was the well-known entertainer Mademoiselle Renée Lelouche, at that time enjoying her most successful season ever at the Casino de Paris, where her sultry Mediterranean charm and her appealingly husky voice had won instant acclaim. She paid little heed to the dictates of high fashion – her raven-black hair was full and long, she made no attempt to disguise the fullness of her breasts – indeed, on stage she revealed quite three-quarters of their rotund charm by the extensive décolletage of the gowns she wore.

Apart from her beauty, which all the world admired, what Jean-Albert found particularly entrancing about her was her secret tattoo – a most inappropriate decoration for a woman! On the inside of her shapely left thigh, high up where the public never saw it, there was tattooed in red and blue against her creamy skin a butterfly with exquisitely spread wings! The first time he saw it, when Mademoiselle Renée bared herself for his examination, Jean-Albert was astounded and entranced. When he knew her well enough to enquire about it, she explained with her famous throaty chuckle – for by then she trusted him completely – that her career as an entertainer had commenced not upon the stage but in an establishment of a certain type in Marseilles, she being fifteen years of age when she made her debut. The majority of the establishment's clients were sailors, and since tattooing is popular among men of that calling, she had swiftly come to accept it as a normal form of personal decoration. It seemed to her the most natural thing in the world to visit the tattoo artist who had his studio next door one day after she had enjoyed a bottle or two of wine.

'It is beautifully done,' said Jean-Albert. 'The man was a true artist. How much did you have to pay?'

'Don't be a fool,' Renée said, 'I didn't pay money for it.'

'Of course. But tell me, now that your lovers are no longer sailors but men of wealth and style, how do they respond when they catch their first glimpse of this delicate little fantasy on your thigh?'

'The same way you did – it fascinates them. Men are all the same, even you.'

During this conversation she was lying on Jean-Albert's examination couch without her frock and shoes, wearing only silk stockings and a thin slip of hyacinth-blue – and that pulled up round her waist to expose for his attention the dark-haired little mound on which her career had been founded.

'There is much in what you say,' Jean-Albert admitted, his sensitive fingers slowly caressing the little butterfly.

'It's the plain truth,' she asserted, 'I've known them all, from sailors to Cabinet ministers, and there's only one thing on a man's mind most of the time.'

'You exaggerate a little,' Jean-Albert protested with a smile.

'Is that so? Well then, tell me what you're doing at the moment – examining me or feeling me?'

Jean-Albert smiled more broadly and brought his mind back to his work.

'Examining you, of course. I was checking to see how the tattooing process had changed the texture of the skin, that's all.'

'Really? Listen, doctor, I don't mind if you do both. That way I won't have to pay you any money.'

'I appreciate your generous offer – believe me I do – but I have an inflexible rule which prevents me from accepting

90

the favours of my patients in return for my professional services. Even, alas, a patient as alluring as you.'

'What a pity,' Renée said with regret. 'But surely you allow a discount for cash?'

'For you, naturally.'

'Good – to work then, dear doctor,' she said, satisfied that she had obtained at least some financial benefit from him.

Jean-Albert examined her tender shrine with loving care and was able to reassure her that her fears of pregnancy were unfounded and that he could prescribe for her irregularities. He wondered briefly, while his fingers were within that cherished entrance, which minister of the Government was indulging his delight with Mademoiselle Renée – and what it was costing him, in money or in favours, or both.

A patient of a different sort was Madame Marie-Paule Boyer, a talented actress of about thirty, who had aspired to the heights of playing in real drama at such theatres as the Boulevard Repertory and the Châtelet. Not for her the sequins and daring costumes of Renée Lelouche; Marie-Paule's appeal to her audience was not based on the allure of her body. Nevertheless, she had looked after that body well and had been married and divorced twice in ten years, on both occasions to actors.

Jean-Albert found it pleasing to examine her – from a strictly medical standpoint, of course. He adored her extravagant personality, though he was secretly wary of her high opinion of herself as an actress. He did not find in her the frankness which delighted him in Mademoiselle Renée, for instance. The truth was that Marie-Paule had convinced herself that her skills on the stage were the sole reason for her success. She had conveniently forgotten that the role which had launched her career before she was twenty had been offered to her by a theatrical producer whose interest had been aroused by the charm of her lustrous brown eyes and her neatly rounded bottom. This particular man was notorious, even in theatrical circles, for his rate of consumption of aspiring young actresses, yet Marie-Paule had been able to retain his interest for several months and had emerged at last from his embraces as a rising stage star.

Her clothes were always high fashion – she had arrived on one occasion in a frock of moss-green with thirty-five buttons down the back, from the collar to a point between the cheeks of her bottom – that foundation of her success! Jean-Albert employed no female attendant to be present during his examinations and this, though unethical, was part of the reason why he inspired confidence in his patients – for there was no second pair of ears present to listen to potentially embarrassing secrets. He assisted Marie-Paule out of her frock with the ease of long practice, discovering in the process that only the top twelve buttons could be opened and the rest were decoration.

'Why have you come to see me?' he asked when she was stretched out before him, her ivory silk and lace cami-knickers unfastened from between her legs and pulled up round her waist, 'some particular reason – or merely a routine check?'

Marie-Paule kept herself in trim. Her breasts had the firmness that daily applications of cold water produced, her belly was flat enough to be chic and just round enough to be desirable. The little fur coat between her legs was rich brown in colour and neatly trimmed.

'I propose to marry again,' she announced grandly, 'perhaps you have heard?'

'No, I assure you. I have seen nothing in the newspapers yet. But my congratulations! Who is the man to be honoured so greatly?'

'Then it is still a secret! There are certain difficulties, you understand. His process of divorce is not yet final – I cannot name him for that reason.'

'I understand. He is someone of importance.'

'Naturally,' Marie-Paule said, amazed that so obvious a statement was necessary.

Jean-Albert made a mental note to ask his many friends in the theatrical world who Marie-Paule had been sleeping with recently. Someone would know – there were no secrets at all behind the scenes.

'Then if you will raise your pretty legs, I will check that all is well for the delights of married life,' he said. 'Good – but wider apart, if you please. I am sure you are familiar with the position.'

'I doubt if that remark is in good taste,' Marie-Paule said, but she smiled as she complied with his request. 'Let me take you into my confidence a little. My fiancé has no connection with the theatre. I wish to give him children – is there any reason why I should not?'

'None that I know of. Has he children by his first wife?'

'No, it seems that she is infertile.'

'That is very sad,' said Jean-Albert, palpating her smooth belly thoughtfully.

'And I – am I infertile?' she asked.

'As to that, there is only one way to find out,' said Jean-Albert, 'and you need no intruction from me in that, I am sure.'

She chose to ignore his remark and asked if he had seen her in her latest role at the Théâtre Antoine.

'I was there for your first night,' he replied, 'you were superb!'

She took praise as her natural right and Jean-Albert knew that he could keep her soothed with flattery for as long as he chose.

'The clothes you wore were enchanting,' he continued, 'most particularly the tango frock in the last Act.'

'I selected that myself,' she informed him. 'The director wanted me to wear something absolutely unsuitable – I put my foot down very firmly, I can assure you. I simply refused to wear it.'

'Naturally,' said Jean-Albert, folding back the petals of her secret rose with tender care, 'he must have been a fool to argue with you.'

'Ah, you understand me so well,' she said approvingly.

Another of Jean-Albert's patients with somewhat elevated pretensions was Mademoiselle Blanche Pasigny, a tall and slender woman who pretended to be twenty-eight

93

but who was five years older. She appeared with reasonable frequency on the stages of the better-known theatres, as did Madame Boyer, though in less important roles. Her face and nose were a trifle longer than was generally thought beautiful but she was undeniably charming, if at the same time a little eccentric.

Whenever she found occasion to visit Jean-Albert, she invariably stripped herself completely naked except for her stockings and shoes. Jean-Albert had no objections, though it was by no means necessary. Mademoiselle Blanche had a secret which she revealed only to her lovers and to her doctor. A secret which Jean-Albert respected – and more than that, which he cherished. When she disrobed her secret was revealed – the pink tips of her pretty breasts had been pierced and thin gold rings inserted! Gold loops as wide across as the first joint of Jean-Albert's thumb, for he used that as a unit of measurement.

'Was it a doctor who did that for you?' he asked, the first time he was privileged to see this truly astonishing mode of adornment.

'Naturally,' said Blanche, glancing down at her ornaments.

She was standing in only her silk stockings by the side of his couch and the movement of her body caused the gold loops to sway.

'But – if I may ask – why?'

'You don't like them?'

'As for that, I find them enchanting. But the idea is an unusual one, even among people of the theatre.'

'Have you never seen a woman with gold rings in her breasts before?'

'Never, I must confess. I have a patient who is of the Indian nobility and she has a diamond set in one side of her nose – it would seem that her husband the Rajah likes it. But jewellery for the breasts!'

'Then you know something now you didn't before.'

'I am grateful to you for that. But do they not cause you discomfort?'

'Not the least. Naturally, it was painful when they were pierced, but that wore off in a few days.'

'But – how shall I put it to make myself clear – when you are with a lover and become aroused, so that those little buds become firm – is there no discomfort then?'

'The sensation is very pleasant – not precisely pain, not even discomfort, but a certain tingling which makes me even more aroused.'

'You surprise me.'

'I see that you do not believe me,' said Blanche amiably, 'then see for yourself.'

She took his hand and put his palm against her left breast – a delicious handful of smooth-skinned flesh. Jean-Albert instantly forgot his medical ethics without the least qualm as he took up her offer to see for himself. He used both hands to delight his senses by the feel of her pliant breasts until, before long, her rose-bud tips were pointing proudly outwards and the gold rings hung clear of her skin.

'Evidently there is no discomfort,' said Jean-Albert in delight.

'On the contrary, I assure you,' Blanche replied, her dark eyes half-closed.

He continued his gentle massage, the reason for her presence forgotten.

'Now what am I to do,' Blanche sighed, 'once I am aroused like this the rings make it impossible for me to stop. I was a fool to let you touch me there. An application of cold water is the only way to calm them down.'

'There is another way,' said Jean-Albert, who had thoroughly aroused himself by caressing her oddly-adorned breasts.

'What do you mean?' she asked with a touch of slyness.

'Cold water on such enchanting breasts is cruel – a denial of their natural rights and a frustration of their ordained pleasure. The better and kinder way is to continue with what we have commenced, you and I, to the culmination of the desire which fills us both.'

'But you – a doctor – can suggest this to me?' she

95

sighed, moving her body so that her breasts rubbed against his hands.

'Chérie – I am a man and you are a beautiful woman. What more is there to be said?'

'I always believed that the medical profession were able to preserve a distance between themselves and their women patients,' said Blanche, her finger-tips stroking Jean-Albert's face.

'Do not be deceived – being a doctor is how I make my living, not how I live my life.'

'I cannot resist you,' she sighed and draped her naked body across his examination couch, her legs widely parted.

Jean-Albert stood beside her, his hands roaming freely over her body from her slender neck to her dimpled knees, his emotions aflame. The smoothness of her belly and the satin skin of her thighs caused his senses to whirl and it was the hand of a lover, not that of a doctor, which touched her dark-fleeced mount of Venus. He perceived that she had told him no more than the truth about the effect of the gold rings – the entrance to her tender alcove was open and ready to receive him. He shed his jacket quickly and lowered himself onto her as she lay on the narrow examination couch, his virile part at full stretch. He tugged at his trouser buttons and felt them give – then without any guidance from his hand or assistance from Blanche his trembling stem of flesh found its way to the portal it sought and, with one easy push, he lodged it fully in her moist warmth.

'That's so good,' Blanche murmured. 'Ah, chéri, if you knew how good that feels!'

This was not, by any means, the first time that Jean-Albert had made love to a patient on his couch. Some of the younger women who came to consult him were so disarmingly enticing that he was unable to prevent himself from bringing into play all his considerable charm to persuade them to share this great pleasure with him. Usually this happened with show-girls, whose youthful grace of face and form was, it must be confessed, their only talent for the stage. The process of persuasion was rarely difficult, as these young women generally had the same casual attitude towards love-making as Jean-Albert himself. Besides, from their point of view it made good sense to cultivate his friendship – after all, who could tell what misfortune might arise to threaten a budding career – and who better than Jean-Albert to deal with such annoyances expertly and in confidence?

When a woman proved to be exceptionally pleasing on the couch, Jean-Albert continued the liaison in more regular surroundings – suppers in good restaurants after their performance, dancing at interesting and fashionable night-clubs, scenes of delicate passion in his apartment. These intimate liaisons never lasted more than a few weeks, neither party being deeply involved, but they afforded pleasure and entertainment of a high level at the time and frequently led to lasting friendships of a semi-platonic type.

In due course many of these beautiful showgirls formed more permanent relationships with men of wealth and status after a year or two on the boards. Occasionally one even managed to marry well, usually to a rich foreigner – South American millionaires were popular for this purpose. Jean-Albert experienced feelings of pride – an almost proprietorial pride – in these circumstances. When the beautiful Madame Santa Cruz came to consult him, for example – he had first made her acquaintance as Mademoiselle Josette Leduc, an elegant twenty-year-old dancer at the Folies Bergère. He and she had been lovers for a whole month, a time he recalled with extreme delight. She had succeeded in marrying one of her stage-door admirers, an amazingly rich though not particularly intelligent foreign land-owner. Naturally he preferred the civilised life of Paris to the simplicity of his ancestral hacienda and peasants.

That all of Jean-Albert's tender encounters were enjoyable, it goes without saying, though some were perhaps less so than others. A few of his non-theatrical patients, women who had passed their fortieth birthday – passed,

97

not celebrated – a few of these pressed their favours upon him as soon as they had bared their intimate parts for his professional inspection. He was, it has to be said, a man of distinguished appearance and wide-spread reputation. It may be that the husbands or lovers of these unhappy ladies were remiss in their attentions. Whatever the reason, the touch of Jean-Albert's hands on their inner thighs, as he prepared to examine their secret shrine, brought long sighs of tremulous anticipation and murmured invitations to set aside the Hippocratic conventions for the time being, to make at that warm shrine the offering which the promptings of passion readily suggest.

These were women of elegance and influence. Age notwithstanding, Jean-Albert obliged them cheerfully. To make love was to make love. A simple closing of the eyes took away the need to contemplate little lines about the eyes or mouth, incipient wrinkles on the neck or thinning hair. To his burrowing part the sensation was the same, whether the receptacle which contained it snugly was twenty years old or forty-five years old. The pleasure was the same and, since ladies like this never queried the specially high fees he charged them, it could with truth be said that to make money in this way was better than working for a living.

The moment that Jean-Albert had inserted himself fully into Blanche Pasigny's delicious little pocket, he knew that she was worth cultivating further. Her legs were crossed over his back and her dark-brown eyes were half-closed as he slid in and out at a measured pace. Her soft breasts were flattened under his chest and he could feel, even through his shirt, the pressure of the gold rings against him. How would it feel if he were naked, like her, he wondered – would they be cold on his skin at first or did her own body heat affect them? How strange a fancy for a pretty woman to have her nipples pierced with loops as if they were her little ear-lobes! He must find out why she had done it.

Such speculations were no more than fleeting and exciting images in his mind, suffused as it was at that time

98

with sensuous pleasure – nothing more than tiny irrides-
cent bubbles in a mounting wave of passion. He thrust
more urgently at Blanche, feeling her grow hotter beneath
him as she sighed continuously and dug her fingers into
the tight cheeks of his bottom. The tidal wave of emotion
reared itself up to a vast height, hung trembling for the
interval between two heart-beats, then broke and crashed
over in a fury of white spray.

'Yes!' Blanche shrieked as her back arched off the
couch.

'Yes!' Jean-Albert gasped as he delivered his ecstatic
tribute.

That night he took her to supper and dancing at the
Acacias and afterwards, in the comfort and privacy of his
own bedroom, made some interesting discoveries about
her gold loops. Blanche had a way of trailing then down a
man's bare belly that was remarkably exciting. When he
had suitably rewarded her for that by sending her into
squirming ecstasy, she reawakened his passion by dangling her pretty breasts over his limp part and shaking them
in such a way that the gold loops beat gently against it and
roused it from its lethargy to such effect that his essence
gushed tumultuously over her breasts and made her laugh.
Thus was initiated a friendship which endured for a very
long time, even after they both had moved on to other
lovers.

In the natural order of things – for who can ever say
with complete sincerity that life has given everything the
heart desires – not every desirable young woman who
sought Jean-Albert's professional advice was susceptible
to his virile charm, however much he might desire her.
There was Mademoiselle Christiane Cartier, for example
– oh the names theatrical people give themselves! There is
a quality of hallucination about the theatre that trans-
forms a girl born in a back-street and baptised plain
Jeanne or Marie by her parents into a creature of glamour
and excitement with a name to match! Mademoiselle
Christiane was in her third season at the Folies Bergère,
though, it must be admitted, only in the chorus line as yet.

She was a tall, exquisitely formed creature, still only nineteen. Her hair was by nature a very light brown and she had improved upon this by becoming blonde. In order to maintain this pleasing illusion, the neat little fur coat between her legs was bleached to the same shade. Stretched out for examination, her long dancer's legs up and apart, she was one of the most desirable sights Jean-Albert had ever enjoyed in his years of viewing beautiful women. He never failed to express his admiration, in words of total honesty, for he thought this no more than her righful due.

But, even as he spread her blonde-flossed and delicate pink petals to commence his internal inspection, he knew with great sadness that only his fingers would ever enter Christiane's endearing little pouch of love. No man had ever been privileged to worship there. The truth was that Christiane had no liking at all for men in that respect – she sought and found her delight in the arms of other women.

A tragic waste, that was Jean-Albert's secret opinion, but naturally he kept it to himself.

'Who is your friend now?' he enquired casually as he paused to admire for a moment the enchanting pink shade of her interior, 'When I saw you last it was a night-club singer from Lyon.'

Christiane shrugged as prettily as she could, lying on her back.

'She's with someone else now. I cannot tell you the name of my present friend – it would to too indiscreet.'

'Ah, little mysteries,' said Jean-Albert, 'well, at least tell me whether she is a singer or a dancer, then I can have the pleasure of guessing.'

'Neither.'

'An actress, perhaps?'

It is difficult for a woman to refuse anything to a man who has two fingers inside her secret place, even if he is not a lover but a doctor – especially if the fingers were those of Jean-Albert, who behaved like a lover and a doctor at the same time.

'It is a great secret,' said Christiane, 'but I will tell you this – she is the wife of a very important person.'

'Important in the theatre?'

'What else?'

'A director or an impressario?'

'I'm not going to say any more.'

'There is no need. I am pleased for you, Christiane. I can already see you as the star of your own show before long, with a connection like that. But please assure me that she is kind to you, your new friend.'

'She adores me.'

'Naturally. But is she kind to you?'

'Kind and tender. When we are together she covers my body with little kisses, right down to my toes. Before she touches me, she looks at me with pleading eyes for permission. And afterwards, when she has done everything she wants to me, she asks me in a soft little voice whether she has really pleased me. Ah, you cannot imagine how marvellous it is to be with her.'

'That's good to hear. Your last friend treated you roughly – you came here once to seek my assistance for an unpleasant bite-mark on this little blonde treasure of yours.'

'Don't remind me! It was sore for a week. I had to go without underwear.'

'It was an act of cruelty, to bite you so fiercely.'

'Ah, yes,' Christiane murmured, 'but at the time, it was incredibly exciting!'

Jean-Albert laughed at that.

'Put your clothes on,' he said, 'everything is in good order. I do not understand why you came to see me.'

Christiane sat up on the coach and crossed her long legs, her flat belly and slender thighs still on view to him – and her little blonde tuft.

'For advice,' she said, 'I have heard that a woman can become pregnant if she makes love with another woman who has been with her husband. This worried me. Is it really possible?'

101

'I have read this myself in medical journals,' said Jean-Albert, 'but I have never encountered such a case.'

'But surely there are well-known instances of women conceiving without the direct aid of a man – everyone knows that.'

'Then everyone does not include me. It is true that over the years I have examined more than one young woman – usually very young – who has insisted that she has not been with a man, even though she was obviously pregnant.'

'There you are then!'

'But the tearful insistence was really for the benefit of the angry mother who brought her here. Not one of these sad young girls was a virgin, I assure you.'

'Then you are saying that there is no risk?'

'Only the Church knows of examples of virgins becoming pregnant. For the rest of the world, including you, it is necessary for a man to insinuate his penis between your thighs, if not actually inside you.'

'There is no danger of that,' Christiane said firmly.

'Then enjoy yourself with your new friend. Accept her kisses and her . . . whatever else she bestows on you. I shall follow your career with interest. I saw your performance at the Folies only a month ago and thought that you were marvellous. Ah, those beautiful long legs of yours, those slender thighs! You stood out from the other dancers like a rose in a cabbage patch. I fell in love with you all over again and, if you had the least interest in men, I would be at the stage-door waiting to take you out every night.'

Mademoiselle Christiane leaned forward to kiss him on the cheek.

'You pay the nicest compliment,' she said, 'if ever I wanted a male lover, you would be the first.'

Mademoiselle Nadine Vallette, a ballerina of some distinction and public acclaim, was a performer in a more elevated category of art with whom Jean-Albert enjoyed a brief, though memorable liaison. She was a lean and dark-haired woman with enormous lustrous eyes. It must

102

be said that, perfect as was her face, she had hardly any bosom worthy of the name and her hips were as narrow as those of an adolescent boy. In her favour, however, was the indisputable fact that she adored making love and she had beautiful thighs, their sinewy development speaking eloquently of her years of training from childhood on. If that were not enough to endear her to a man, her entire body was so supple that Jean-Albert was able to devise extraordinary ways of making love to her.

Nadine could, for example, stand with her legs apart and bend forward to put her hands flat on the floor – all this without the least inconvenience! In this stance, totally naked, she presented from the rear to a discerning lover the taut cheeks of her bottom and, set between her long and strong legs, a tender fruit about the size of a large peach, ripe for splitting.

Jean-Albert found great interest in approaching her closely from behind when she assumed this posture for him, to steep his stiff appendage in the sweet juice of her fruit and enjoy the pulpy feel of its warm flesh enclosing him. Nadine, steady as a rock, withstood all the amorous pounding which his male part subjected her to – more than that, she found it most gratifying. She took the view that any woman could lie on her back for a lover but only she, Nadine, could offer herself to love's pleasure in this unusual way. From the standpoint of Jean-Albert, she was somewhat less than a real person in this position, for her head was down between her knees and all that she presented to him was the essential channel of love. He accepted that quite cheerfully, Nadine being not entirely his ideal of a woman, for reasons which became more and more obvious during the course of their affaire.

Apart from the the delights of this acrobatic trick of hers, Nadine was very willing to follow all Jean-Albert's suggestions. The truth was that she found interesting the variety he introduced into their encounters, being herself too unimaginative to have until then explored the astonishing possibilities of her own lithe body.

She was also able, Jean-Albert ascertained when they

had known each other for some time, to cross her legs behind her head! On the first occasion she demonstrated, in a state of total nudity, this rare feat to him, Jean-Albert was astounded – and fascinated – as who would not be? While she was locked in this bizarre position he picked her up from the bed and carried her to an armchair, there to balance her upright on the cushion. The exertion caused a charming crease across her flat and muscular belly and, below that, she gave the impression of being totally open to him – as indeed she was! Her great shining eyes stared at him in urgent invitation as he stood imprinting on his memory the unique spectacle before him.

'Jean-Albert – do not keep me waiting,' she whispered.

He was already as naked as she was, one tender passage between them having taken place earlier that evening. He knelt before her chair almost in reverence, took her high-arched feet in his hands and penetrated her secret recess with a skilful push. Nadine put her hands on his shoulders – she could reach no further round her upright thighs – and closed her eyes in anticipation. The subtle pressures on her nervous system brought about by her posture seemed to accelerate her sensual feelings remarkably – she shrieked out twice in delicious crisis before Jean-Albert attained his rapturous release.

The problem with Nadine, from Jean-Albert's point of view, was not that she had no imagination – he himself had enough of that for them both, as he demonstrated during their liaison. It was rather that she was completely without humour. To another man this might not have been of the slightest importance when weighed against the satisfying pleasures her body afforded. But there was an element of frivolity in Jean-Albert's character that predisposed him towards laughter, even in the most serious moments of love. He alone understood the slightly ridiculous nature of their love-making in the extraordinary positions Nadine's suppleness permitted. He alone appreciated the comic grotesquerie of it. Poor Nadine was far too intense to be aware of the piquancy of the ludicrous. She could not share the joke with him. Inevitably,

104

Jean-Albert began to experience a slight boredom after some weeks, when the novelty of what they could do together wore off.

In consequence he was more than pleased – he was also relieved, the day she confessed to him in her very earnest way that she had met another man and had fallen in love with him. As befitted the occasion, Jean-Albert played the comedy through to its end with all the correct emotions. He told her of his undying devotion to her, of the true joy she had brought into his life, of the memories of her he would treasure until his dying day. He assured her that he would not reproach her, for love strikes like a thunderbolt and no one can say where it will strike next. He said with great nobility that it was her happiness that must come first. Nadine took all this nonsense at face value – she was, after all, without either imagination or humour – and they parted the best of friends.

If, in some impossible tribunal, Jean-Albert had been questioned on solemn oath and required to name the person for whom he had done most in his professional capacity, he would have answered '*Madame Pascal*' – and this without any serious pause for reflection.

Charlotte Pascal had been long retired from the stage when she consulted Jean-Albert. He was recommended to her by friends who knew of his connections with the theatre and his sympathetic handling of the annoying little problems which can complicate matters for entertainers. Fifteen years or more had passed since she last performed in public, but her legend endured and Jean-Albert was honoured when she arrived for her appointment with him. What he knew of her was no more than all the world knew, that she had been born in the Dordogne, the seventh or eighth child of miserably poor parents. At fifteen she had run away from home to seek her fortune – or so her publicity said – and on her own had secured a job in Paris in a cheap cafe-concert. She could sing a little and dance a little in an untrained manner, but above all, her engaging personality, vivacious and impudent, shone out boldly and enchanted all who saw her little performance.

Better offers were not long in presenting themselves. She sang and danced in more impressive establishments for more money, her path ever upwards. Only five years after her first appearance in Paris she enjoyed a season of phenomenal success at the Moulin Rouge! Her fortune was made, even though she was never outstandingly pretty and her talent on the stage was limited. She was of middle height, with light brown hair, and her figure was the ideal of the Belle Époque – full-bosomed, tiny waist and well-rounded hips and bottom. Rich men were soon jostling each other for the privilege of being her companion – and for that she had real talent. From her throngs of admirers she acquired over the years property, money, furs, jewellery – all the trappings of success. Her tours of New York and London were triumphs, from which she returned with millions of francs.

The War changed all that, alas, as it changed so much else. The public which had once delighted in her type of entertainment wanted something modern and different. The directors of the Moulin Rouge, the Casino, the Folies Bergère, gave it to them – pretty young girls with bare bosoms, tall head-dresses of ostrich plumes and a narrow band of glittering rhine-stones to conceal the genuine bijoux between their thighs. Madame Charlotte retired to live on the income of her considerable investments. Unlike some of the stars of those far-off pre-War days – Polaire and Caterina Otero, to name but two – Charlotte had not gambled away her vast earnings from performances on the stage and in bed.

Her loves were also legendary. She had married three or four times – Jean-Albert could not remember precisely – and her lovers had been too numerous to count, even by her. The thought in Jean-Albert's mind as he contemplated with respect the tender parts bared for examination on his couch – the thought was of the formidable legion of important men who had entered this little pleasure-palace and revelled in it. If only it were possible, he thought, to preserve it forever as a monument to the Golden Age of France! He touched it with

106

great reverence, almost as if it were a holy relic in a church.

'I find nothing wrong with you, Madame. Why have you come to consult me?'

There was an expression of dejection on her famous face and dark shadows under her eyes, as if she had not slept properly for some time.

'For the best reason in the world,' she said, 'I can no longer enjoy the pleasures of love.'

According to Jean-Albert's secret calculation she was about fifty. Apart from the air of dejection, she seemed to him to be in good health.

'For how long has this unfortunate condition persisted?' he asked.

'Nearly a week! Tell me candidly – am I too old for it?'

'Of course not. You have twenty years yet of the pleasures of love ahead of you.'

'But I cannot do it anymore, that's the problem, however hard I try.'

Jean-Albert arranged her legs flat on his couch and pulled her skirt down over her thighs – still firm and unblemished, whatever her age. He pulled up a chair to sit beside her and talk.

'Tell me about your usual range of amorous activities, Madame, so that I can form a picture as a preliminary to diagnosis.'

Madame Pascal talked to him very freely, as women always did, and it was with a feeling approaching awe that he came to understand the force of her sexual drive. After parting from her last husband, five or six years ago, the poor man being depleted in body and purse by the continuous demands she made on him, Charlotte had made provision for herself by installing in her home a succession of strong young men – sometimes Spanish, sometimes Italian. Each lasted, as far as Jean-Albert could ascertain, no more than six months at the outside. In turn, each was sent away with the fine clothes and trinkets Charlotte had bought him, and a parting gift of money. The arrangement seemed a most sensible one for a woman in her circumstances and Jean-Albert offered his congratulations on its logical simplicity.

'Since I must know everything in order to determine where the problem lies,' he said, 'Tell me how often you require the services of these young stalwarts.'

'Not as often as when I was in my prime,' she answered sadly. 'It is a melancholy truth that middle-age slows us all down. Even so, the young men of today lack stamina – a few months and they are useless.'

'Your present companion – how long has he been with you?'

'Manuel? A month or so, no more than that.'

'And are his abilities satisfactory to you?'

'In the sense that he is ready at any time to carry out the little duties I require of him, he is satisfactory – so far. But he can no longer satisfy me, whatever he does. Nothing happens, you understand.'

'To you, to him, to both?'

'To me, of course. He is only a good-looking animal. He does it on command.'

'How frequently do you command him to perform this little duty?' said Jean-Albert, coming back to the question she had earlier evaded.

'Since you insist on knowing my personal affairs, no more than three or four times, in general.'

That number of times a week was good for a woman of her age, Jean-Albert considered, for surely her ardour had been cooled somewhat by the years.

'Every week?' he asked.

'What are you saying – week? I am not a decrepit old woman yet. Every day, I mean.'

The revelation explained for Jean-Albert why her young men were dismissed after a few months – they were probably too worn out to carry their own luggage when they departed!

'I see,' he said thoughtfully, 'and until quite recently you were able to enjoy the full delights of love as regularly as that?'

'Of course I was!'

'Some years ago, Madame, when you were twenty-five, for example, what then? Much the same?'

'Ah, those marvellous days when my name was on posters all over Paris! My appetite for love was larger then, I assure you.'

'How large?'

'I needed to be loved six or seven times a day, at the very least.'

'Not by any one man, I am sure of that.'

'I never met a man who could satisfy me for more than a day. I always needed several lovers to keep me happy. Because of that I met so many charming men – dukes, bankers, industrialists – and everyone of them insisted on making me the most interesting presents! A house here, an apartment there, a small chateau in the country, a race-horse or two, diamonds enough to fill a bucket – it was an enchanted time for me! But see what I am reduced to now – a useless body that does not respond to a man's touch.'

She wept a little and Jean-Albert patted her hand to soothe her distress.

'Calm yourself, Madame. Did this misfortune occur gradually or suddenly?'

'All at once! It was incredible. Last Thursday Manuel was particularly vigorous – he surpassed himself that day, the dear boy! He transported me to Paradise again and again, then we fell asleep in each other's arms and I remember that I promised him a solid gold cigarette case with his initials on it as a special reward. In the morning . . .'

'One moment,' Jean-Albert interrupted. 'Had you been making love all through the day?'

'Naturally! In the morning before we got up. Then again while I was in my bath. And after lunch when we returned home, and before dinner while I was dressing for the evening. And naturally when we went to bed that night after an hour or two dancing in the *Boeuf sur le Toit*. It was a marvellous day.'

'I see. Please continue.'

'Where was I? Ah yes, the gold cigarette case. I fell asleep with that thought in my mind. I was so happy. Then in the morning, after my maid had brought in the coffee, I turned to Manuel and he loved me with passion, as he always does. But I – I lay there absolutely numb, feeling nothing at all! Imagine my horror!'

Jean-Albert nodded sympathetically.

'What then, Madame?'

'I was terribly upset – I cried for an hour! Then I pulled myself together and told myself that it meant nothing, that it was a small reaction from a surfeit of love the day before. I kept away from Manuel all through the day – I think that was the hardest thing I've ever done in my life – and at ten that evening I took him to bed, certain that all was well again.'

'And was it?'

'No – it was exactly the same as in the morning. Nothing!'

'Since then you have tried again, of course?'

'Naturally – three or four times every day, hoping desperately that the ability to enjoy the sensations of love would be restored to me. But my body remains numb and unfeeling.'

'Yet you still feel the urge to try?'

'More than ever before! You must understand that this rapture of the senses has been the most important thing in my life since I was sixteen. To be deprived of it so cruelly after all these years is more than I can bear! For the past five days I have hardly slept more than an hour or so at a time and I cannot eat at all from nervous anxiety. I am totally exhausted and I cannot go on. If you cannot cure me, I shall kill myself.'

'There is no need for that,' said Jean-Albert firmly, 'I am certain that a cure can be effected if you will place yourself in my hands.'

'You have my complete confidence! Cure me and you may charge any fee you like.'

'As to that, we shall see,' said Jean-Albert. 'First we must make you well, then we can discuss fees. But understand me, Madame, when I said that you must place yourself in my hands, I mean without reservation. The treatment, you see, will be unpleasant.'

'Not a surgical operation!' Charlotte exclaimed in horror.

'Nothing so drastic, I promise you. But once started, you must go through with the treatment, even if you are tempted to abandon it halfway. And to that end I shall require you to sign certain legal documents giving me permission to proceed with such treatment as I think best, with no possibility of action by you in the courts.'

'Good God,' she whispered, 'Your words terrify me.'

'Let me assure you that in all that happens I shall have your best interests at heart,' said Jean-Albert with his most engaging smile.

'Can you guarantee a total recovery?'

'What doctor can give a guarantee in so serious a case? But I will say this, Madame, I have every confidence that your powers of love can be restored.'

'Tell me about the treatment, so that I can gather the courage to stand it.'

Jean-Albert shook his head gravely.

'You have my word that it will not be painful,' he said, 'apart from that I can say nothing.'

'How long will it take – at least tell me that much,' she pleaded.

'A week, perhaps, no more.'

'I will bear anything that will restore me to normal,' she said with determination, 'when can we begin?'

The following day Jean-Albert escorted her to an establishment owned by a medical colleague of his, where special arrangements had been made for her reception. It may be thought ironic that the place in question was a residential clinic where well-to-do families concealed young daughters who had the misfortune to become pregnant without the benefit of marriage. That was not Charlotte Pascal's problem, to be sure, but the clinic was discreet, secluded, well-managed – and in so distant a

111

suburb that no person of style would regard it as being a part of Paris at all.

Madame Pascal was installed there in a small but charming room, well away from the young ladies awaiting their big event. She was put to bed with a sleeping-draught prescribed by Jean-Albert that kept her soundly asleep for the next twelve hours. She awoke to find herself in the care of a woman of thirty who wore a plain grey frock and was burly enough to be a Grenadier! This woman, Ernestine, supervised her regime – which consisted of nourishing food, two glasses of wine a day and plenty of sleep, either natural or induced.

There was nothing seriously wrong with Madame Pascal, Jean-Albert knew, only a nervous exhaustion brought on by years of excessive indulgence in the pleasures of the bedroom, too many late nights, too much champagne – and all this made worse by her own natural anxiety and insomnia when her body failed the first time to respond to the touch of a lover. In the clinic she had no choice but to rest, eat properly and remain chaste. Ernestine was with her throughout the entire day, seemingly a companion and maid but in truth a jailer. At night, to her chagrin, Charlotte's body was enclosed in a thick quilted bag that fastened above her breasts and her hands were enclosed in similarly thick gloves, tied at the wrists! This, she realised with some embarrassment, was to prevent any attempt on her part to ascertain whether the power of sensation had returned between her legs!

Jean-Albert visited her twice a day, morning and evening. On each visit he asked her to lie naked on her bed while he took her temperature, checked her pulse, palpated her breasts lightly, opened the tender petals of her sex and probed delicately inside with his fingers. None of this had the least medical significance, of course, but it reassured Charlotte that she was receiving constant expert attention. As the days passed, the feel of his fingers on her breasts and, even more so, between her thighs, became increasingly exciting – and increasingly frustrating!

112

On the sixth morning, as he started to go through his routine, he asked, as usual, if she had slept well.

'No,' she replied, 'I had such dreams that I kept waking up all the time.'

'What sort of dreams?'

'They were so vivid – yet I can remember only the final one. Isn't that strange?'

'Then tell me that.'

'But it concerns the most intimate matters!'

'So much the better – it may be a sign of recovery. Tell me about it.'

'If you insist. I dreamed that I was on stage at the Moulin Rouge, just like the old days – playing to a packed house. How they clapped and cheered when I made my entrance! There was a man in full evening dress on stage to greet me and introduce me – as if *I* needed any introduction to audiences! But he was tall and very handsome and he took me by the hand and presented me to the applauding audience as if I were an unknown. I found this very strange and puzzling, though I did not become angry, as I would have done in real life.'

'Was this man someone you knew?'

'I thought that I knew him but I couldn't think of his name.'

'What happened then?'

'There was a divan on the stage. He led me to it and I sat down, then he stood behind me so that we were both facing the audience – it was so strange, and yet it was as if we had rehearsed all this together. He put his hands on my shoulders and made me lie down – with my legs up in the air! My frock slipped to my waist and I knew that I had no underwear on! And he, the man who was making me exhibit myself in this way, he announced loudly that here at last the management of the theatre presented, regardless of expense, the sight which all Paris had been waiting to see! Ah, how they clapped and shouted their appreciation – what a triumph!'

'A most interesting dream, Madame,' said Jean-Albert, smiling as he looked down at the naked body of Madame

113

Pascal on the bed. Her breasts had lost the firmness of youth and lay slackly, spreading outwards, but her skin, through continual massage and treatment with lotions, preserved its smooth sheen. Her thighs were good, only a little fleshier now than when in her great days she had clasped many a rich admirer between them. The little tuft of hair that covered her much-loved treasure-box was a rich brown colour, though that might have been aided by a touch of colouring, as on her head. But what of that?

Within her curly fleece Jean-Albert's sensitive fingers encountered the soft lips which had been the object of so much desire – and a certain moistness that informed him that in relating her dream she had become aroused. She sighed very softly, her eyes half-closed, as he felt a little further inside. Beyond all doubt, she was distinctly aroused! That was to be expected – she had been compelled to remain chaste for a longer period than at any time in her life since she attained the age of sixteen.

'Jean-Albert,' she murmured, using his name for the first time, 'I shall die if you don't let me do it!'

His finger-tip was on her firm little bud of passion.

'The course of treatment should last a full week,' he said, 'To cut it short now might undo all that we have achieved. Have you considered that?'

'I don't care!' she exclaimed, 'I'm cured – I know I am. You must not torment me any longer, I implore you!'

Tiny tremors ran across her belly and her thighs were trembling.

'Then you are of the opinion that I should let you return to your home to resume your pleasures with your Spanish friend?' Jean-Albert asked.

'I cannot wait that long! It must be now!'

'Like this?' he asked, his fingers moving in her open furrow.

'You are a man – do it properly!'

Madame Pascal was almost at her last gasp as Jean-Albert positioned himself, fully clothed, between her wide-spread thighs. Her fingers tore at his trousers, pulling off three buttons in her haste. Then she had him by his

114

rigid part and pulled it into her, her loins rising to meet him. A dozen fast strokes – no more – and she shrieked and thumped the bed with her heels and fists in ecstasy. There was no more for Jean-Albert to do but wait for her long and profound transports to end in shudders and sighs.

When at last she was calm again, she looked up into his eyes with an expression of deep gratitude.

'You have cured me,' she said, 'there are no words adequate to thank you.'

'The restoration of your abilities is thanks enough,' he said.

'But you, dear friend – you were not satisfied. How could you be – it was so fast.'

'As to that,' said Jean-Albert, easing himself off her, 'do not disturb yourself on my account. What I did was in my capacity as your doctor, to find out in the only possible way whether the proper sensations had returned.'

'I understand. But it would be ungrateful of me to permit you to depart in a condition of frustration. Take off your clothes and lie here with me and we will do it again.'

Jean-Albert stroked her hand and smiled, trying as best he could to make his trousers cover him decently, even though buttons were missing and his part was upright and prominent. He had no intention of remaining frustrated for long, but Madame Pascal's kind offer was not to his inclination. A scientific experiment was one thing, but to do as she proposed would imply another sort of relationship between them. He had no wish to become one of those hard-worked persons who relieved her emotions on a regular basis.

'Let me give you some advice,' he said to her, in a manner that was equally friendly and professional, 'all is well now – you may leave her as soon as you are ready. They will order a taxi to take you to your home. But – please listen to me carefully – you must regard yourself as cured but convalescent for the next few weeks and not overtax yourself. Otherwise, who can say what might occur?'

115

'What are you saying?' she asked in evident dismay. 'That I must live like a nun even though I am well again?'

'Not at all. What I want you to do is to reduce the frequency of your lovemaking for the next month or so, that's all.'

'Reduce! Good God – I really am getting old!'

'You're still in your prime, but you must take care of yourself a little. Come and see me in four weeks and tell me how things are with you.'

'But to what must I reduce?' she demanded. 'Tell me!'

'I suggest to not more than twice a day for the present.'

He could hear her moaning softly to herself as he left the room.

Perhaps she would follow his advice – she had been deeply shocked by what had happened to her and would not want to risk a repetition of that sad condition. But Madame Pascal's future behaviour, now that she was fully recovered, had little interest for Jean-Albert at that moment. Despite all his talk of scientific methods, the truth was that it had aroused him to touch her – and had aroused him even more to penetrate her, however briefly. It would have been simple enough to continue from that position of advantage, but his fantasy required another type of realisation just then. Madame Pascal was, after all, an averagely attractive woman of fifty or thereabouts. Jean-Albert's fancy embraced other possibilities.

He had it in mind – bizarre though it may seem – that he would find it prodigiously interesting at that moment to roll about on a bed with Ernestine, the muscular woman attendant who had taken care of Madame for the past few days. Through her grey frock Jean-Albert had discerned breasts as big and round as water-melons – and haunches that would not have disgraced a blacksmith. Her thighs – ah, they must be like the trunks of smooth trees, he thought, columns of marble to support so magnificent an edifice. To revel in Ernestine's mountains of flesh – what incomparable joy! To lay bare that which was concealed between her thighs – unimaginable pleasure! Would it be on the same heroic scale as the rest of her – a fleshy

116

mound as big as a clenched fist, covered by a mat of hair? He wanted very much to find out, and from the glances he had exchanged with her on his daily visits to Madame Pascal, he guessed that this Amazon would deny him nothing.

THE SELF-ESTEEM OF MARCEL CHALON

When a woman changes lovers, it may mean little more to her than changing her stockings – and perhaps for much the same reason. But the shock to the discarded lover's self-esteem may prove to be catastrophic. At first he refuses to believe what she has said, then, when he realises that she is in earnest, he becomes angry. Many crimes of passion have been committed in these moments, no one can be unaware of that, though the average man does not murder his former beloved out of hand but contents himself with shouting at her before he storms out of the door. Anger is a fatiguing emotion and after a time the discarded lover subsides into bitter disappointment. Eventually he recovers and finds another mistress, so that life and love may continue.

Marcel followed the classic route after Yvonne Daladier informed him that their affair of a year was at an end. With him the anger continued for three days, during which time he roamed around the Grand Boulevards, getting drunk in bars, smashing glasses and insulting complete strangers. More than once he was evicted by force, until at last he went home by taxi, dishevelled and bruised, his anger spent and bitter disappointment setting in.

Why had she done this to him? he kept asking himself. He was a good-looking man of twenty-six, he dressed well and was a lively companion. In bed he was more than adequate to make a young woman happy. He had independent means and had maintained her in good style. Their months together had been happy for them both. In short, there was no possible reason for her to have behaved in so disgraceful a manner.

Yet she had abandoned him for someone else! Indeed, she had moved out of the apartment where they had enjoyed many delightful hours together and had taken up

118

residence elsewhere! It was incomprehensible – and it was intolerable!

After he had slept off his drunkenness and changed his clothes, Marcel made his way with a sad and heavy heart to what had been Yvonne's apartment for one last time. What was in his mind, who can say? Perhaps he would die there alone of a broken heart. Perhaps he would get drunk again there in order to forget her. Anything was possible.

He let himself into the deserted apartment with his key and looked around. It was only three days since she had told him of her decision and already half the furniture and pictures were gone. She herself had not been there in all that time, he knew, having made innumerable telephone calls from public bars to vent his rage. The maid had answered once or twice and had told him that Madame was away. Away she certainly was! Away somewhere with her new lover – perhaps in a hotel, perhaps in the country. Not, surely, at Deauville, where at the start of the relationship Marcel had taken her for ten days of interrupted delight together! But, perfidious as she had shown herself to be, he told himself painfully, she might well be at Deauville with her new admirer, leaving the maid to pack up and move her belongings to her next apartment.

He wandered into the bedroom. The bed was still there – that piece of furniture on which they had given each other so much pleasure. A groan of agony escaped Marcel's lips as he stood and looked at it, recalling happier times. The fragrance of Yvonne's perfume still clung faintly, making the scene unbearably poignant.

He pulled open a drawer of the dressing table, expecting to find it empty. To his surprise it was half full of her things – stockings, underwear. Yes, he concluded mournfully, she had taken only a small suitcase of clothes with her – enough for a brief stay in a hotel somewhere until everything had been transferred to wherever she was going.

In a sudden burst of anger, Marcel pulled out every drawer and spilled the contents on to the bed. There was a dazzling profusion of elegant lingerie – little silk chemises

119

and lace-edged knickers in rose-red and dusky-pink, myrtle-green and eau-de-Nil, hyacinth blue and cornflower blue. There were sleek pairs of camiknickers with hand-embroidery at the yoke, inlet with Chantilly lace. There were at least a dozen pairs of silk stockings, of every shade from flesh to dramatic black.

He plunged his hands into the sumptuous array of intimate finery piled high on the bed, his mind ablaze with confused emotions. He had adored her so much – her soft skin and tender thighs, her pouting mouth and little face, her delicious breasts . . . poor Marcel thought he would go insane with these reminders of what had once been between him and Yvonne. Three days without her! Even worse – three nights without her and the pleasures of her body! It was more than he could bear.

He hardly knew what he was doing as he tore off his jacket and threw himself onto the bed, his fingers fumbling with his trousers and underpants until he wrenched up his shirt front and pressed a handful of Yvonne's silk underwear to his hot belly. The thrill of that moment made him gasp aloud. His male part stood stiffly erect, trembling of itself even before he began to caress it with the coloured silks he held.

'Yvonne . . . Yvonne . . . I adore you . . .' he groaned aloud, feeling himself to be within instants of fountaining his desperate passion for her into a fistful of her underwear.

In the madness of longing that had seized him he was deaf and blind to the whole world, unaware that someone else had entered the apartment and, attracted by his moans, was heading towards the bedroom. How could he? He was at that moment of divine folly when the body knows that it is committed to a convulsion of ecstasy that nothing can prevent.

In that very moment Yvonne's maid entered the room and halted, wide-eyed with amazement at the spectacle before her. There lay Marcel on the bed, his trousers round his knees and his shirt round his waist, rubbing a double handful of Madame's underwear against himself!

Marcel stared back, open-mouthed, at the maid in her hat and street-clothes, her hand still on the door-handle. It was a moment of incredible tension for both of them.

Embarrassment, shame, anger – a most complicated mixture of emotions coursed through Marcel's mind at this ill-timed intrusion – but it was beyond human remedy to avert his oncoming crisis. His distended part twitched furiously and discharged into the wad of flimsy underwear that concealed it from the maid's view. He attempted to suppress the spasms that were racking his body, but he was helpless until at last the process was completed.

The maid watched him shake and gasp through his anguished climax, her agile mind at work on the question of how to turn this astonishing event to her own advantage.

'Wait outside, Cécile,' said Marcel when the power of rational speech was restored to him, 'I will explain everything to you in a while. Just go outside. You will not be the loser, I assure you.'

'But Monsieur Marcel,' she answered, advancing into the room, 'there is no need for you to be embarrassed. I can understand your feelings and I am not in the least put out. Besides, it seems to me that at this moment you are in need of some assistance to clean you up.'

Her sympathetic manner soothed Marcel's agitation at being discovered in so unlikely an act. He had got to know Yvonne's maid well enough during his short liaison and had always found her to be an understanding woman. Moreover, he had been accustomed all his life to being waited upon by servants who prepared things for him and tidied up after him. Not that one had ever performed this particular service for him before, but there was a first time for everything.

He lay back easily on Yvonne's bed and closed his eyes while Cécile removed the sodden pad of tangled garments from his belly.

'My,' she said, 'you have given me a lot of extra washing and ironing to do, Monsieur Marcel. You must have been in a terrible state.'

121

'To think I have been brought to this,' he murmured in self-pity, 'she knows that I love her with all my heart and yet she denies herself to me for the sake of another man. It is too much!'

'Heart-breaking,' Cécile agreed, 'lie still while I fetch a towel.'

She brought a cloth dipped in warm water and a fluffy towel. While she was attending to him she said in a friendly way:

'May I ask you something personal, Monsieur Marcel?'

'Of course. I know that I can trust you, Cécile.'

'It's easy to see why you did what you were doing when I came in just now unexpected. To have Madame's underwear against your skin was the next best thing to having Madame herself, yes?'

'A poor substitute,' he said.

'That's what I wanted to ask you. It produced the right result, but was it any good? I know I came in at the wrong moment and took your mind off things, but suppose I hadn't – what then?'

Her ministrations were not unpleasant. She washed Marcel's deflated part as gently as if she was bathing a baby and patted it dry with the soft towel. Marcel began to appreciate her attentions.

'Your entrance made no difference, Cécile. As soon as those moments of madness were over I would have lain here in an agony of disappointment. To tell you the truth, I might have burst into tears of frustration. You have saved me from that and I am grateful.'

'Oh Monsieur – it is too sad to think about! Don't you feel any better for the relief you gave yourself?'

'Worse, now that it is over. For a few moments those delicate underclothes gave me an illusion of her presence, but at the critical moment, I was alone.'

'Even though I was here?'

'I think that made my loneliness even more unbearable, Cécile. My heart is broken – what more can I say?'

'It is tragic,' she sighed. 'What will you do now?'

'I? There is only one course of action open to me to

calm down my jangled nerves and bring tranquillity to my mind and body.'

'What's that?'

'There are certain establishments men visit – I am sure you have heard of them – where a dozen obliging women are available at a price. I shall go to one of them and stay there, paying woman after woman, until I faint from total exhaustion. Then at last my broken heart will be at peace.'

'You mustn't do any such thing,' Cécile said firmly, 'Have some regard for your health, I beg you.'

'There is no other way.'

'Perhaps there is. I have an idea. If it fails, nothing is lost. If it succeeds, calm will be restored to you.'

'Tell me!'

'Will you trust me, Monsieur Marcel?'

'Implicitly. You have shown yourself to be a person of profound sympathy.'

'Then close your eyes and keep them closed. This is most important, Raise yourself a little so that I can remove the rest of Madame's underwear from under you.'

She gathered the frothy little garments he had strewn on the bed and went to the dressing-table to fetch a perfume spray.

'Are your eyes closed? Now stay still and accept whatever happens.'

She draped an item or two of silk and lace over his face and gave them a quick spray of expensive perfume.

'Ah,' Marcel murmured, 'that fragrance! I could almost believe that she is here with me.'

Cécile said nothing. She stood beside the bed observing the effect on him. His limp part was stirring – that being the art of the perfumer, to arouse a man's feelings. She dangled a black silk stocking so that the toe just brushed over the head of his lengthening and thickening staff. As it grew stronger yet and raised itself from his belly, she trailed the stocking along its whole length.

'Oh my God!' Marcel whispered through the scented garments over his face.

123

Cécile continued, trailing a dainty chemise over his bare belly to make the lace hem tickle him delicately.

Ah . . . ah . . . ah . . .' he sighed.

She wadded up the black silk stocking and pushed it gently between his thighs so that he would feel the touch of it against his dependents and then flicked at his jutting part with a pair of eau-de-Nil coloured knickers. Only a few moments of this were needed to render Marcel incoherent with pleasure. She wrapped the garment loosely round his trembling part, so that more sensation woud arise from the intermittent contact and so carry Marcel further towards his goal.

That done, she stood back from the bed to remove her hat and outdoor coat – and then her skirt and knickers – very plain and uninspiring when compared to Madame's frilly silks. She was ten years older then Yvonne Daladier, which made her thirty-four. She was not unattractive, in her way, but as a servant she had little time to herself and her pleasures had necessarily been with men of her own class and therefore lacking in finesse. She envied her mistress the succession of handsome and elegant young men to whom she formed attachments.

No one can say, of course, what was uppermost in her thoughts as she got on to the bed to straddle Marcel. The opportunity to try out for herself the joys of one of Madame's lovers – it may have been partly that – in addition to her natural desire for money. Pleasure and greed are two strong motives which frequently march together.

Because he was blindfolded by the underwear draped over his face Marcel saw nothing of her broad bared belly and its thick muff of black hair, nothing of the fleshy lips she drew apart with her fingers. He felt the caress, as soft as a whisper, of the silk draped around his upstanding part gently pulled away, to be replaced by warm flesh that slowly took him into itself.

'Yvonne!' he exclaimed, 'I adore you!'

Cécile was careful not to touch him directly with her hands in case he could distinguish between Yvonne's skin

124

and her own work-hardened skin. She balanced herself above his loins and rode gently up and down, hearing him babble on and on as his excitement grew stronger.

Men are complete idiots, she thought; show them a pair of drawers and they take leave of their senses. What stupidity!

'Yvonne!' Marcel moaned.

'Yes, chéri, yes,' Cécile whispered back, making her voice as much like her mistress's as she could in the circumstances.

She need not have given herself the trouble. Marcel was far beyond the point at which he could distinguish between one woman's voice and another. She continued to ride him slowly and his loins rose by degrees from the bed, pushing deeper, as he hung tremulously on the brink of rapture.

'Oh yes . . . oh yes . . .' he whispered, until his words changed into a long muted wail as he discharged lengthily, deep inside Cécile's convenient receptacle.

Though she was only mildly aroused until then, Cécile gasped and clutched at her own breasts through her blouse as Marcel's warm douche flicked her into a brief climax.

Still riding up and down easily, she waited for his spasms of delight to fade, watching his quivering belly in surprise at how long they were lasting. The men she had known until then were finished in five seconds when their emission began. Marcel continued to shudder and gasp in ecstatic release long after he had emptied himself into her. Now that, she thought, would do wonders for a woman properly prepared in advance to share it with him. Perhaps she had discovered the secret of Madame and her lovers – perhaps it was an intensity of passion prolonged for a long time.

Only when Marcel at last lay still did she climb with care off the bed, to wipe herself before donning her underwear and skirt in silence. An occasional tremor still shook Marcel's body, she noted, as, properly dressed again, she slowly removed the chemise from his face.

His eyes opened slowly to take in his surroundings

125

before focusing on the friendly face of the maid standing beside the bed.

'Oh, it's you, Cécile,' he said, smiling at her, 'I had a most marvellous dream.'

'Did you, Monsieur Marcel? What was it?'

'She was here with me and we made love. It was incredible! I feel so good – so calm.'

'I'm very pleased to hear that. Do you want to sleep for a while?'

'I believe that I will. You won't go away, will you?'

'No, I have plenty of work to do around the apartment. I shall be here when you wake up. I'll draw the curtains to help you sleep.'

For the next couple of hours Cécile busied herself with hand-washing and ironing the expensive underwear which Marcel had made use of for his first solitary attempt to summon up the remembrance of past pleasures. Her little ruse had proved to be a success beyond her expectations. It had calmed Marcel down and without question that alone had earned her a considerable tip from him when he woke up. In passing, he had given her unawares a brief pleasure which she had not expected – and an insight into the ways of those with more money and leisure than herself. But that apart, she was cheered by the thought that Marcel would without doubt be generous to her and that led her to speculate on the possibility of making more money from him to add to her savings, before the lovelorn young man recovered his wits and found himself another woman – a matter of a week or ten days at the most, in Cécile's estimation. Madame Daladier had never been a generous employer and there was little to be squeezed out of the household budget. Cécile's savings came from tips given to her by Madame's admirers for little services.

She woke Marcel at six in the evening with a glass of tea with a thin slice of lemon in it. While he was sipping at it gratefully she attended to his exposed part, now soft and small, washing and drying it in the most matter-of-fact way.

'Has your sleep refreshed you?' she asked.

126

'Yes, I am eternally in your debt, Cécile. When you found me here, I wanted to die. Now I am ready to live again. I can never repay you for your kindness.'

'As to that, Monsieur Marcel . . .'

'Of course! If you will be so good as to pass my jacket to me . . . there, I know that mere money can never repay the devotion you have shown me today in my hour of need, but I hope that you will accept this as a small token of my gratitude.'

'You are too kind,' Cécile said politely, tucking the bank-notes quickly down her blouse. 'If only I could do more to help you through this time of anguish.'

'Perhaps there is a way to help me,' he said slowly, 'though I hesitate to impose my misery on you.'

'You have only to mention it.'

'Because of you I enjoyed a dream of such exquisite pleasure that I shall never forget it. I would like to dream that dream again, if you could bring yourself to assist me.'

Between them it was arranged that Cécile should return to the apartment on the next day at three. She left her hat and coat in the entrance hall and went to the bedroom, where the door stood slightly open. Inside, the curtains were drawn to dim the room and Marcel was in bed, his eyes closed as if he were asleep.

'Yvonne – it's you at last,' he whispered, not stirring.

Without a word, Cécile took from her capacious hand-bag a tiny chemise the colour of Parma violets and spread it gently over his face. She had already sprayed it with Madame's perfume and the familiar fragrance caused Marcel to sigh loudly.

'You are so adorable, Yvonne! To be with you is happiness beyond imagining.'

Cécile had brought the spray with her. She squirted a cloud of fragrance on to the silk to intensify its effect.

'Chérie!' Marcel moaned.

She drew the coverlet and sheet away from him and down to the foot of the bed. He was naked and his projection was at full stretch.

127

'See how impatiently I have been waiting for you,' he murmured.

Cécile delved into her bag for a pair of silk stockings and trailed them slowly the length of his body, from throat to thighs, then upwards along his strong shaft from base to tip. This caress, many times repeated, brought about a trembling in his limbs and made his upstanding part twitch.

'It is so thrilling when you tease me,' he whispered, 'you will drive me mad with pleasure. Don't stop!'

She continued the treatment until she judged the moment right – Marcel was squirming in delight and muttering little endearments. She wound the stockings loosely around the portion of him that throbbed so urgently, gripped it high up between thumb and forefinger and flicked a few times.

The result was dramatic. Marcel convulsed as if an electric wire had touched him and a torrent into the stockings announced the arrival of the climax of his pleasure. But, Cécile observed, the duration of his passion was much shorter than the day before. Evidently he required something more to bring him to full release.

His words confirmed her deduction.

'Ah, chérie,' he said, 'No one has ever aroused me as you do. I dream incessantly of your beautiful body.'

As before, Cécile bared herself below the waist and took up her position, kneeling above his loins. His firmness had only partially relaxed and a few flicks of her short finger-nails on his nipples soon restored it sufficiently to guide into herself. The warmth of that contact brought back Marcel's vigour in full measure.

It was in Cécile's mind that on this occasion she might benefit equally with Marcel from the union of bodies. She therefore slid up and down very slowly so as to give herself time to respond physically to the feel of what was inserted in her. Marcel trembled and sighed as she worked away steadily – his satisfaction was assured and she could take thought for her own.

She had been told that the positions of love are numerous. She had seen illustrations in a book of engravings that demonstrated the possibilities that existed when a man and a woman had the time and inclination to experiment with such diversions. Nevertheless, the only ones Cécile had experienced herself were two in number – flat on her back or standing against a wall, according to circumstances at the time. To find herself sitting above a man on his back was unfamiliar, of course. She experienced a strange sensation – not of doing it to him instead of him doing it to her, which she would have expected – but almost of doing it to herself! That was of no importance, however, for she was pleasing him and at the same time she was giving herself pleasure.

When the spasms in Marcel's body warned her of the imminent arrival of his spate of passion, she thought that it was too soon for her. This momentary disappointment proved to be false – his prolonged quaking brought her to a turbulent climax. She heard herself squeal in gratification as her eyes bulged and her nipples tried to burst through her blouse.

So that's what Madame enjoys two or three times a day, she thought when the exquisite sensations died away.

The bizarre liaison between Marcel and Cécile continued for three more days. The routine was not changed. He was there naked and in bed by the time she arrived. She covered his closed eyes with perfumed lingerie and teased him with silk stockings on his skin until he discharged for the first time, then prepared herself and mounted him to give him – and herself – a great felicity. After that she became the attentive servant again, properly dressed and polite as she washed and dried his satisfied part. And each time, before she departed, Marcel made her a handsome present of money.

On what proved to be their final meeting in Yvonne's abandoned apartment, matters proceeded differently. The customary sigh of pleasure was absent when she covered his face with a pair of lilac silk camiknickers and sprayed on the perfume. He said nothing and did nothing. There was a tiny frown on Cécile's face as she drew down

129

the bed covers to expose his naked body. He was aroused, that was a good point, she thought. Yet he seemed to be ill at ease. No longer was he allowing himself to be enchanted by the illusion of Yvonne's presence.

His first gratification was unusually slow to arrive, however long Cécile trailed the edges of soft underwear over the skin of his belly and along his rigid part – not even when she made it sway from side to side by flicking at it with a pair of cyclamen red knickers. His continued silence was a further indication which she could not fail to understand – his mood of the past few days was changing. All the same, there was a service to be performed if she hoped to benefit again financially from his gratitude.

Eventually, to facilitate matters, she drew a silk stocking over his stem to encase it and his bulbs fully, then took it boldly in her hand and stroked up and down in a fast rhythm.

That had the intended effect, to be sure! He gasped and writhed in pleasure and then squirted his passion into the stocking. But, Cécile's watchful eye noted, compared with what she had seen him do before, his climax of delight was brief. His body had responded to her stimulation, but his heart and mind were untouched.

Since he made no comment of any kind but just lay on his back as before, she prepared herself to complete the regular performance. There too she encountered a new problem! By the time she was in position above him she found that his hitherto unflagging part had become limp and small.

Yes, she thought, we are fast reaching the end of the little comedy we have played out together!

Even so, the only indication she had of his desires was that he lay waiting for her to continue. Now assuredly Cécile did not possess one-tenth of the skills of her mistress in arousing the passions of a failing lover. She did what she could, guided only by her instinct – rubbing, squeezing and tugging – until at last the sleeping part was awakened and rose up. In great relief she inserted it into the portion of herself ordained by a kindly providence for

130

that purpose. At once she began to move up and down forcefully, her consideration being that brisk stimulation seemed to be necessary to retain the interest she had stirred with much difficulty. It would be a catastrophe if she permitted this interest to droop before the final act was accomplished!

Marcel raised his hand and pulled the lilac silk underwear from his face and stared her full in the eyes.

'But this is ridiculous!' he exclaimed, 'I'm doing it with you, not *her*.'

Cécile said nothing, for there was nothing to say. The dream was evidently at an end and Marcel had woken up from his torpor. His next words surprised her.

'So then, if it's you, it's you – and why not? We'll do it properly this time, Cécile.'

He reached out to unbutton her plain white blouse and in his hurry he pulled one button right off. His hands went up under her chemise to take hold of her breasts and squeeze them.

'Not a bad pair at all,' he commented, speaking more coarsely than would have been suitable if he had been with Yvonne.

Cécile shrugged. It wasn't much of a compliment but it was the only one she had ever been paid on her bosom.

'You've done me a favour or two these last few days,' he said, 'now I'm going to do you one. Swing your backside – let's have some action to warm you up!'

It was true that he was hard inside her and for any man that meant that he would want to complete the process that had been commenced. So much was obvious to Cécile, but beyond that she wondered what she had stirred up in him. This was a new Marcel she was seeing – vigorous, demanding – one might even say dominating. She obeyed his instructions and moved her hips to and fro hard, becoming more and more aware of the fleshy protruberance on which she was impaled – and of the pleasant sensations it was giving her. Under her chemise Marcel's hands kneaded her breasts and tugged at her nipples to intensify her passion. Before long, Cécile was

131

out of control. She moved fiercely, her whole being straining towards the point of rapture which she felt was very close.

'That's good,' Marcel urged her on. 'Faster! I want to see it happen to you.'

The tightness of his grip on her breasts was almost painful, except that even pain was a pleasure to her at that moment. She thumped down on him another six or seven times and his wish was fulfilled – he saw it happen to her. Her head went back until her face was directed towards the ceiling, the muscles of her belly clenched like a fist – and from her wide open mouth there came a long throaty groan of pure ecstasy.

'More!' Marcel commanded her, jerking himself sharply upwards into her.

Without question it was the best she had ever experienced. It was in a totally different category from the pleasure other men had given her and it took some time for the tremors in her body to cease. Her head fell forward and she was looking into Marcel's face and there she saw a smile of triumph.

'Good enough for a start,' he said to her. 'Now I'm really going to show you what it's like.'

'Oh, Monsieur Marcel! I'm as limp as a rag already.'

His hands left her breasts and took her by the hips. An agile twist of his body reversed their positions, so that she was underneath him, her thighs outside his legs and his belly pressed flat to hers – and this he accomplished without losing his place in her fleshy cleft.

She thought that he would attack her as if with a battering-ram and had no relish for it. Here again he surprised her. He pulled her chemise up around her neck to expose her breasts and stroked them softly.

'Did I treat them roughly?' he asked, smiling down at her.

'It felt nice, whatever you did.'

'You must understand, Cécile, the moods of love change quickly. After the wild pleasure you have just experienced you need a different sort of approach.'

'Do I?'

'Believe me, I understand these things.'

He moved inside her with long and slow strokes to give her a little time to recover from her recent exertions, but not too much for her to go cold. She appreciated the tenderness he was showing her, though in her heart she did not believe that it would do anything for her. In this she was judging from her own limited experience, in which the few men she had been with had wanted to do it fast and hard and then go to a bar for a drink. Marcel had been taught the ways of love by a succession of beautiful young women who knew how to savour love to the very last drop – women like Yvonne who expected a lover to be able to entertain them in bed for several hours at a time.

It was not until sighs of pleasure from Cécile indicated that she was responding correctly to what he was doing that Marcel changed his pace from a gentle canter to a brisk trot.

That Marcel, an average selfish man, devoted all this attention to the sensual gratification of a maidservant was an indication of his unusual frame of mind at that time. As she lay on her back with her clothes round her neck and her legs encased in cheap black stockings, she was not beautiful. Her face was broad, her eyebrows unplucked, her complexion uncared-for. All this he had seen for himself when he had removed the blindfold from his face and stared at her. Her breasts, it must be said, were flabby, she had no discernible waist. Worst of all, the unkempt bush of black hair that grew from her groins halfway up her belly demonstrated that she was devoid of the slightest idea of how to make herself attractive to a lover.

Truth to say, Marcel did not understand his own motives in making love to her as if she were the most desirable woman in the whole of Paris. He was obeying the promptings of his own heart and it was not necessary that he should understand them. What he was doing made him feel good, that was what mattered. Not just physically good – that was the result of the exciting friction of joined sexual parts – but good in his heart.

133

'Oh my God!' Cécile moaned, 'It's incredible!'

'Ah, but it gets better still,' Marcel gasped.

It was as he promised, until she was reduced to a body quivering uncontrollably at the spasms of pleasure that shook her. But there is a limit to the intensity of pleasure a man or a woman can sustain. Of this Marcel was well aware, and in good time his measured trot became a gallop. The bed on which they lay was creaking to their efforts. His belly smacked against hers again and again and by now Cécile was thrusting upwards simultaneously with Marcel to plunge him to the limit each time.

When the moment came she screamed in delight and Marcel cried out aloud with her as the surge of his passion flung them both into ecstatic release. For Cécile it was as it she were watching a Fourteenth of July firework display – the whole night sky ablaze with exploding rockets, blinding white star-shells and coloured rains of fire.

For Marcel it was his ticket to freedom from Yvonne and he revelled in the relief of it, his movements extending Cécile's pleasure beyond anything she thought possible. He was still pumping away at her, though more slowly, long after she was lying limp and almost unconscious beneath him.

On this occasion it was she who wanted to doze for a while. Marcel was too exhilarated to think of sleep – he wanted to go out into the street and see people and visit friends and reactivate his life.

He roused Cécile by shaking her shoulder gently. She opened her eyes and saw that he was fully dressed and ready to depart. A moment later she remembered that she was lying naked on her back and she closed her legs modestly – though what *modesty* signifies after what had taken place between the two of them, who can say? Marcel smiled briefly, at her reaction.

'Cécile,' he said, 'I am going now and I shall never come back to this apartment. I want you to have this,'

'Thank you,' she said, taking the money without even looking at it, 'if there is any way in which I can be of

134

service to you in the future, Monsieur Marcel, please let me know. I mean that.'

'You have done more for me than you realise. The rest I shall do for myself.'

'Then good luck, Monsieur.'

Almost six months passed before Marcel and Yvonne spoke to each other after their parting. Of necessity they caught sight of each other by chance from time to time, how could it be otherwise? They had the custom of dining in the same half dozen restaurants favoured by good society, they frequented the same half dozen theatres. And being young, they danced in the same half dozen fashionable establishments. On these occasions Marcel made no attempt to avoid Yvonne, but it was obvious to him that she was avoiding him. She pretended not to notice him, or looked the other way – or even became engrossed in conversation with her companion whenever Marcel was within ten metres of her. She was always with her new lover – a dark-complexioned man with shiny black hair parted exactly in the middle. Marcel knew that his name was Pierre Aubernon and he had learned a little about him but had never made his acquaintance, nor wished to.

Imagine then Marcel's astonishment when out of the blue one morning Yvonne telephoned him at his home with the suggestion that he should take her to lunch. He gave the suggestion a little thought, but not too much, before deciding that he was free to meet her. After all, he was not a complete fool. If she wanted to meet him then she had some sort of plan into which she hoped to fit him. To her own advantage, naturally.

They met and talked over a particularly good meal. Yvonne was wearing a simple green frock of panné velvet and a hat with a turn-down brim. She looked remarkably chic. She behaved towards him quite charmingly and displayed not the least sign of embarrassment at what had happened. Indeed, an observer at another table in the restaurant might well have received the impression that an

135

affair of the heart between these two was about to commence!

'Are you happy?' Marcel enquired, not greatly interested in the matter, one way or the other.

'But of course. And you?'

'As always.'

'I thought I saw you in the crowd at the theatre last week. Were you there?'

'I was twice at the theatre last week. Which one were you at?'

'The Champs-Élysées.'

'Yes, I also caught a glimpse of you. With Monsieur Aubernon, I believe.'

'Ah, is that a reproach?' she asked with a smile. 'Since we parted I've seen you in public with at least three different women.'

'It was not a reproach, merely an observation. If it is of any interest to you, though I cannot imagine how, then there have been four women in my life since we parted, as you so tactfully put it.'

'Four in less than six monthes! You certainly have been amusing yourself, Marcel.'

'Of course,' he said, smiling back at her.

Towards the end of the meal she said:

'You still live with your mother? I don't know why, but I half-expected not to reach you there when I telephoned.'

'It would be too cruel to leave her alone.'

'What happened to the little apartment I lived in? Do you still have it?'

'I gave it up after you moved out.'

'Really? Then where do you take all these new friends of yours?'

Marcel shrugged and made no reply.

The lunch ended and still nothing of significance had been said. Marcel paid the bill and the head waiter bowed them all the way from their table to the door. They stood on the pavement outside and both knew that the moment of truth had arrived.

'Shall I put you in a taxi?' Marcel asked politely, leaving the initiative with Yvonne deliberately.

'A taxi? Yes,' she answered, seeming a little put out that he had not offered to escort her home.

'There's a cab rank on the corner. Let's walk down to it. Where do you live now, Yvonne?'

'Rue Bosquet. Don't tell me you didn't know.'

'I didn't know. That must be off the Avenue Bosquet, I suppose.'

'Yes – a charming little street, very quiet and peaceful.'

They were at the taxi. Marcel opened the door for her to get in and remained on the pavement himself.

'Au revoir, Yvonne,' he said, 'it has been delightful to see you again.'

'Oh!' she pouted, 'come with me. You must see my apartment.'

'But what of Monsieur Aubernon?'

'He is in Brussels. Come with me, Marcel, there is something I wish to ask your advice on.'

The taxi driver was an unshaven individual, slumped behind the steering wheel. He had heard similar conversations between men and women a million times and they bored him.

'Well . . .' said Marcel, 'only for a few moments though. I have an appointment later on.'

He got in the back of the taxi with Yvonne and told the driver where to go.

'This matter on which you want my advice,' he said, taking one of her gloved hands into his, 'is it important?'

'Very. And most confidential.'

To see what her reaction would be, he slipped a hand under her skirt and gently stroked her thigh. She smiled at him and sighed as if in pleasure.

Her apartment was on the first floor. Cécile opened the door to them and stared in surprise at Marcel. When she took his hat he winked briefly at her and she gave him a quick grin, unseen by Yvonne, who was taking off her hat in front of the hall mirror.

Cécile followed them into the sitting-room.

'Is there anything you would like, Madame?'

'No, thank you. I have important matters to discuss with Monsieur Chalon. Please see that we are not disturbed for any reason.'

'Very good, Madame.'

'You have a nice apartment,' said Marcel.

The furniture was all new and expensive. Two of the pictures on the wall were presents from him to Yvonne and had previously hung on the walls of the other apartment.

Yvonne was at last betraying signs of nervousness now that the moment had arrived for her to come to the point.

'You know that Monsieur Aubernon has been a dear friend of mine for some time now,' she began.

'I am aware of the fact,' Marcel answered non-commitally.

'He is involved in high finance – did you know that?'

Marcel shrugged his shoulders.

'I had heard something to that effect from a friend who is an expert in such things,' he said, 'but I did not pay much attention.'

'What expert?' Yvonne asked quickly.

'Why do you ask? It cannot be of any importance.'

'Perhaps it is. Will you tell me, Marcel?'

'Certainly. It was Charles Brissard. Do you know him?'

'I have met his wife and I know a little about the Brissard family and their financial interests. What did your friend say about Pierre Aubernon?'

'That he was involved in high finance.'

'No more than that?'

'Yvonne – what is this about? Surely you did not invite me here to cross-question me about the business activities of a man you know much more about than I do? Tell me the point of your questions and perhaps I can be of some assistance.'

'Did your friend mention that Pierre is involved with Alexandre Stavisky?'

'Stavisky?' said Marcel thoughtfully. 'Yes, I seem to recall that the name did crop up in the conversation.'

138

'What was said of Stavisky?'

'Yvonne, this is becoming an irritating conversation. I am not a witness in a court of law.'

'Please – I have a reason for asking. What did Charles Brissard say?'

'I don't think that I should repeat it. After all, it was a confidential conversation.'

'Tell me, I implore you!' she exclaimed.

'Since you wish it . . . he said that Stavisky is a swindler on a big scale and that he will end his days in prison. Unless . . .'

'Unless what?' Yvonne asked breathlessly.

'Unless his secret partners in the government have him murdered first to save their own necks. Understand me, I know nothing of these things, I repeat only what was said to me.'

'Oh my God!' Yvonne gasped and burst into tears.

Marcel moved across to perch on the arm of her chair. He put an arm about her shoulders to comfort her and pulled the silk handkerchief from his breast pocket to give to her.

'I'm lost!' she sobbed mournfully.

'What do you mean? How does this affect you.'

'I will tell you everything.' she said through her tears, 'Aubernon has gone – run away before the scandal breaks. He is deeply implicated in Stavisky's business affairs. He went without telling me – it was only yesterday that I discovered that his clothes are gone and his other belongings. He said nothing to me except that he had to go to Brussels on business. But he's cleared out and left me behind.'

'Good God,' Marcel said as sympathetically as he could.

'He'll never dare show his face in Paris again. He has left me nothing – not even my jewellery – that's been taken too. I don't know what I am going to do. This morning I learned that the rent of this apartment is already overdue. And there are outstanding debts everywhere.'

'Can you return to your parents at Ivry and live with them?' Marcel asked.

'It is out of the question . . . you see, on my advice they allowed Aubernon to invest their money for them in Stavisky's bonds. They will have nothing – and it's all my fault!'

'How very awkward,' said Marcel, 'I don't know what to advise.'

At that she uttered a heart-rending sob. Evidently she expected him to resolve her pressing problems for her.

'You must stop crying,' Marcel said firmly, 'or you will make yourself ugly.'

That dried her tears at once. She dabbed at her eyes with his handkerchief and gave it back to him.

'I have ruined my make-up. Excuse me while I repair the damage. I will only be a minute.'

While she was gone Marcel resumed his seat and pondered the implications of her position – and his own. Her desertion of him had caused him to suffer atrociously. He still recalled the numbness of heart and the sense of futility that he had felt. By good fortune, the services of her maid had been of tremendous assistance in reviving his normally robust vital forces. Plain though she might be, the maid was a woman who understood a man's grief and offered practical comfort. In retrospect, the afternoons he had passed with Cécile in the abandoned apartment seemed most strange – yet undeniably the touch of her hand on his masculine part and the use of her body had been extraordinarily healing to his bruised heart.

Now, it seemed, he could have Yvonne back for the asking – if she didn't do the asking first! That surely was the entire purpose of the meeting. The question was, after so much had happened, did he truly want her back? She was beautiful, that went without saying, and very desirable. When he put his hand on her bare thigh in the taxi, above her garter, the touch of that delicate skin had brought back a flood of very tender memories. But then,

140

Paris was full of beautiful and desirable women. He had enjoyed the intimate friendship of four in the past six months. And at no greater cost than that of entertaining them to dinners and theatres and a shopping trip or two – a frock for one, a dozen pairs of silk stockings and gloves for another, a string of pearls, some frilly underwear – nothing very serious.

That was not Yvonne's style at all. She expected far more. This apartment, for example, she would surely not want to move out of it and the rent was bound to be higher than he had paid before to house her. She was expensive to dress too, and she had a collector's instinct for pictures, not to mention jewellery.

To set against that was the fact that she was adorably entertaining. Not today, perhaps, because she was immersed in her troubles. But ordinarily, her wit and charm were unfailing. In bed she was unparalleled, at least in Marcel's experience. To explain why was not easy. Her body was pretty, though perhaps not exceptional. She had little pointed breasts set high and a narrow waist. Her arms and legs were very slender – if ever she lost any weight they might even become thin. No, it was the instinctive use she made of her body that was so enchanting, the sophisticated enthusiasm she brought to the act of love, however often repeated.

Alone in her bedroom, Yvonne did far more than touch up her tear-ravaged make-up. When her mirror told her that her face was perfect again, she took off all her clothes and sprayed herself from head to foot lightly with the perfume that Marcel found so exciting. She checked that the lacquer on her carefully groomed toenails was unblemished and brushed the small patch of russet hair between her legs downwards into a neat little point.

She put on her newest négligée, a flimsy creation of silk and lace so fine that her body was almost visible through it. A little experiment with the tie-belt produced the effect she wanted – a deep décolletage that exposed enough of her breasts to rouse a man's interest and still

141

left something for him to uncover for himself when matters had proceeded that far. The négligée had another advantage – she could make it fall open when she was sitting in a way that exposed one leg to halfway up her thigh.

Marcel still desired her, she knew that for certain, as women always know these things. Shè had known it in the restaurant while they were eating, though nothing had been said by him that would reveal his feelings. In the taxi, when he had slipped his hand up her skirt to feel her thigh – an old gesture of his from the time when they were together – that had only confirmed what she already knew. Perhaps she should have moved her legs slightly at that moment, in a manner she understood well enough, to bring his finger-tips into fleeting contact with the soft hair that graced the tender lips between her thighs. That used to have a most encouraging effect on him in the old days.

Yes, he still desired her. Very well – the time had arrived for her to show him how very desirable she could be when she put her mind to it. He would go hard in his trousers the moment he saw her enter the room dressed as she was – or should it be undressed – in her enchanting négligée. A few moments sitting on his lap, her bottom rubbing against his hardness, a hand inside his shirt to tickle his nipple – and he would beg her to return to him. She would appear to hesitate, saying that her problems were too great to impose upon a friend, even so intimate a friend as he had been. He would be so eager by then to get inside her that he would sweep away her objections and insist that they resume their affaire.

She returned to the sitting-room, having been away for no more than ten minutes to make her preparations. Marcel was not there! Yvonne rang for her maid.

'Cécile, where is Monsieur Chalon?'

'He's gone, Madame.'

'Gone? But that's impossible!'

'He asked me to give you a message.'

'Then give it to me at once.'

142

'He said that he regrets that he had to leave for his appointment elsewhere.'

'Is that all?' Yvonne demanded in a shrill voice.

'No, Madame. He also said that he hoped you would be able to settle your problems satisfactorily.'

NICOLE LIBERATED

The first time that Nicole Brissard permitted another man to enjoy the intimate privileges reserved by decree of Church and State for her husband alone, she was acutely nervous. So much so that she was not able on that memorable occasion to attain the climactic release which is the natural result of the exercise of those intimate privileges.

The setting was too unfamiliar, perhaps – not the comfortable security of the marriage bed but the rear seat of Pierre de Barbin's shiny automobile, parked under the trees of the Bois de Boulogne after dark! For a woman of Nicole's station in life such a setting for an act of passion might seem extraordinary – grotesque even – but then, de Barbin was an extraordinary person. From the moment he had been introduced to her, not more than two weeks before, he had been most persistent, calling on the telephone to propose little meetings, as if she were unmarried and he a suitor. At first Nicole was surprised, then she was flattered. Eventually she agreed to meet him for lunch. He was amusing and charming – so much so that she fled away quickly after lunch before he could suggest a visit to his apartment, if that was what was in his mind, as she supposed. For at that moment she was not certain that she would have the good sense and prudence to say 'No'. And if she were to accompany him to his apartment and he embraced her, would she have the strength of character to resist temptation? The answer to that question being unclear in her mind, Nicole decided that discretion was the better part of valour and so she took her leave of him.

That afternoon, safe in her own home, she recalled a conversation she had had perhaps a month previously with her sister-in-law Jeanne Verney. They were drinking coffee together on the terrace of the Café de la Paix, two beautiful and elegant women pausing for a moment during

144

a shopping expedition. Their conversation had turned to the subject of the less than satisfactory ways of husbands in general.

'But why do they do it?' Nicole demanded.

'It is their nature,' Jeanne replied, amused by the question.

'That's no answer. Why do married men chase after other women?'

'Really, Nicole – it is the way of the world. You speak like a convent girl. How long have you been married to Michel now – it must be seven years.'

'Yes, but that is no reason. Am I ugly? Am I cold-blooded? Am I undesirable?'

'That has nothing to do with it, as you well know. In all those seven years have you never enjoyed a little adventure of your own? Be truthful now.'

'Of course not!' Nicole exclaimed, 'what are you suggesting? That I have been unfaithful to my husband?'

The word that best described Nicole was *appetising*. At all times she looked sleek, well-fed and healthy, her chestnut-brown hair shone, the skin of her broad-cheeked face was flawless. When she was pink with indignation, as now, she was so attractive that men sitting at nearby tables turned to stare at her in open admiration.

'My dear, be calm,' said Jeanne. 'You believe that Michel has a little friend he visits. That does not surprise me in the least. Michel is a Brissard, and so am I. We share the same passionate nature.'

Nicole pursed her red-painted lips and stared hard at Jeanne.

'I've certainly heard rumours about *your* little adventures,' she said virtuously, 'though naturally I refuse to believe them.'

Jeanne laughed at that.

'Perhaps someone has been indiscreet,' she said, 'but it is of no importance.'

'No importance? How can you say that? Suppose that these rumours came to the ears of your husband – what then?'

145

'Who would tell him? And if someone did, do you think that he would pay any attention to them? His interest in my charms was never very strong and it expired some time ago. What is of importance to Guy is to be married to me.'

'Because you are a Brissard, you mean?'

'Precisely. Guy cannot afford to offend my family.'

'That hardly applies to me,' said Nicole, 'I am a Brissard only by marriage to Michel.'

'Then discretion is even more important.'

'Discretion in what?'

'In any little adventure you may decide to embark upon.'

'Jeanne – what are you saying? I have no such intention, I assure you. I am a married woman with children.'

'You, me, Marie-Thérèse, Lucienne – we are all women with good marriages and children. If our husbands have a roving eye – well, that's the way of things. They never stray far and they preserve the decencies. There are no scandals, no dramas. Why should we complain?'

'Because we are wives, not kept women!' Nicole replied hotly.

'Assuredly, but since the world is not perfect, we must be practical as well as virtuous.'

'Ignore a husband's infidelity, you mean?'

'Ignore it, of course. And arrange one's own little pleasures. What could be less chic than a wronged and grieving wife?'

'But I could never bring myself to contemplate going with another man. I am a good Catholic.'

'We are all good Catholics – it is expected of us. I must arrange for you to meet some charming and unattached men to take your mind off Michel's little arrangements.'

'Never!' Nicole declared, and she meant it.

That notwithstanding, it was through Jeanne that she met Pierre de Barbin not long afterwards – that extraordinarily persistent man who had taken her to lunch and charmed her with his conversation to the point where she fled in dismay.

Unabashed, de Barbin tried again, this time proposing

an afternoon drive. Nicole accepted, for on reflection she was sure that she could deal with him if he attempted to extend their friendship into forbidden territory. Pierre's automobile was impressive – a great gleaming maroon-coloured Panhard-Levassor open tourer. It had huge lamps on the front like the eyes of a predator and the strength of a score of horses to speed it along. Nicole sat beside Pierre on the black polished leather upholstery, warmly wrapped against the wind, as he drove out of Paris in the general direction of Alençon. It was a fine day in early autumn and, once clear of the suburbs, Pierre put the big machine through its paces for her. The engine roared its bass note of power, the trees on either side of the road whipped past them and Nicole's long silk scarf trailed behind her like a banner in the slipstream. How exciting it was, that headlong rush! And when Pierre, his leather-gauntleted hands clamped to the steering-wheel, put back his head and howled out a song to the open sky – ah, what intoxication! Nicole's heart fluttered wildly in her bosom as if she were a young girl again.

When the exhilaration of speed at last burned itself out, they turned back towards Paris, but by a different route. Pierre drove more reasonably now, maintaining a ready flow of amusing conversation which Nicole found irresistible. When the light began to fade he switched on the big headlamps and sent long lances of yellow light piercing the darkness before them. That too was fascinating, though in a different way from the outward journey.

As it happened, Nicole's husband was away from home that day, on business of some importance in Bordeaux, or so he had said, and there was no need for her to be home in time for dinner. When they reached Chartres Pierre stopped and they dined together in a restaurant he knew there. Before they resumed their journey towards Paris, he put up the folding hood of the car to protect Nicole from the night air. By the time they reached the outskirts of Paris it was after nine o'clock and Nicole was thinking that her children would have been put to bed by the servants and she would not see them that night.

They were passing through the Bois de Boulogne when Pierre pulled off the road, set the hand-brake, switched off the engine and headlamps and, before Nicole was completely aware of his intentions, had assisted her out of the car and back into it in the rear seat. In the dark his arms went round her and he kissed her passionately. Replete with good food and good wine, Nicole allowed him to do so, for the experience was undeniably pleasant. But when she felt his ungloved hand on her thigh under her coat and skirt, naturally she protested at once. But not too much. After all, her heart said, the man embracing her in the dark might almost have been her husband. The hand stroking the soft skin of her bare thigh above her garter might almost have been Michel's hand. Her conscience insisted that it was not, but the touch was so *interesting* that she listened to her heart. After all, nothing irrevocable was going to take place here in the open air, of that she was sure.

But in fact, the moment was a critical one for Nicole, whether she chose to recognise it or not. Almost without her awareness the hand that was touching her thighs so tenderly soon gained ground and arrived inside her silk underwear! And in another moment or two it was caressing her closely-guarded *bijou*! She uttered a little gasp and tried to squeeze her thighs together, but Pierre's hand was too well-placed to be so easily dislodged.

'No, no!' she exclaimed. 'you must stop that !'

Pierre silenced her protest with a long kiss, while his fingers gently parted the soft lips they had caressed and touched her tiny bud as delicately as a bee kisses a flower in its search for nectar.

'Ah,' Nicole sighed.

An idea had become fixed in her mind, one which grew ever more obsessive as her passions kindled under Pierre's sure touch. In the whole of her adult life she had known only one male part – that of her husband, of course. The question in her mind was – were all men the same in this respect, or were there differences? What sort of differences could there possibly be, she wondered as she

148

thrilled to Pierre's intimate caress – differences of length, of thickness? An opportunity to find out might never again present itself!

She put a trembling hand to Pierre's lap and encountered a hardness through his trousers. But that told her nothing except that he was in a state of acute arousal, as was to be expected in view of what he was doing to her with his fingers.

Her determination grew. She hooked her fingers into the opening of his trousers and jerked the buttons open in one hard pull. Then it was Pierre's turn to gasp as she delved under his shirt and into his underwear until she held his stiff pride firmly in her kid-gloved hand.

Nicole's mind was ablaze with her new-found discovery – yes, there was a difference! In her years of marriage to Michel she had come to know his body well, especially that part of it which gave her the greatest delight. Of course, when they were first married her girlish shyness had permitted her to glance at it only surreptitiously during their love-making. To reconcile her deepening affection for that upstanding part with her modesty had been something of a struggle for her. But as she became on terms of familiarity with it and her appetite developed for the pleasures of the marriage bed, she soon learned to look at it openly, to touch it, to caress it affectionately and then to kiss it.

The darkness prevented her from seeing what she held in her gloved hand but she knew it to be different. To avoid the possibility of mistake in this, she hastily removed her gloves and grasped it again in her bare hand. Yes, it felt somewhat thicker than the one she knew best. A little shorter, perhaps, but thicker. That being established, the next question that formed itself in her excited mind was – if simply by holding it she could distinguish a variation of shape and size, would the sensations it gave her also be different? In the hypothetical and unthinkable event of it being permitted to enter her, that was, her prudence hurriedly added.

While Nicole debated this question in her mind, Pierre

was sighing with pleasure at the touch of her hand on the part of him which formed the subject of her speculation.

'Nicole, chérie,' he murmured between kisses.

'Oh,' she said in disappointment as his hand withdrew from between her thighs.

But it was only to unfasten her coat. Then he had her by the waist with both hands and lifted her from the seat beside him as if she weighed no more than a feather. He seated her across his lap, facing him, her legs straddled wide.

'What are you doing?' she gasped as he groped between them to pull aside the loose leg of her expensive silk knickers and so bare her *bijou*.

Even as she asked her wholly unnecessary question, a wicked little voice in her mind was suggesting to her that it was a great pity that because of the darkness Pierre was unable to see and appreciate the sheer beauty of her silk underwear – the delicacy of oyster-grey crêpe-de-chine patterned all over with charming pink rosebuds and trimmed around the wide legs with a narrow band of fine lace. And before the little voice could be suppressed, it went on to add that it was an even greater pity that for the same reason Pierre was equally unable to see and admire the elegance of the *bijou* he was stroking so ardently, with its tender pink lips and neatly clipped tuft of dark brown fur.

That such thoughts should enter the mind of a happily-married young woman may be thought utterly reprehensible – worse than that, sinful if one is a good Catholic, as Nicole undoubtedly was. But as all the world knows, such thoughts do enter the heads of even the most happily-married women, though naturally they never admit this to anyone else. Even more reprehensible – or sinful – according to how one looks at it, is that a beautiful young woman like Nicole should find herself in the back of an automobile in the Bois, with a man not her husband – and he with his fingers caressing her inside her secret feminine sanctum! Yet such things happen, not rarely, but with great frequency, most especially in Paris, though undoubtedly in every other city in the whole world.

150

Something warm and firm pressed against the delicate skin of the lips between Nicole's thighs, and this time it was not Pierre's fingers. What a short time ago had been merely hypothetical now became reality, and what had been unthinkable was now fact as Pierre slid his stiff part into her. Nicole's conscience complained bitterly that she should never have allowed matters to reach this stage. Moreover, it insisted that she must take immediate action to prevent the natural outcome. 'Smack Pierre's face and get off his lap at once', her conscience shrilled.

But really . . . the unfamiliar male part moving boldly inside her was extremely pleasant – thrilling, one could say. And if the question was to be answered completely as to whether lovemaking with another man was truly different, than a little more time would be necessary to appreciate the subtler point of difference. These matters could not be decided in an instant.

Pierre's hands were up her skirt, clasping her by the cheeks of her bottom, to pull her closer into his lap. To drive himself in deeper, Nicole thought. The plan was a logical one – after all, if his part were a little shorter, as she suspected, then she would need to get closer to him to experience it to the full. In the interests of the experiment, she assisted him by pulling her skirt up around her belly and eased herself forward with her feet up on the car seat on either side of him, her knees up level with his shoulders.

One difference was already noticeable. Michel talked almost without stop when he made love to her – little endearments and words of admiration and pleasure. In contrast, Pierre had hardly uttered a word since they had got into the rear of the car. Now that was interesting.

'But you must stop him at once,' said the voice of conscience in Nicole's ear. 'This is infamous! If you allow him to continue doing that to you for one more minute it will be too late! Just feel how tightly he's gripping your bottom – he's nearly ready to do it!'

The insertion of Pierre's slightly shorter, though undeniably slightly thicker, part had imparted a most exquisite

151

warmth to Nicole. She could sense her face glowing pinkly in the darkness, while inside her clothes her body seemed to be bathed in delicious heat. The rhythmic motion to which Pierre was subjecting her initiated tremors of delightful sensation that sped from her spread thighs up through her belly to her breasts, making their engorged tips tingle. How very enjoyable it was to make love, she thought, even with a comparative stranger.

'Stop him,' her conscience exclaimed in alarm. 'He's going to do it now!'

'*What if he does*?' Nicole replied silently and she shrugged, so silencing the voice of conscience.

Her shrug achieved more than that. The movement transmitted itself from her shoulders through her body to Pierre's busy male part and brought on his crisis. His fingernails dug into the soft flesh of her bottom as he cried out and discharged his rapture forcefully.

When the power of rational speech was restored to him, he protested that it was little short of tragic that she had not shared in his momentous delight. With a thousand apologies and expressions of self-blame, he withdrew from her frustrated body his limp sprig, replaced it with his agile fingers and in seconds had her gasping in her emotional crisis, determined that he should not leave her unsatisfied.

Nicole was to learn in due course that Pierre de Barbin was a most unusual man. All that she knew of him at that moment was what she had observed and what she had been told – in short, his outward characteristics. He dressed well, was a clever and amusing conversationalist, had a large circle of friends, he was to be seen at all the appropriate parties and entertainments. For years he had been a target for many a mother with a daughter to marry off. But at thirty he was still sauve, still charming, still amusing – and still unmarried.

To doting mothers of eligible daughters he was an enigma. All the world knows that a man of means requires a suitable wife to manage his household and to give him children. His avid and continuous interest in pretty women was no secret. Well then? To those who knew him well, Pierre was also an enigma. Outwardly he conformed to the manners and customs of polite society – yet he readily explained to his intimate friends, men and women, that he despised all that. His intention was to break every rule, to defy convention – and never to be discovered doing so. The reason he gave for this curious intention was that if he were to be recognised for the social anarchist he was at heart, then he would be indistinguishable, except for his income, from the shabby crew of bohemians who haunted cheap cafes and changed their women more often than they changed their shirts. The *rabble*, as he described them.

'I shall destroy the system from within, by bringing as many young women as possible to my way of thinking' – that was his boast. When asked who was to know that he was destroying the system if he always stayed in the shadows, he answered with pride: '*I* know.'

In short, Pierre was the worst kind of romantic, lacking even the usual excuse of being a writer or dauber of some sort.

A day or so after the drive in the country he invited Nicole to accompany him on an afternoon walk along the riverside. That, at least, was what he said on the telephone. When she accepted and asked where they should meet, he at once proposed his apartment in the rue de Cléry. Nicole's analysis of the situation was that the suggestion of a walk was merely a ruse to get her into his bedroom. In this she was mistaken, for she as yet knew nothing of his secret life of rebellion. She agreed to meet him that afternoon at three.

Naturally she had her reasons, though she would have died rather than admit them to anyone. During the encounter in the Bois de Boulogne she had detected, she believed, certain variances in the configuration of men's proudest parts. The belief – perhaps half-belief would be more precise – had been to some extent confirmed by tender connection with her husband since then. During the mutual caressing which preceded the marital act, she had made a point of handling Michel's stiffness for some time, to impress its general size and shape on her memory. In due course it had made a deep impression on her elsewhere, an event which she remembered with pleasure and, in addition, with a detailed review of the sensations it had provided.

An opportunity now offered itself to investigate further – to formulate a definite opinion about the comparison. In effect, it would be interesting to determine if the comparison was valid or not, this affair of the length and thickness of two different stems of hard flesh. More important still, this was an opportunity to discover whether Pierre's adjunct produced sensations of pleasure more intense or less intense that that of Michel. Of that she was far from certain – in the unfamiliar confines of the rear seat of a car she had not responded fully. In Pierre's apartment, in the comfort of his bed, she would be at ease and therefore able to concentrate her mind on the matter in hand – and after it had been in hand long enough, between her legs.

From these secret speculations it may be judged that Nicole had passed beyond the ordinary considerations of a married woman's duty to her husband and that she was already contemplating the commission of actions which may be described as – if not immodest – then indiscreet.

She arrived at Pierre's apartment a little after three, not wishing to make herself appear too enthusiastic, yet telling herself that politeness dictated that she must not be more than ten minutes late. The autumn afternoon was almost at an end, the street-lamps were already lit. Pierre greeted her with kisses on both hands and then on her lips. She had dressed with care for this meeting – her impressive full-length silver fox coat over an afternoon frock in pale turquoise that looked simple yet had the touch of a master couturier in its cut, the ensemble topped by a pretty little close-fitting hat of the same delicate turquoise.

Pierre maintained a ceaseless flow of compliments as he drew her into his bedroom and began to undress her as if he were her maid. After the hat and coat were off he unbuttoned her frock at the back of her neck and lifted it

154

taxi turned onto the Boulevard de Sébastopol with its brightly lit shops and cafes. They crossed the rue de Rivoli and drove over the bridge to the Île de la Cité. She recognised with feelings of despair the Palais de Justice to their right and the Prefecture de Police to their left. Automatically she crossed herself quickly, praying silently that she would not be required to attend at either building as a result of this insane escapade of Pierre's – for she was sure that it must be in some way illegal to drive about the streets of Paris in only a coat and with no knickers. They crossed the bridge on the far side of the Cité and the taxi stopped in the Place Saint Michel . . .

'Here we are,' said Pierre cheerfully.

'No, please take me back at once,' she begged, 'I can't get out of the taxi.'

'But certainly you can,' he insisted, his hand under her elbow – and she found herself standing on the pavement while Pierre paid off the driver.

'We'll go this way,' he said, taking her by the arm.

This was total madness, she told herself as she allowed him to lead her along. How had it come about that she, Nicole Brissard, had put herself in this position – naked but for stockings and shoes under her fur coat and walking in public with this strange man? He was taking her along the Quai St Michel, the river to their left. Already it was nearly dark and the book shops along the Quai had their lights on to attract passers-by.

Against her bare skin the silk lining of her coat felt unfamiliar and yet comforting. In some indefinable way, she realised, it had the touch of a lover almost. The movement of her walking caused the silk to caress softly her naked breasts and to brush lightly against her thighs and the cheeks of her bottom. She thought that she would feel cold, but she did not. The truth was that the unaccustomed touch of the coat-lining on her body and the incredible fact of walking about in a state of concealed nakedness – and with a man who knew – these conspired to arouse her eroticism and to make her flushed and warm.

157

Nicole was aghast when she identified her own emotions. She was also an honest person.

'This it not so intolerable as I thought it would be,' she said.

'As I told you, only the first step is difficult. I am teaching you to enjoy freedom.'

'From what?'

'You are learning to cast off the fetters that exist in your mind – the fetters imposed upon you by your staid upbringing and conventional marriage.'

'How absurd! You are attempting to make me a libertine like yourself.'

'I am no libertine – I am a free spirit. You are here of your own free will. Be truthful now – the reason you are here is that you want to discover what it is that I have to teach you.'

'I fear that you can teach me nothing except infidelity, Pierre.'

'That is not true – not in the least true. I can show you how to find your innermost self.'

'How – by making love to me?'

They had reached the Petit Pont that runs across the river to the Place du Parvis in front of the grandiose facade of Notre-Dame cathedral. Pierre glanced quickly about to make sure that no one was approaching them. He turned Nicole to face him and put his hand inside her coat to fondle her bare belly. He was not wearing gloves and his touch was cold on her skin. She gasped once in shock, then gasped again differently, for the cold fingers were suddenly very exciting.

'You do not understand yourself at all,' he said, 'you defer to the opinions of others and the wishes of your husband. When will you awake to your own needs and desires?'

His hand slid down to the mound between her thighs, squeezed it gently and was withdrawn from her coat. They strolled on, side by side but not touching, past the bridge and along the Quai de Montebello. To their left, across the river, the huge bulk of Notre-Dame reared up against the dark sky.

158

Nicole said nothing for a while, engrossed in her own thoughts. What he had said was ridiculous, of course, yet perhaps there was a small element of truth in it. Could it possibly be that she was too much concerned with her family duties and gave little thought to herself as a separate person, she asked herself. That she should even think in this way showed that she was already half-seduced by the memory of Pierre's cold fingers stroking her belly.

'You are silent,' he said eventually, 'is your mind troubled by what I said – it was no more than the truth.'

The light rub of the silk lining of her coat against the pink rose-buds of her breasts was really quite delicious, Nicole was thinking. If more women knew about it, Paris would surely be full of women in furs wearing nothing underneath – for she was sure that the sensation would, if she permitted it and walked far enough, lead to a crisis of delight!

So occupied was she with her own sensations that she paid no attention to what Pierre was saying. Needless to say, it was some nonsense about his extraordinary views of life – nothing which a sensible person could take seriously. More important to Nicole was the question of when he would decide that their strange promenade had lasted long enough and find a taxi to take them back to his apartment, where he could appease the desire he had aroused in her. The sooner the better, she thought.

Something he said caught her attention.

'What?' she said, not sure that she had heard him correctly, 'you want to go down onto the towpath?'

'*Sous les ponts de Paris*,' he half-sang, the words of the old song about the lovers of Paris and where they met.

'Out of the question!' Nicole said firmly, 'what am I – a girl picked up in a cheap cafe and taken under the bridge to be mauled?'

'No, you are not that,' he replied quickly, 'let us walk back to the Place St-Michel – we can get a taxi there.'

At last, she thought, as they turned around and headed back in the direction they had come. In spite of the early hour it was almost completely dark. There was not much

159

traffic on this side of the river and few pedestrians, though the time for home-going was close for those who were compelled by their circumstances to work for their living. Pierre guided her across the road and they were soon not far from the old Tour d'Argent restaurant. From there to the Place St-Michel would take not more than a few minutes.

The best intentions go most often wrong, as Nicole was to discover. Her state of mind was no secret – Pierre understood well enough that her eroticism had been savagely awakened by her uncommon circumstances and he was content to stroll along by her side, sure in his mind that he would have his way. Once the volcano of sensuality comes to life and announces its powers by little shakes of the ground, nature will take its course. As well try to bottle up Vesuvius as to check the rising pressure in a human being at this stage. The eruption is inevitable – the onlooker has only to wait.

They were perhaps halfway along the Quai St Michel when Nicole halted, her knees trembling so violently that Pierre had to put an arm around her and support her. Her open mouth and staring eyes told him all that he needed to know – she was almost in a state of ecstasy from the touch of her coat on her bare body and the wild imaginings brought on by her nakedness.

A few steps ahead of them a narrow street – no more than an alley – led off the Quai. He led her round the corner and twenty steps or so into the semi-darkness of the deserted little street. She was without strength to protest as he placed her with her back to the ancient building behind her and stood close, his feet between hers.

'Not here!' she pleaded as he opened her coat to give himself access to her body.

Even in speaking the words she knew that they were futile. What choice had she? Her excitement was at fever-pitch and there was no possible way of avoiding the critical moment she knew to be fast approaching. Perhaps it was better if Pierre brought it on swiftly and so ended her marvellous torment.

160

He opened his expensive camel-hair overcoat, then his jacket, and finally his trousers. Nicole sighed and shook in a mixture of pleasure and apprehension as she felt the blunt head of his stiff projection touch the soft lips between her thighs and then push slowly upwards into her. To do it here on the street, like dogs coupling – it was monstrous, shameful, she thought – yet she was powerless to prevent it. More than that, unless it happened speedily she felt that she would explode. Pierre's hands were busy with her firm-pointed breasts for a while, rolling and squeezing them. The touch sent waves of unbearable pleasure through her, for his hands were like cold fire on her skin. Then his hands slid round her sides and downwards as his thrusting became more insistent, to grasp the cheeks of her bottom and hold her steady.

To preserve the last shred of decency Nicole held the sides of her coat as far round his body as they would go, as if to enclose him in it with her. She knew that it would be only moments before her climax of passion arrived – already she was experiencing in her breasts and belly the tingling which was the prelude to the act of high drama itself. She hoped fervently that Pierre would be equally quick, so that they could abandon this dangerously compromising encounter in a public place.

There were footsteps from her right. She stared wide-eyed over Pierre's shoulder as a man approached in the gloom. He walked straight past without even a glance, for in Paris no one pays any attention to lovers huddled together in a dark corner.

Pierre was strong and forceful, as he had been the first time with her in the rear seat of his automobile. She had been too nervous then to respond but now, in infinitely more risky circumstances, she was responding all too well! With joy – and it must be added, with relief – Nicole abandoned herself to the tremendous upsurge of sensation in her body. She moaned in her ecstasy and clung tightly to Pierre to squeeze her belly tight against him and drive him deeper into her.

He too was only a heart-beat or two away from his

zenith. His hands unclenched themselves from her bottom and moved outwards to force her arms away from him, until he held her by the wrists. He pinned her arms to the wall at shoulder level, so that she felt almost as if she was being crucified against it! He leaned backward away from her until only their loins touched, her fur coat fell open and her entire body was revealed in its nakedness, round breasts, smooth belly, and parted thighs! He stared down at all this tender white skin gleaming in the darkness of the alley, his mouth drawn back to show his teeth in a grimace. The effect was more that of a wolf's snarl than a human expression of tenderness at this most intimate of moments.

Nicole groaned aloud in horror at being so exposed. She fought against his grip in an attempt to free her arms and push him away from her. Let him fountain his passion against the wall – she wanted no more of him. But her struggles were of no avail. He held her easily, his natural strength reinforced threefold by his raging emotions. Fortunately for Nicole, her mental anguish was brief – a few more fast lunges against her set off Pierre's rapturous spasms and she felt the evidence of his release flood hotly into her most secret place. Seven times she counted his urgent convulsion within her, then he relaxed his hold on her wrists, sighed deeply in satisfaction and smiled in the darkness, a real smile this time, not a grimace. The instant he took a step away from her, Nicole wrapped her coat tightly round her and pressed it against her still trembling body with her arms, seeking its protection.

In retrospect, the episode had been exciting, she decided later on, however distasteful it had seemed at the time. Pierre de Barbin had twice treated her as casually as if she were a street-walker, pulling her into the back of his car, standing her up against a wall – all for his very curious pleasure. He was, without doubt, a most unusual person. Who else, in his right mind, would strip a beautiful woman, walk her about the streets and make love to her in such limiting and uncomfortable circumstances? It must be admitted that no woman would find a liaison with him boring – quite the opposite! Yet, to be frank, such encounters were necessarily somewhat less than satisfactory – at least to Nicole. She prefered the comfort and privacy of a proper bedroom, and enough time to savour love's pleasures to the full – not these snatched moments of raging passion in unsuitable places.

Obviously Pierre thought that far too conventional to be of interest to a person of his liberated tendencies. That is all very well, Nicole decided, but as far as I am concerned he is an unsatisfactory lover. Unless he can be made to understand my point of view, I shall stop seeing him. He shall have one more opportunity to understand me, an undertaking which will require great effort on my part – and on his!

For almost a week she refused his invitations to meet him while she gave serious thought to the best way of bringing him to her point of view. When she was ready, she met him for lunch one day – not in any of the fashionable restaurants where she might be recognised, but in a small and charming place on the Left Bank. He was already installed at a discreet table when she arrived, he rose to bow and kiss her hand and she behaved towards him in her most pleasant manner. Over an aperitif and the ordering of their meal Pierre talked easily and without stopping, telling her how much he had missed her, how beautiful she was, how chic her hat was – the usual thousand little things men say on these occasions. Halfway through the meal, as they were enjoying their steak *au poivre* with a salad of chicory and endives, Nicole set in motion the plan she had formulated. Under the table, hidden from all eyes, she slipped off one of her elegant shoes and stretched out her leg towards Pierre. He paused in mid-sentence, his loaded fork halfway to his mouth, and a thoughtful expression appeared on his face as a silk-stockinged little foot inserted itself between his thighs, under the linen table-napkin spread over his lap.

'Go on with what you were saying,' Nicole encouraged him.

'Yes . . . where was I?'

'You were speaking of the importance of disseminating your ideals of true personal freedom. I find the subject of great interest.'

The proximity of her foot to his treasured part was very pleasant and Pierre expounded his thesis of liberty, equality and fraternity cheerfully. Meanwhile Nicole was probing delicately with her toes. She located a soft bulge within his trousers, alongside his left thigh, and pressed it with the ball of her foot until she felt it harden.

Pierre interrupted his discourse once more to say softly.

'Chérie – what you are doing is delightful. But the time and place are not appropriate. Later, yes?'

Nicole arched her plucked eyebrows in surprise.

'Why inappropriate?' she asked. 'You spoke a moment ago of total liberty to express our feelings.'

'I was making a general point, you must see that.'

'I understand perfectly. But there is something I would like to have explained to me. It is this – in your ideal republic of complete freedom from restraint, do you envisage women as equal citizens with men? Or will it be complete freedom for men and subjection for women?'

'I see women as equal citizens, of course!' he protested. 'How could you think otherwise?'

'Your protest at my freedom of expression made me suspect that you were not entirely serious.'

'But surely you see that I was speaking of different circumstances,' he said, glancing around the restaurant with a worried expression.

'Are you certain that you are not being hypocritical?' Nicole asked.

He was, it may well be imagined, in some discomfort, both physical and mental, at that moment. The physical discomfort he resolved by setting down his knife and fork and reaching under his table napkin to free his standing part from the pressure of his trouser-leg, so that it could assume a more natural position upright against his belly. The mental discomfort was not so easily dealt with.

'Nicole – we are in a restaurant, surrounded by people,' he said urgently.

164

'Did you think that I hadn't noticed?' she asked pleasantly. 'The last time we met we walked along the Quais – you fully dressed and I naked except for my fur coat and stockings. That too was a public place – there were passers-by. Yet you took it into your head to arouse me. More than that, you opened my coat and made love to me against a crumbling wall.'

'Ah, it was magnificent!' said Pierre. 'The setting was so exciting – for you as well as for me. You cannot deny that it was pleasant – you gave me proof of your pleasure long before I gave you proof of mine.'

Nicole's little foot had crept forward between his thighs, her heel on the chair cushion, until the sole rested against the swelling inside his trousers.

'I admit it,' she said, smiling at him, 'the experience was bizarre and yet very enjoyable. In the same way, do you not find it enjoyable to be aroused by me now?'

Her foot was pressing rhythmically against its trapped quarry. Her question posed a dilemma for the preacher of liberty from restraint.

'As to that,' he answered slowly, his face pink, 'it is impossible to deny that I enjoy what you are doing.'

'Exactly – the signs are unmistakable. How hard and strong you are, even through your clothes.'

'But that is the point – the signs of a man's excitement are very obvious. When we walked along the Quai, no one could observe that you were aroused.'

'But you knew,' Nicole countered, 'and I certainly knew. So why is it any different now?'

Pierre's face was flushed under the stress of the emotions stirred in him by the gentle but insistent massage of her foot against his most sensitive part.

'Nicole – I beg you to stop,' he said breathlessly.

'Give me your reasons.'

'Because this is too much . . . I must leave the table until I am calm again.'

'If you must – but dare you stand up in your present condition, Pierre? Dare you walk across the restaurant like that? In my opinion the friction of your clothes will

165

produce an interesting crisis before you are across the room.'

'My God, it's true!' he murmured, 'I cannot risk moving from this chair.'

'Then you must sit and listen to me for once.'

'Stop what you are doing, I implore you!'

Her foot ceased its movement and rested lightly against him.

'The theories you explained to me during our walk,' said Nicole, 'I have thought about them and I find them without value. They are no more than a thin disguise for your desire to subjugate women to your will.'

'That is a monstrous thing to say!'

Her foot resumed its exciting but embarrassing motion against him.

'Do not interrupt,' she said, 'or it will be the worse for you. How will you leave the restaurant if I keep you in your present state?'

'I won't say another word,' he assured her quickly.

The erotic pressure stopped.

'If you really believed in your own theories,' Nicole continued, 'then you would not be in the least perturbed when someone else pursued the same logic. You would accept that as a tribute to the validity of your ideas. In short, my friend, you would not at this moment be in the least embarrassed because I have touched you with my foot and caused you to become stiff.'

Pierre opened his mouth to say something, but a warning pressure between his legs silenced him.

'Suppose we follow this thought to its conclusion,' said Nicole, 'we reach an interesting prospect, I believe. If you were sincere in your beliefs, then that sincerity would demand that instead of objecting to my initiative, you would happily co-operate with it. Is that not so?'

'Co-operate?' he gasped, his face a bright red.

Pierre's circumstances were peculiar indeed at that moment. Her foot was still, and for that he was grateful. Nevertheless, its earlier caressing had stirred his passions to an almost intolerable extent. Not just the physical

166

caress, for as all lovers know well, in these matters the physical aspect provides perhaps a third of the excitement and the mind provides the other two-thirds. The thought itself of Nicole's foot caressing his upstanding part in so public a place – the incredible prospect of what it might make happen if she continued – his imagination had seized on these considerations and aroused him to an incredible extent.

'Do you need to ask how?' she said. 'Obviously, you would undo your trouser buttons at once.'

'To let your foot enter?' he gasped.

'More than that.'

'What?'

'Undo your trouser buttons for me, Pierre, pull up your shirt and let your big strong stem out so that I can rub it with my foot. Surely that does not shock a person of your advanced opinions?'

'Oh . . .' Pierre sighed.

'Imagine how very pleasant it will be – the thrilling touch of my silk stocking against the tender head,' she whispered across the table.

Pierre stared down into his lap. Her words had captured his imagination completely. In his mind's eye he envisaged his stiff pink part poking out of his open trousers, its head purple with passion. Nicole's foot pressed firmly against him and he uttered a tiny half-stifled moan of pleasure.

From the other side of the table Nicole gazed humorously at his flushed face and into his eyes – half-open but seeing nothing, blinded by the turmoil of his emotions. She rocked her foot backwards and forwards on her heel as fast as she could, confident now that he was unable to resist any longer. He was entirely in her power, as she had been in his on the Quai St-Michel.

'Ah . . .' he sighed.

Her foot rocked – only a few moments of this treatment were required to push him beyond the limit of endurance. He jerked upright in his chair, one hand flew to his mouth and he bit his knuckle to prevent himself from crying out

aloud as the torrent of his passion was suddenly un-
leashed. Against the sole of her foot Nichole could feel
the vibration of his straining part as it discharged itself
inside his shirt. She smiled as he shuddered and fought to
control himself through his climactic pleasure.

She withdrew her foot and slipped it back into her
shoe as a waiter approached the table. He enquired if
everything was to their satisfaction, a small gesture of his
hand indicating the unfinished meal.

'Yes,' said Nicole, smiling brightly at him, 'Everything
is to our satisfaction. The food is delicious but we
became so engrossed in conversation that we both forgot
to eat.'

She took up her knife and fork and resumed her meal.
Pierre, his face averted, did the same.

'Thank you, Madame,' said the waiter, topping up
their wine glasses.

He departed, convinced that they were so deeply in
love that nothing else was of importance to them – a
circumstance he had encountered often enough. Such
couples annoyed the chef de cuisine, as one would
expect, but in the waiter's experience a liberal tip was
usually forthcoming when they left.

'Have you recovered?' Nicole asked sweetly.

'My God – what have you done!'

'Surely you have more reason than I to know that.'

'But if someone had seen! The waiter seemed suspi-
cious.'

'Calm yourself. He knows nothing and suspects nothing. Finish your lunch.'

'I cannot eat now. We must leave at once.'

'Where are we going?'

Pierre surreptitiously groped inside his jacket to pull
his wet shirt away from his skin.

'To my apartment – I must change out of these
clothes.'

'And then?'

'What do you mean?'

'When I accepted your invitation to lunch it was because

I thought that you had planned some new and outrageous way of enlightening me further in the ways of freedom,' said Nicole, 'don't tell me that you have lost interest, Pierre?'

THE SOLICITUDE OF PAULINE DEVREUX

Taking Gisèle home by taxi, Roger put his arms about her without hesitation and kissed her. She returned his kiss warmly, for at eighteen the whole of life was waiting for the two of them to explore and enjoy. The kiss lasted a long time and during the course of it Roger's hand moved up the girl's side until it touched, then gently clasped, a small and soft breast through the thin material of her frock. Gisèle sighed into his open mouth and the tip of her tongue touched the tip of his tongue. This was not, to be sure, the first time Roger had ever kissed her, nor the first time he had fondled her prettily little breasts. He was encouraged by her sigh and took it to signify that his attentions might proceed further without the hindrance of maidenly reticence on her part.

Could it even be, he asked himself as the kiss continued and his hand stroked her breast until he felt the tiny nipple grow firm through her frock – could it be that Gisèle was not a virgin? His experience, brief though it was, told him that well-brought-up girls of her age quite often were virgins still, and always claimed that they were. This, naturally, was a matter of considerable annoyance to a young man whose blood was hot from kissing and touching, only to be halted in his tracks by a querulous or timid 'No, you mustn't do that!' Ah, those terrible experiences of youth, when nature made it imperative to leave a reluctant young virgin and make one's way – in great discomfort from the pressure of a bulge in the trousers, to the house on the Boulevard des Italiens and there to pay a woman of the house for the privilege of using her warm body to satisfy the raging desires aroused by some eighteen year old girl who refused to spread her legs!

But with Gisèle he felt that matters might turn out differently. Her mouth was hot upon his and her body was responding to his caresses. He gasped as her hand found

170

its way into his lap and tested the extent of his arousal. Her mouth pulled away from his at last, she giggled and swung her legs up so that they lay over his thighs. Could there be a more open invitation to proceed? Roger's hand abandoned her breasts and slid under her frock and up her leg until he touched the smooth flesh above her stocking-top. At that very moment he fell in love with her for the generosity of her response to him. He knew with complete certainty that she would deny him nothing that evening.

The practical question of where the final act in this drama of the passions could take place was almost driven from his mind by the surge of emotion let loose in him by the satin skin of her thigh under his hand. Not in the back of a taxi trundling through the streets of Paris! Yet as his trembling fingers eased forward inside her underwear to encounter the silky floss covering her warm and secret treasure, Roger was so transported by desire that he would have been capable of making love to her right there in the taxi, even under the sardonic eye of the driver, if need be. But good sense prevailed and with her warm prize firmly in his grasp he whispered,

'We'll go to a small hotel I know behind the Opera. When do you have to be home?'

'There's no need for that,' she whispered back, 'there's no one at home.'

She swung her slim legs off his lap and sat upright a moment before the taxi stopped and the driver announced 'Avenue Montaigne.'

The apartment was dark and silent. Gisèle switched on no lights but led Roger by the hand along the hall and into the salon. The long curtains were undrawn and the street-lamps outside provided the only illumination.

'Is your mother away?' Roger asked as she drew him down to sit beside her on a long sofa.

'She's out with her friend Larnac.'

'But what if she returns and finds us here together?'

Gisèle giggled.

'She won't be back before two in the morning. She goes

171

to his apartment with him after dinner and he brings her home when they've finished.'

Further enquiries on his part were made impossible by Gisèle's mouth finding his. In moments they were lying side by side on the sofa and the enchantments of her young body were his to explore and enjoy. In a very short space of time matters had progressed to the point where Gisèle's frock was up round her waist and her underwear discarded. Her left knee was bent and raised to permit free access to her most tender secret and her busy hands bared his quivering appendage to guide it home.

'Ah, chérie . . .' Roger breathed as warm folds accepted him and he eased forward into this delicious haven.

The events of the next few seconds were confused. A scream of rage erupted from somewhere behind Roger, he was seized by the hair and dragged away from Gisèle so violently that he fell off the sofa and landed painfully on the floor. He looked up, bemused by the fall, to see – with what horror can only be imagined – Gisèle's mother standing over him. She was shouting angrily but it took some moments for the import of the scene in which he was an unwilling participant to register fully in his mind. He glanced over his shoulder at Gisèle, just in time to see the pale gleam of her belly and thighs vanish as she pulled down her frock and scrambled off the sofa.

'Go to your room!' her mother shouted, 'I'll deal with you in the morning!'

As Gisèle ran from the room, Madame Devreux switched on a standing lamp beside the sofa.

'As for you,' she raged at Roger, 'my God, Roger Tanguy – it's you!'

'Madame Devreux,' he said hurriedly, 'please, I implore you, do not leap to conclusions.'

'Conclusions!' she retorted, 'I find my daughter lying here with her clothes round her neck and you beside her in *that* condition. What conclusions should I reach then?'

Roger looked down at where her accusing finger was pointing and became aware that his trousers were wide

172

open and his male part thrusting stiffly out, fully exposed to Madame Devreux's angry stare.

'Excuse me,' he murmured in embarrassment while he hastily concealed the offending member.

'Get off the floor and sit properly,' she ordered, 'there are things which must be said before you leave.'

Roger seated himself on the sofa and Madame Devreux sat at the other end of it, as far from him as its length allowed. She was wearing a long saffron nightdress over which she had thrown, evidently in a hurry, a white negligée and she was barefoot. Obviously she had been in bed when Roger and Gisèle arrived at the apartment. Could it be, Roger wondered, that she had brought her lover back with her and that even now he was in Madame's bedroom? If so, that would make the predicament slightly easier to get out of, if he used his wits.

'I hardly know where to begin,' said Madame Devreux in an icy voice, 'to find my daughter in the very act with the son of a close friend . . .'

'But surely that is preferable to finding her with a complete stranger?' said Roger.

'Is that meant to be funny?'

'Why no, not at all. What I meant was that it is better for Gisèle to have a dear friend who is someone you know and whose family you know than for her to form a friendship with a person of uncertain origin.'

'You are suggesting that my daughter is in the habit of casual fornication?'

'Certainly not! Gisèle is a beautiful girl and I am a man. What more natural than that we should be drawn to each other in mutual esteem, however deplorable you as a mother may find it.'

'You have a slippery tongue. Do you love my daughter or do you merely wish to sleep with her?'

'I adore her!'

'Do you wish to marry her?'

'Marry?' said Roger in dismay. 'Why Madame, surely she and I are far too young to contemplate so important a step.'

173

'Too young to marry but not too young to enjoy the pleasures of the honeymoon – is that it?'

'As to that . . .' and Roger's mind began to work faster as little incidents from the past presented themselves from the depths of his memory, 'surely it is you, Madame Devreux, who would be pleased to see me marry Gisèle. I think that you have wanted that for some time.'

'Why do you say that?' she asked, her tone softening.

'The way in which she and I have so often met each other by chance – or so it seemed then – here or at my home and at other places. It was your doing – confess it – you have been pushing us towards each other for a long time.'

'You exaggerate. Of course, I am not saying that I would be unhappy if you and Gisèle wished to marry each other.'

'Because my father is a Senator?'

'No, no! Because your mother is a close friend and because you are a most handsome and acceptable young man.'

'But too young to marry for some years yet, I must remind you. My father would never agree.'

'I don't mean this year, Roger – perhaps not for several years. But it would please me to think that the possibility existed.'

'I thought you had a greater regard for my cousin Gérard – and he is some years older than me,' Roger teased her.

'Oh without doubt Gérard is a fine young man and the Brissards are a family of note and distinction. But I've always preferred you to him. Now, tell me frankly, Roger, how long has this *affaire* been going on between you and Gisèle?'

'To be truthful, tonight was the first occasion on which I . . .' he broke off and shrugged.

'I see. So tonight my little girl has become a woman.'

'As to that, I can make no comment, Madame.'

'What are you saying? That she has been with someone else?'

174

'I have nothing to say on that, but I remind you that Gisèle is a beautiful young woman and must have had admirers before me. How could she not be beautiful, being the daughter of so elegant and attractive a mother?'

'Flatterer!' said Madame Devreux, passing one hand lightly over her hair, 'Yet it is true, Gisèle has her looks from me, everyone says that. Of course, she insists on pursuing this ridiculous modern fashion of looking like a bean-pole. She starves herself to skin and bone and hides her figure to make herself resemble a boy. Twenty years ago it was very different when I was her age. We young girls then were proud of having figures like an hour-glass. The ideal was to have a full bosom and rounded hips.'

'I have not the least doubt that you were the ideal of every man who saw you, Madame Devreux. You have preserved your voluptuous figure in spite of the dictates of dressmakers.'

'Ah, you understand me,' she sighed, 'yet to you I must seem terribly old.'

'Not at all,' said Roger gallantly, confident of himself now that the point of the conversation had shifted away from himself and his frustrated little adventure with Gisèle, 'vogues come and go according to the whims of expensive couturiers, but the fundamental beauty of woman remains and is unaffected. The Venus de Milo in the Louvre has not ceased to be the ideal of feminine beauty simply because some idiot has decreed that women should flatten their breasts and disguise their hips. On the contrary, we men cherish the ideal in our hearts and wait patiently for the day when women will again display their true and natural charms.'

'To find such good sense in one so young!' said Madame Devreux. 'How refreshing – even, I may say – how encouraging!'

Although Roger was aware of no change of position on her part, the fact was that she was no longer at the other end of the long sofa. Indeed, she was quite close to him, close enough for him to detect the musky fragrance of the perfume she wore.

175

'You credit me with good sense,' he said, 'but I pride myself on my good taste. It is apparent to me, as to any man of discernment, that your breasts are most beautifully shaped.'

Her response to his boldness was not unexpected.

'Do you think so, Roger?' and her hand smoothed her bosom gently upwards.

'Without question. As you have said yourself, the young women of today have no breasts. In some manner I cannot understand they have transformed nature so as to deprive themselves of what should be a woman's most enchanting attributes. It is sad – tragic almost.'

'Quite beyond belief,' Madame Devreux agreed, her hand still gently smoothing her own bosom through her negligée.

'Dare I say it?' he exclaimed. 'Yes, your understanding has given me the courage to say what otherwise I would never dare – I would consider myself the most fortunate man in Paris if you were so gracious as to permit me one glimpse of these delights. There, it is said!'

'I can scarcely believe what I am hearing! A young man half my age asking me to reveal my bosom!'

'Not asking, Madame, pleading for an opportunity to be made aware of the glories of one who has the courage and strength of will to ignore the fleeting silliness of the crowd and remain staunchly loyal to herself.'

'How can I refuse so enchanting a plea?' she sighed.

She slipped negligée and nightgown off her shoulders and exposed to him a pair of full round breasts.

'Magnificent!' Roger exclaimed, 'I can never thank you enough for this rare privilege.'

'You are not disappointed then?'

'You do yourself an injustice to ask that question. Your breasts are incomparable.'

'Then you do not find them large and inelegant?'

'A thousand times no! They are sensuous in the extreme. May I dare to hope that you will allow me to signify my admiration by saluting them with a respectful kiss?'

'Roger! How can such a thought enter your head? Not a

176

quarter of an hour ago you were lying here with my daughter.'

'I can assure you that the incident has been utterly wiped from my memory by the splendours you have been so good as to reveal to me.'

With great tenderness he imprinted kisses on each of her soft breasts. They were warm to his lips, the skin delicate of texture, creamy-white with tiny and delicious blue veins faintly visible through the translucence of the skin. Her nipples were already firm in the centre of red-brown discs almost the size of the palm of his hand.

'You go too far,' she murmured coquettishly as his wet tongue flicked at them.

'Such opulence of warm and tender flesh,' he replied, 'Ah, the foolishness of women who crush such delights brutally inside tight clothes – and the total foolishness of men who admire women with chests like boys! You have given me a glimpse of a world I never knew existed, Madame, and I shall be eternally grateful to you.'

Roger was certain now that Larnac was not in the bedroom. Evidently he and Madame Devreux had parted early for some reason. There was something else of which he was sure – Madame Devreux had been emotionally stirred by the unexpected sight of her daughter and a man in the act of love. She had displayed her emotion in the form of outraged anger, that being what morality required – to say nothing of a mother's instinct to protect her child, even against the child's own wishes if need be. But in truth, as the events of the last few minutes had proved, the anger was only a disguise for a more profound emotion – one which had embarrassed her in the presence of her daughter. Now that Gisèle was no longer in the room, there was no need for disguise – or only such flimsy disguise as would conform to polite convention. The emotion burning fiercely within Madame Devreux's heart was desire. Larnac had been remiss in his duty as a lover, Roger thought to himself as he continued to play with her breasts.

'This gratitude you spoke of,' she said, her voice trembling.

177

'You may rely upon it.'

'Then you may demonstrate it by resolving a question that troubles me.'

'What is it you wish to know?'

'It is difficult for me to explain without seeming to . . . what I mean is . . .'

'Please speak freely, I beg you, Madame.'

'When I came into the room, half asleep and half awake, to find you and Gisèle lying on the sofa together, I naturally pulled you away from her.'

'Very forcefully,' Roger agreed.

'I was upset, you must understand.'

'I understand perfectly.'

'Well, when you fell to the floor I could not help noticing . . . your trousers were undone, you see.'

'You noticed a certain part of me, you mean?'

'Yes . . . only very briefly, of course.'

'Of course.'

'What I am trying to put into words – the question which troubles me – is this. Had you actually reached the point with Gisèle at which you . . . no, I cannot say it.'

'I understand,' Roger assured her in his most soothing tone, 'do not distress yourself. You put an end to the tender passage between Gisèle and myself some seconds before either of us had reached that point. There, does that relieve your distress?'

His hands on her breasts were doing quite as much to relieve any distress she might feel as any words he could utter.

'Not entirely,' she murmured, 'my mind is still uneasy on another matter.'

'Then allow me to calm it. Tell me the cause of your anxiety.'

'That certain part of you which I happened to see quite by accident – well, Gisèle is very young and very slender. What I saw seemed out of proportion – I fear that you must have hurt her.'

'She gave no evidence of discomfort, Madame, only of pleasure.'

178

'I find that impossible to believe, Roger. I must ask you to show me plainly what I only glimpsed before so that I can judge for myself what condition she may be in. After all, medical attention may be necessary.'

'Really, Madame Devreux, what you are suggesting is most improper,' said Roger, smiling broadly.

'Not in the least. I am Gisèle's mother. I have a right to know to what she has been subjected. You cannot deny that.'

'You make it sound as if I raped her. I can assure you that she participated willingly.'

'How could she know what was involved, she is only a child.'

'She is eighteen.'

'A mere child. Good heavens, to what has she submitted in her youthful innocence!'

Without further permission, Madame Devreux began to unfasten Roger's trousers. He allowed her to proceed. For one thing, fondling her plump breasts had spread a diffused sensation of pleasure through him which was now beginning to concentrate itself in the part of his body she wished to examine. And for another, the interruption of his love-making with Gisèle only seconds from its culmination had left his nerves outraged to the point where, unless something else happened, it would be necessary for him to seek the solace of a professional woman in the house on the Boulevard des Italiens before going home to bed. And also, though he was not consciously aware of it, he was undoubtedly flattered by the degree of interest in the source of his masculine pride that so elegant a person as Madame Devreux was displaying.

'Very well,' he said, 'it shall be as you wish. I will conceal nothing from you, Madame.'

By then her busy fingers had laid him bare and she was staring round-eyed at his taut stem.

'Heavens!' she said faintly, 'it is not possible.'

'What is not possible?'

'That this huge and distended organ could have been lodged in the tender body of my poor daughter.'

179

'But she is fully grown in every respect. We encountered no problems.'

'No, it is impossible. Why, the circumference is such that I can only just get my hand round it.'

She suited the action to her words and clasped it warmly.

'Yet I give you my word, Madame, that there were no difficulties of the type you are suggesting.'

'She must have suffered, my poor daughter. Why, the length is monstrous – there is no way in which it could have been accommodated.'

Roger encountered no resistance as he gently urged Madame Devreux to lie full-length on the sofa with her head on his lap. Indeed if the truth were told, she displayed a certain enthusiasm in approaching her face so nearly to the object of her interest, in order to examine it more closely. Her enthusiasm was, of course, tempered with dismay at the size of what she beheld, though Roger knew beyond a doubt that in this respect he was averagely endowed and that her expressions of dismay were wholly false. He continued to stroke her exposed breasts during the lengthy time when she was eyeing his equipment.

'Your touch is very exciting,' she breathed, her face pink with emotion.

'To caress *you* is very exciting,' he responded, 'it appears to me that you and I have progressed to a level of communication when words would be only a barrier to the exchange of understanding between us.'

'Yes, what you say is unquestionably true.'

Roger's hand moved slowly down under her nightgown to her belly and he stroked it in a gentle circular motion.

'Do you not find me too plump for your modern taste?' she asked, 'I'm not a skinny creature like . . .'

'Like your daughter, you mean, Madame?'

'Please . . . you must call me Pauline. Formality is ridiculous now that we have revealed everything to each other.'

'Not quite everything, Pauline,' and his hand slid further down her warm belly until his finger-tips touched her hidden patch of crinkly hair.

'Ah no – that is presumptuous of you!' she exclaimed and her hand grasped his wrist to prevent his exploring further.

'But why?'

'What sort of person are you, Roger? I discover you with your *hand* between my daughter's legs and immediately you attempt to thrust it between mine.'

'But with good reason,' he answered, 'between hers I encountered the charms of a young girl. Between your thighs I am certain that I shall discover the warm and generous delights of a fully grown woman of the world. Do you blame me for this?'

'Such a comparison can never be permitted! It would be unnatural,' she protested as his finger-tips gained another centimetre or two against the restraint of her hand encircling his wrist. He touched the top join of the fleshy lips under a covering of hair.

'How can that be?' Roger asked, 'I am a man of good appetite. The hors-d'oeuvre was snatched away before I had finished it. Is the main course to be removed before I even begin? If so, I shall leave with my hunger totally unsatisfied.'

'You beast!' she moaned, 'to compare Gisèle and me to the courses of a meal – it is abominable!'

Perhaps she believed her own words, perhaps they were merely a token protest. What is sure is that her grasp loosened on his wrist and his fingers found the vantage point they had been seeking. Madame Devreux gasped loudly as he pried apart those soft folds of flesh and penetrated her citadel.

In all this, Roger's intention was to arouse and please her to the point where she would offer no further resistance, then hoist up her long nightgown and board her as she lay on the convenient sofa. But her degree of arousal was greater than he had realised and he had utterly forgotten the proximity of her face to his free-standing part. Scarcely had he begun to caress her moist bud than she rolled her head in his lap and took his full-stretched device into her hot and wet mouth.

181

'Take care!' he said jerkily, made suddenly aware of how excited he had himself become during the process of playing with her big breasts.

His warning went unheard and unheeded. Madame Devreux moaned in her throat as she pressed home her assault on his most sensitive part. Her back lifted off the sofa and she thrust herself hard against his rubbing fingers. In one moment more Roger was overwhelmed by sensation and his essence was sucked from him. Through his delirious pleasure he was vaguely aware of his companion's legs and bottom thrashing against the sofa cushions as she too underwent her climactic experience.

When she had recovered herself a little, Madame Devreux sat up and put her feet on the floor. She moved away from him, pulled her nightgown up and slid the straps over her shoulders, then closed and tied her negligée.

'Thank God I was able to prevent the final infamy,' she announced.

'What do you mean? There can be no infamy in love between a man and a woman.'

'Between you and me it would have been infamous.'

'But why?'

'You know perfectly well why. Half an hour ago you made love to my daughter. And then you attempt to do it to me. This is infamous, to employ the same organ on a mother and her daughter.'

'I have only the one,' Roger pointed out reasonably.

'This is not a subject for mockery.'

'My profound apologies.'

'You must leave now, Roger, and never come back. You are not to see my daughter again. Is that understood?'

'Do not distress yourself, Madame. I shall take my leave.'

He rose and bowed politely, only then remembering to tuck away his *infamous* organ and to fasten his trousers. To his surprise Madame Devreux also rose to see him to the door, her arms folded firmly across her bosom as if to protect herself from an attack.

'Try to understand my feelings, Roger,' she said to him in

182

the entrance hall. 'It is my duty to protect Gisèle from the consequences of her folly until she finds a husband.'

'I do understand,' he replied, giving her his most charming smile, 'a mother's duty is sacred. May I kiss your hand in farewell?'

She stretched out her hand and he kissed the back of it lightly but with feeling.

'Ah, if only . . .' he sighed.

'If only what, Roger?'

'If only I had dared to direct my attentions towards you rather than towards Gisèle . . . what pleasures you and I might have enjoyed together. But it was quite unthinkable for me to raise my eyes in the direction of so exalted a person as yourself, whatever the urging of my heart.'

'You are an impudent young man,' Madame Devreux said softly, 'I am twenty years older than you. My daughter is your contemporary.'

'Yet what are a few years difference between lovers when their deepest sentiments are engaged. I should have been bolder.'

Her hand was on the door knob, yet she paused at his words.

'Since it is goodbye,' said Roger, 'permit me to kiss you respectfully on the cheek as a sign of peace between us.'

'Do it and go.'

Roger put his hands lightly on her shoulders and kissed her cheek, then the other cheek – and then her mouth, his arms about her to press her body close to him. For a moment she resisted, then as the tip of his tongue insinuated itself between her lips, she relaxed and enjoyed the embrace. After all, it was only a kiss – nothing more would happen.

What did happen was that Roger's hands slid down her back, smoothing her thin nightgown and negligée against her skin, until he could grasp and hold the fleshy cheeks of her bottom.

'No!' she exclaimed, breaking off the kiss, 'you must not do that!'

With half a step Roger turned her so that her back was

183

against the door and his foot between hers. Short of screaming for help, she could do little to prevent him from proceeding further, if that was his intention. As indeed it was, for with one hand he hitched up her loose clothes at the back and with the other he parted the cheeks of her bottom and probed with his fingers until he was touching her furry mound. Madame Devreux attempted to get her hands between their bodies in order to push him away, but he was pressed too close for that.

'Stop it at once!' she commanded nervously.

His finger-tip was within the warm and secret place he had previously stimulated when they were together on the sofa. Madame Devreux's resistance was not long sustained after that. What woman of her age could reject the attentions of a handsome young man once his skilful fingers had penetrated the citadel of her passions? Only the most determined, and in the circumstances in which she found herself, Madame Devreux was not excessively determined. Deep sighs of pleasure squeezed her full breasts against Roger's chest, stimulating her even more. Her hands descended to his narrow hips and held him, perhaps even pulled their bodies closer together, if that was possible.

'I surrender,' she murmured, hardly aware of her own words.

Thus encouraged, Roger hauled her night clothes up around her waist.

'Raise your left leg,' he instructed her, even as he dealt one-handed with his trouser buttons.

'My God, not here! Surely you do not intend . . .'

He cut off her feeble outcry by pressing his mouth to hers in a long kiss. Her foot left the floor, her knee bent upwards and outwards. Roger steadied her against the door while he positioned his firm part at the entrance to her secret spot, then bent his knees a little and pushed slowly and yet inexorably upwards until he was fully embedded. With one arm around her waist and the other supporting her raised leg, he had her fully under control.

The unfamiliarity of the position – or perhaps the

184

strangeness of her plight – affected Madame Devreux deeply. Her whole experience of the delights of love until that moment had been limited to lying comfortably on her back on a bed, with a partner lying on her. For her, the bizarre nature of what was taking place had a distinctly aphrodisiac quality. Tremors ran through her body, from the centre of her joy up to her breasts and down her legs. But for the support afforded her by Roger she would surely have fallen to the floor. The door against which she was pressed rattled as if sharing in her delight, until Roger shuffled a foot forward against it, without missing a single thrust, to silence this inanimate witness to Madame Devreux's pleasure.

'I'm there!' she exclaimed, her belly shaking against his, 'oh God!'

But Roger was not. Only a very short time had elapsed since their curious passage on the sitting-room sofa and though he enjoyed the recuperative powers of youth, he required a little longer to scale the heights a second time.

Madame Devreux's dark head lolled back against the door, her face flushed and yet content. Her body was limp as Roger drove on towards his goal. She still held him by the hips, no longer pulling him towards her but in submission to what he was doing to her.

Had Roger not been at that moment utterly enrapt by the tremendous sensations coursing through his body, he might even have discerned a certain affection and pride in his prowess in the manner in which she held him while she waited for him to run the last lap of the course she had already completed.

The critical moments, when they arrived, were formidable. Roger panted and jolted and stabbed furiously into her submissive body, beside himself in the sharp joy of the male's conquest. Or seeming conquest – for who is the victor and who is the victim in the encounters of love? He was still trembling and breathing heavily in the afterglow of passion when Madame Devreux reached up to smooth back the lock of hair that had fallen across his perspiring forehead.

He eased himself away from her with care and courtesy, her long night clothes descended to her ankles, concealing all.

'I don't know what to say,' she murmured while he was adjusting his own clothes.

'What should you say, Pauline? Together we have enjoyed a momentous experience and it is for me to express my fervent gratitude to you for making it possible.'

'But I didn't want it to happen, you know that!'

'That is all in the past. There is no reason for regret, only for joy that so enchanting an encounter could be shared by you and me.'

'Perhaps you are right,' she said, smiling at him, 'regret is absurd. Goodnight, then, Roger.'

'I hope that you think better of me now than earlier this evening.'

'I hardly know what to think of you – or of myself. But one thing is for sure – every time I pass through this door in future I shall be reminded of what happened to me against it.'

On the next day Roger met Gisèle by arrangement at Fouquets in the Champs Élysées. His thoughts became more and more complicated as he sat waiting for her at a table on the terrace, but the moment he caught sight of her walking towards him, his spirits lifted. She looked extremely pretty and very young in a sleeveless frock of bright pink with a long yellow scarf tied under the collar and floating with her movements. The late spring sunshine made her light brown hair gleam, so that she was altogether enchanting.

Roger stood to greet her with a kiss on the cheek and she gave him a radiant smile.

'Whatever did you say to Mama last night?' she asked the instant she was seated.

'Why, how was she this morning?'

'Not one angry word – can you believe it? I expected her to be furious and scream at me all morning. I was dreading it.'

'What *did* she say?'

'She said that finding us like that had shocked her but that on reflection she had come to realise that I was no longer a child. She said that I must be treated like an adult and that I must behave like one. She said much more than that, of course, but that's what it amounted to.'

'Did you find out how she came to be there? You told me she was out.'

'Apparently she had a tremendous quarrel with Larnac in a restaurant and walked out on him. I gather that he won't be calling any more. I felt quite sorry for her – I mean, to lose your lover and find your daughter with a lover all on the same evening, it's too much for any woman. No wonder she was angry and upset. How did you manage to calm her down? Or did she just throw you out?'

'I stayed to talk to her for some time. It was not easy, but I urged reason upon her and eventually she took my point.'

'I think you're brilliant, Roger. If we weren't in a public place I'd hug you.'

'I would enjoy that. After all, we were interrupted last night at an unfortunate moment.'

Gisèle giggled at him.

'It would have been better if we had gone to a hotel as I suggested,' said Roger.

'Yes. My little visitor made his entrance and then ran away before I could make him properly welcome. That was very sad.'

'He was settling in very comforably when events forced him to retreat,' said Roger.

She was delightful, he thought – witty, amusing – and so very pretty with her slightly turned-up nose and shining brown eyes. He felt that he loved her to distraction.

'Are you free this evening?' he asked, touching her hand with a gesture that spoke eloquently of intimacies to be shared.

'No, Mama and I are invited for dinner at the Colombes. It will be boring.'

'Then tomorrow? Say yes, or I shall burst with love.'

'Not even tomorrow,' Gisèle answered sadly.

'Why not?'

'I have to vist my cousins in the country.'

'But this is terrible! When will you be back in Paris?'

'We could meet on Sunday.'

'And be together in a hotel?'

Gisèle nodded and smiled.

'Yes, I'd like that, Roger.'

Events were to prove themselves more complicated than Roger imagined. He was, after all, only eighteen years old and for all his assumed *savoir faire* he had everything still to learn about the ways of the world – and especially the ways of women. A pressing invitation from Madame Devreux took him to her home after dinner on Saturday evening.

She opened the door to him herself, from which he deduced that the servants had been given the evening off. On this occasion she was wearing a simple evening frock in silver grey with emerald clips on the neckline about where her collar-bones were. The hem was discreetly below her knees, longer than the styles worn by Gisèle.

'Sit down, Roger,' she said, 'will you take a little glass of something?'

'Cognac, if you please.'

He seated himself on the famous dusty-rose coloured sofa on which his consecutive encounters with Gisèle and her mother had taken place. Madame Devreux poured the cognac, handed one of the glasses to him and sat on a chair out of arm's-reach.

'We must talk very seriously,' she announced, her tone pleasant but firm.

'I am at your service.'

'Where to begin . . .? The truth is that I have been upset and worried since the other evening. You cannot imagine how upset I have been, remembering what occurred. I do not blame you, Roger, for anything. It was I who should have known better than to let myself be swept away by unseemly emotions.'

188

'My dear Pauline,' said Roger boldly, 'what use is this self-reproach? What happened was the natural outcome of the proximity of a man and a woman in circumstances which were, though unusual, extremely provocative. We both responded to the urgent dictates of our hearts, nothing more.'

'Ah, but you are young – you can dismiss from your mind an event which to me is a heavy burden.'

'A burden of guilt, you mean?' he asked in some surprise.

'Guilt, yes – but worse than that, a burden of jealousy.'

'I find it hard to understand what you mean.'

Madame Devreux's expression was woeful.

'Why should it be so difficult to understand?' she asked, 'Am I so old that I cannot be jealous of my own daughter? Am I not a woman too, with a heart as susceptible as that of a young girl? Did you leave me the other evening with the impression that all passion has withered in me?'

It would have taken a man older and more experienced than Roger to distinguish between the real and the false in Madame Devreux's anguish. If, that is, any man ever could. Like all women, she was sincere and yet at the same time had a concealed purpose. She was capable of honest emotions and deceit at the same time – without herself being able to tell the difference. In short, she was a woman.

Oblivious to this, Roger was on one knee before her, kissing her hand.

'Dear Pauline,' he said, 'how could I imagine that you could be interested in me in that way. I am deeply honoured.'

She stroked his cheek fondly.

'What a tragedy we are involved in,' she said, 'if only I were twenty years younger and you were not in love with my daughter!'

'It is true that I adore Gisèle. But believe me, there is a deep and enduring affection in my heart for you.'

'That may be – but how cruel!'

'Cruel?'

189

'Affection is not the emotion which you have awakened in me. Your feelings do not match mine, that is evident.'

'But I used the word affection in order not to risk offending you. Since you have shown me the way I will speak more openly – I adore you too. The truth is that you stir my profoundest passions.'

'Roger, take care what you say!'

'I have gone too far now to retreat. To be completely frank with you, once I had experienced the delights of your love I knew that I must find a way to return to you for more.'

'But what about Gisèle?'

'I love her too and I must possess her, as I must you.'

'But this is unnatural!'

'For me it is the most natural thing in the world to want to make love to the two women I adore. If you cannot accept that, you must tell me to leave.'

'My God, what will become of us,' she murmured, leaning forward to kiss his face.

'Only that which we desire for ourselves,' he replied, his hands on her waist.

'How can I tell my confessor that I have erred with my daughter's fiancé?'

'Tell him nothing,' said Roger instantly, 'what he doesn't know won't disturb his sleep.'

'But what of my conscience?'

His hands were on her breasts, moulding them through her frock.

'In matters of the heart there is no place for the quibbles of conscience. That is for priests and old women, not for lovers. I want you now, Pauline.'

'So young and already so forceful,' she sighed, her hands on his, pressing them more tightly over her breasts.

In her bedroom she took off the elegant silver-grey frock and stood revealed in a white lace slip and over it, from just below her bosom to her bottom, a white satin corset laced down the front.

'A sign that my youth is past,' she sighed, observing his interest in this garment, 'does it disgust you?'

'Why no, no such thought entered my head. Rather I was thinking that this is a disguise for the exuberance and bounty of your body. I find it strangely exciting.'

'Do you? You will change your opinion as you grow older.'

'Let me undo it!'

He knelt before her to puzzle out the cross-lacing and to unfasten it. When the corset fell away he ran his palms lovingly over her plump belly through her lace slip, then pressed his cheek against it.

'So warm and soft,' he said, 'how delightful!'

He stood up again, his face flushed red, and gently pulled the slip up over her head and threw it onto the bed. Beneath it she wore a bandeau brassiere of open lacework to restrain her large breasts. She turned to let him find and undo the hooks and eyes which held it at the back. Once that was removed, he leaned against her back and reached round to fondle her breasts for a long time before pulling down her loose-legged silk knickers and planting kisses on the fleshy cheeks of her bottom.

Madame Devreux sat on the side of the bed to remove her shoes and stockings, while Roger tore off his clothes, scattering them across the carpet, before hurling himself on the bed beside her and clutching her fiercely in his arms.

With all the surging virility of eighteen, he gave a convincing account of himself in every way. As for Madame Devreux, she was delighted to have acquired a lover half the age and with twice the strength of Henri Larnac. That Roger had only a fraction of Larnac's finesse was a small matter that could be put right by a suitable course of education in bed.

After the third passage at arms she lay limp and contented, a faint sheen of perspiration between her breasts and over her broad belly.

'Do you really love me, Roger?'

'Madly,' he replied, 'Can you entertain the slightest doubt after the proof I have just given you?'

'And Gisèle?'

191

'She has not yet enjoyed the evidence of my love as you have. But she will, and soon.'

'Do not torment me!'

'Do not torment yourself, Pauline. Afterwards I shall return to you, to reassure you of my devotion.'

'What – you intend to pass backwards and forwards between us?'

'Why not?'

'You are proposing a conspiracy between you and me, no less.'

Roger shrugged and smiled, confident of his powers. He leaned over Madame Devreux to imprint gentle kisses on the insides of her thighs, her soft belly and the tips of her breasts.

'You are a cynical young man,' she said, 'and an immoral one too. But I find you irresistible.'

Her hand crept between his thighs to appraise the condition of his appurtenance. She also was confident of her powers. In their separate ways she and Gisèle would be able to shape Roger to the pattern they desired.

'Then it is agreed that I shall have you both?' he asked, smiling down at her.

'Why not?' she replied, using his own words.

GUY'S EARLY RETIREMENT

Dr Moulin was a man of good sense, who understood that certain matters should be arranged with discretion, particularly if the Brissard family was in any way involved. When he was summoned to the bedside of Guy Verney, a short examination and a few questions were sufficient to inform him of the reasons of Guy's weakened condition and to start in his mind a train of thought that involved the interests of the Brissards. In consequence, Moulin instructed his patient to stay in bed and rest until his return the next day. He told Jeanne Verney that her husband was suffering from the strain of over-work, a diagnosis which surprised her. Then, without her knowledge, the good doctor arranged an urgent appointment with her brother, Maurice Brissard.

Maurice was amused by what the doctor told him in confidence.

'You wish me to believe that my brother-in-law has been indulging himself in masochistic practices?' he asked.

'His body is criss-crossed with the marks of old and new whippings and other abuse, Monsieur. Of the condition of his private parts I will say nothing.'

Maurice, who had no particular affection for Verney, laughed aloud.

'Extraordinary! But after all, it is his right to amuse himself in whatever way he chooses. Why have you come to me?'

'Perhaps you have not fully understood the gravity of the case,' said Moulin, a little shocked by Maurice's unexpected levity, 'Monsieur Verney's health is seriously undermined. If he should continue in these practices, I fear for his life.'

'As bad as that, is it? He must have been very enthusiastic about his pleasures.'

'You should not joke, Monsieur. How am I to tell Madame Verney of these things?'

Maurice's smile faded, for he was devoted to his sister.

'Leave that to me,' he said, 'what course of treatment do you propose for your patient?'

'Complete rest, for a long time, away from Paris. Somewhere quiet in the country perhaps. He will require a trained nurse in attendance.'

'Then, if you will be so good, find a suitable person at once. I will take care of the rest. And thank you for coming to me – your discretion will not go unrewarded.'

While Moulin made enquiries of his colleagues for a suitable person to undertake the task of nursing Guy back to health, Maurice visited his sister at her home in the Avenue Kléber. He explained everything to her with complete candour. Jeanne was not as amused as he had been, but she was practical, like him.

'He must be looked after properly,' she said, 'but we cannot risk any scandalous gossip – imagine what Papa would say if this came to his attention! Moulin has shown himself to be trustworthy and we may rely on him to find a discreet attendant. But what about the . . . partner . . . with whom Guy has played these violent games. Do you know who she is?'

Maurice shrugged in distaste.

'Guy may have been a regular visitor to one of the establishments which specialise in this type of activity,' he said, 'I have heard that there is such a place in the vicinity of the Stock Exchange.'

'You must talk to him and find out, Maurice. A few thousand francs may stop any idle talk.'

Guy turned his head slowly on the pillows when Maurice entered his room. His face was pale and drawn – he looked much older than his fifty years. Maurice put a chair near the bed and sat down.

'My dear Guy,' he began cheerfully, 'I am sorry to find you unwell. It seems that you have overdone your little pleasures.'

194

'That doctor has betrayed me,' Guy exclaimed, somewhat dramatically.

'He has your best interests at heart, I assure you. There are arrangements to be made and you cannot expect Jeanne to make them, in the circumstances. So he took me into his confidence. You have to go away for a long rest, Guy. Moulin suggested the country – what do you think?'

'I should be dead of boredom in a week. I would prefer Deauville.'

'Why not? Good sea air, good food, proper care – you'll be a new man in a month or two.'

'I hope so. I am so weak that I can hardly get out of bed. When do you want me to go?'

'Tomorrow or the next day – it is a question of how quickly Moulin can find a properly trained attendant for you. Out of interest, will you tell me something?'

'What do you want to know – my motives?'

'Of course not! Your motives are self-evident – you enjoyed it, so you did it. Whatever Jeanne might think, as a man I find your motives require no justification. My question is this – there are not, in so far as I know, many establishments *de luxe* where a man can obtain these particular services. Do you mind telling me where you found them – was it at the Chabanais?'

'Why do you want to know?'

'I will be frank with you. There is the question of family honour.'

'The Brissard family honour, of course,' said Guy acidly.

'And that of the Verney family. Your wife, your children – we must think of their interests, Guy. We must also consider your interests – it would be impossible for you to resume a normal life in a few months if there were an atmosphere of ill-natured rumour about you.'

'You may put your mind at rest. I have not frequented any of the special establishments in Paris.'

'Then where?'

Guy explained. On one of his regular business trips to

195

his factory in Nantes he had made the acquaintance of Madame Yvette Bégard and her friend Mademoiselle Solange. In telling this to Maurice he was intentionally vague about his first encounter with these two, but suffice it to say that he had become aware that Madame Bégard and her friend were enthusiasts of the sexual humiliation of men. After the initial shock, Guy discovered an unsuspected truth about himself – he had a natural aptitude as a victim.

'How long have you been visiting these ladies?' Maurice asked, suppressing a smile at the thought of his brother-in-law in the clutches of two provincial women wreaking their will upon him.

'Nearly two years.'

There was a gleam in Guy's eyes at the memory of his visits to Nantes. He was transported by a surge of enthusiasm and babbled of naked women with tall black hoods over their heads, big soft breasts swaying violently as arms were raised to lash him, strong and cruel female fingers which gripped his excited male part and inflicted delicate tortures on it, shiny black patent leather shoes with high heels which trampled his helpless body. To all this Maurice listened closely. He had heard of such things before, but never from one who had participated in these unusual pleasures.

When Guy's energy ran out, he asked him if he could be sure that his friends in Nantes would be discreet. Guy thought about that for some time.

'I don't know,' he said, 'they are such marvellous and demonic creatures. They seize control of you, body and soul. They do horribly fascinating things to you. You scream in pain and beg for more. I tell you, Maurice, there is no pleasure with any woman that is half as intense as the pleasure they inflict upon you.'

'Calm yourself,' said Maurice, smiling at the new burst of animation with which Guy was speaking, 'what you are saying is that they cannot be relied on to remain silent.'

'I am completely in their power!' Guy exclaimed. 'They control me – they make me experience incredible sensations! They are capable of everything, those beautiful naked she-devils! Perhaps they will seek me out when I do not visit them – seek me out and kill me with ecstasy!'

'Don't trouble yourself about that, Guy. I will arrange matters so that you are not disturbed.'

In this way it came about that two days later Guy found himself installed in a hotel suite in Deauville, under the care of Mademoiselle Ernestine Noiret. She was a woman of about thirty, with a strong and pleasant face and dark brown hair. But she was of the size of a boxer! Out of the short sleeves of her plain grey frock there bulged arms strong enough to lift Guy in and out of bed as if he weighed no more than a small child. The legs she displayed between the hem of her frock and her large-size shoes would not have disgraced a marathon-runner. It was evident that Dr Moulin had selected her as much for her physical strength as for her nursing experience. Yet as Guy was to discover, she had a cheerful temperament and was no fool.

On his second day in the hotel, when he had recovered from the fatigue of the train journey from Paris, Guy had his first taste of Ernestine's methods. At ten in the morning she entered his room and swept the covers to the bottom of his bed with a flick of her muscular wrist. There lay Guy in patterned silk pyjamas – a dome-shaped object, his belly the highest point, curving down to his chest and pallid face on one side and to his chubby legs on the other. She put an arm round his shoulders and lifted him into a sitting position to remove his pyjama jacket before lowering him again. She untied the drawstring of his trousers and pulled them off his legs, so that he was naked.

She eyes him thoughtfully as he lay passive. The hair on his chest was already tinged with grey, his arms were flabby, the expression on his face was apathetic. His belly bulged formidably – the result of too many years of over-eating and over-drinking. The marks of his peculiar interests were apparent to her. There were faint red weals on his fat belly where he had been lashed, even the thin

197

lines of healed wounds. She rolled him over to inspect his back and saw the traces on the wobbly cheeks of his behind of frequent whippings.

Ernestine took note of all this and rolled him onto his back again. Close inspection showed her that his nipples had been stretched beyond the normal size – no doubt by the repeated use of metal clamps. There were curious marks in the soft flesh of his thighs which, she concluded, had been caused by the insertion of steel pins to galvanise his jaded sensations – and yes, the limp penis hanging weakly between his thighs bore the same marks. She took it between two fingers the size of sausages and stretched it a little to see the extent of the marks. Without doubt, she said to herself as she released it, Monsieur Verney had been exceptionally thorough in his pursuit of the dark pleasures.

'Monsieur,' she said, 'it is my function to restore you to health. The matter has been put entirely in my hands by your family and your doctor, so you must accept it. I am very expert and I shall soon have you well again, with your co-operation.'

Guy grunted doubtfully.

'You are too fat,' Ernestine declared, patting his bulging belly with a hand as big as a dinner plate, 'a man must be strong, not thin and feeble, but this – this is ridiculous. This paunch must go. I shall personally supervise your diet. It will be appetising and nourishing, but there will not be an excess of anything, believe me. Starting tomorrow morning, you and I will walk together on the beach for half an hour. As your strength returns, the walk will get longer. There will also be twice daily massage, beginning now.'

Guy groaned inwardly. It had been years since he had walked any greater distance than the width of a pavement into a taxi.

'The day is hot,' said Ernestine, 'you must excuse me if I remove my dress before massaging you.'

Guy became slightly more interested as Ernestine fumbled at the fastenings of her frock with her great capable

198

hands. He sighed gently to himself as it came over her head and she stood revealed in a knee-length white slip.

'You are right,' he said, 'it is remarkably hot for June. Remove your slip too, if you like – it would be a pity to spoil it.'

'Thank you,' she said, 'I didn't like to suggest it myself. But do not entertain any little ideas about you-know-what, Monsieur.'

'How could I?' Guy reassured her, 'You have observed my condition.'

He watched with interest as Ernestine removed her slip to display her huge bare breasts, each the size of a water-melon. Her belly was a wall of muscle in which her navel was visible only as a tiny closed eye, her thighs were those of a weight-lifter, clad in plain grey stockings held by unadorned black garters. Between these two points of interest she wore close-fitting knickers of dark-blue bom-bazine. Not only did Guy' eyes gleam – his limp part twitched once, but only once, then subsided in wretched-ness. Not, of course, without Ernestine noticing.

'Poor Monsieur Guy,' she said, 'of what use are you now to a woman? That little thing won't stand up – and even if it did, you haven't got the breath to exert yourself enough to do anything with it. You have ruined your health and pleasure is only a memory now.'

'But what memories I have!' said Guy.

'I'm sure you do. But now we will start to repair the damage.'

She attacked his naked body with tremendous energy. She pummelled him with her big hands and rolled him about on the bed as if he weighed no more than a feather-stuffed pillow! This was not the easy massage that soothes and relaxes tension – it was a whole course of exercise in itself. She flexed his arms and legs, bending them up, round, behind, over, utterly without regard for his gasps of distress. How she worked, this Ernestine! In a few minutes the perspiration stood out on her forehead from her exertions, on her broad chest – it dripped down her massive breasts and trickled down her belly.

199

What of Guy? Ah, the suffering of that treatment! Not the suffering of distorted pleasure which had reduced him to this condition, but the suffering of muscles and sinews long unused to such employment. His belly ached from the twisting and stretching it received, his back ached from being forced to bend – not until his head touched his knees, for that was impossible, but somewhere towards them. His arms ached, his legs ached – and then ached even more when Ernestine put a stockinged foot into his groin, took him by each ankle in turn and hauled until he felt that his knees and hips had been totally disjointed.

At last it was over and he lay whimpering softly. But it was not over! Ernestine took a large sponge from a basin of water and pressed it to his tortured belly. Guy uttered a shriek – the water was ice cold! She continued relentlessly, wetting the sponge and pressing it into his armpits, his nipples and into his groins. Even to the soles of his feet! Only when he was numb all over did she take a towel and rub him dry – and that too was agony, for the towel was rough and her rubbing was violent.

'There,' she exclaimed, throwing the bed covers over him, 'we've made a start. You may sleep now until it is time for lunch.'

Poor Guy, utterly exhausted, fell asleep instantly.

Two weeks of increasingly long walks in the brisk sea-air, of plain food in small portions, of rigorous daily massage – the regime had its intended effect. Guy's paunch was diminishing and a healthier colour was returning to his face. Other changes were also taking place, a most important one being the strengthening of a bond of familiarity between Guy and Ernestine. He had resigned himself totally into her hands, obeyed her every word – and this was perhaps not surprising. His bizarre experiences with Madame Bégard had taught him the joys of submission. The strange element which must always have been present in his character had been exposed and encouraged until he was obsessed by it. Ernestine – so big and strong – had in his mind taken the place of

200

Yvette Bégard, though Ernestine cared for his well-being rather than trying to destroy it.

To Guy himself it was a sign that he was making progress that he enjoyed his daily view of Ernestine's near-naked body when she submitted him to her rigorous massage. Ah, the sight of her meaty breasts swinging and bouncing as she pummelled and rubbed him! Her thighs, emerging from her tight knickers – how muscular and thrilling! There were nights when Guy dreamed of those thighs. Ernestine was conscious of Guy's slowly growing interest in her – and of his dependence on her – yet she remained respectful. She invariably addressed him as Monsieur Guy and called him Monsieur Verney when she had occasion to speak of him to the hotel servants. For Ernestine, this was, after all, the best-paid job she had ever had, and she meant to keep it.

One day, as Guy lay face-down on his bed while she chopped with the sides of her hands at his flabby buttocks, she observed a certain change in his expression – his head being sideways on the pillow – along with a change in the muscle tone of his body. She rolled him over and observed that his male part, for so long limp, had swollen to a noticeable size and was attempting to stand erect.

'Well!' she said, 'there's a little surprise!'

'Things are improving,' said Guy, looking at his own success in surprise.

'And will continue to do so,' Ernestine assured him.

'I hope so – but there's a long way to go yet. I hardly know whether to laugh or to cry – laugh that something important has happened or cry that it is so poor a shadow of what it once was.'

In the friendliest way in the world Ernestine took his half-hard part between her fingers and tugged it gently. The pin-marks had faded but would never entirely vanish.

'To be truthful,' she said, 'it is not very strong yet, Monsieur Guy. But at least we have proof that its strength may return in time. Poor forlorn little creature – how badly you have treated it!'

'But how it responded to that treatment!' said Guy with a smile.

201

'Tell me, if you regain your strength completely, what then? Will you return to your former pleasures?'

'What else can I do?' Guy said sadly. 'The ordinary pleasure of love is meaningless to me now. But, as you have said, I shall be destroyed by what I most enjoy. Dear Ernestine, what shall I do?'

His misery caused the pink part she held to lose its power and shrink back into lassitude.

'There are many alternatives,' she said sympathetically, 'for the present, put all thoughts of pleasure out of your head. Have confidence in me.'

On Guy's fourth week-end at the sea-side Maurice came from Paris to visit him and see how he was getting on. He was impressed by the improvement in Guy's physical condition and assured him that all was well with his business. Not that Guy cared very much – he had lost interest in business matters a long time ago, when the dark delights of Madame Bégard's torture chamber became an obsession. He was content to leave financial affairs in Maurice's hands so long as he could stay in the private world of his hotel suite and be nursed by Ernestine.

Before he departed, Maurice talked to Ernestine alone and congratulated her on Guy's progress.

'His physical condition is satisfactory, Monsieur, for only a month of care, and it will improve further. But his will – that is another matter.'

'His will to live, you mean?' asked Maurice, slightly puzzled.

'There is no question of his will to live. I mean that he has lost the will to lead the life of a normal man.'

'With women, you mean?'

'I fear that Madame Verney will not again enjoy the pleasures of marriage with her husband, Monsieur. But more than that – I doubt if he will ever regain his interest in directing his business and caring for his family, and the other activities of ordinary men.'

That Jeanne would not again share a bed with her husband was no great loss, thought Maurice. She had never found any pleasure in Guy's embraces. She had endured them as a duty, while seeking gratification in the arms of other men. As for Guy's business, his nephew Christophe could manage that very well, under Maurice's guidance.

'It would seem from what you say, Mademoiselle, that my brother-in-law may remain a permanent invalid in his own home.'

'It is too early to say. Another month or two and I shall be in a position to advise you.'

There they left it and Maurice returned to Paris to inform his sister of how things stood. Guy had never been popular with any of the Brissards and all were happy to leave the arrangements in Maurice's hands, especially Jeanne, so long as Guy was properly cared for.

In the healthy sea-air Guy continued to mend. There came a day when, as Ernestine removed her frock in preparation for massaging him, he made a suggestion which neither shocked nor surprised her.

'Ernestine – we are good friends, you and I,' he began.

'I certainly hope so, after all this time.'

'I have no secrets from you,' he continued, gesturing at his naked body, 'You know everything about me there is to know – even how my poor little pink thing tries to stand up and fails.'

'Not fails, Monsieur Guy. Several times now it has succeeded, though only for moments.'

'Brief moments,' he said, 'but that aside, there is part of yourself which you conceal from me. Whether this is from modesty, I do not know.'

'I understand you. You wish me to take off my knickers.'

'It would be an act of friendship, no more than that, in my condition.'

'Then I shall do as you request. It was not for reasons of modesty that I have kept them on during your massage.'

'What other reason could there be? You are certainly not afraid that I shall pull you onto the bed with me and rape you.'

She laughed at that and he laughed with her.

'I did not wish to upset you by letting you see the part of a woman which has no interest for you,' she told him.

'That won't upset me. On the contrary, it may give me encouragement.'

Without another word Ernestine stripped completely for him. Guy stared with longing at the thick patch of hair which started between the columns of her thighs and ended halfway up her muscular belly. Profuse as it was, it did little to conceal her big fleshy mound and the thick, pouting lips of her sex.

'Thank you, Ernestine,' he said with a sigh.

By the time she had worked on his shoulders and back with her strong fingers, and the still faintly-scarred cheeks of his bottom, she was not surprised on turning him over to find that his pink stem was responding as well as it could. To be sure, the degree of stiffness was insufficient for any practical use. Instead of massaging his paunch, much less prominent now than a month ago, Ernestine took his struggling part between the palms of her big hands and rolled it gently. It seemed to her that a minute or two of this treatment had some effect, though not as much as she would have prefered.

'There is a way in which you can make it stand up like an iron bar,' Guy whispered.

'How?'

'Whip me! Use my braces – anything – the result will amaze you.'

'Absolutely not!' she said, continuing her rolling motion, 'all that is in the past. There is to be no more infliction of pain, do you understand?'

'Just this once, Ernestine,' he pleaded.

'No, no, no! If what I am doing to you is not sufficient, then you must be patient until your health returns completely.'

To distract his thoughts she released his penis and resumed her normal massage, but with a vigour that amounted almost to brutality. Guy was gasping for breath under the attack of her strong hands on his body from shoulders to thighs. His stem did not shrink, as she

204

expected, though he was approaching the point of total exhaustion. Indeed, it appeared to grow firmer! She ground at his flesh even harder and was kneeling on the bed between his spread and plump legs, her fingers tormenting the sinews of his soft thigh muscles, when his engorged limb bounded in a lively manner and let fall one tiny drop onto his belly.

'Ah!' Guy exclaimed, 'Ernestine!'

'Well!' she said softly, 'look what has happened! Our prayers have been answered, Monsieur Guy.'

Guy lay with his eyes closed, breathing heavily. Ernestine climbed over his legs to sit propped up against the bed-head and lift his head onto her massive naked bosom. She stroked his forehead solicitously.

'I am astonished,' Guy said faintly, 'I had given up all hope of ever feeling those sensations again. Thank you, Ernestine, thank you.'

In a little while he fell asleep. Ernestine moved her bulk from under him, arranged him comfortably on the bed, covered him over and left him. The episode had given her much to think about. She had been recommended for her present assignment through Dr Moulin by Doctor Faguet and the understanding was that she would return, when Monsieur Verney was well again, to the clinic at which she had been employed for over two years. It was there that she had met Dr Faguet, who used the clinic's facilities at times for purposes of his own. The meeting with him was one she remembered with pleasure, for in addition to the professional aspect of it, Jean-Albert Faguet had taken it into his head once or twice to make love to her. He had proved to be both energetic and imaginative.

But Ernestine had no illusions about herself. Her size made her unattractive to men in general and the incidents with Jean-Albert Faguet had been no more than a fleeting fancy on his part, alas. She had no desire to return to the clinic now that she had enjoyed the rewards of working for a rich family on a case that required the utmost discretion. The salary was very good and she was living in a first-class hotel! The fact was, however, that her assignment with

Monsieur Verney was nearing its end. Another month at most, she considered, and he would return to his family in Paris – and she would be thanked and dismissed. His little climax of emotion, feeble though it had been, was indication enough that she had done her job well – perhaps too well for the good of her own future prospects.

Madame Verney came to visit her husband a few days after that little event. She was, Ernestine observed, a most elegant and beautiful woman, nearly twenty years younger than her husband. She arrived at the hotel wearing a summer frock of layered petals of a delicate cyclamen colour, with a light coat of shantung silk open over it – and a white hat with a broad brim, very suitable for the sea-side. She was kind and attentive towards her husband and dined with him in his suite, making him laugh a little with her chatter.

After Guy had gone to bed, Madame Verney sent for Ernestine.

'Mademoiselle Noiret,' she began, 'my husband is obviously much better. I am extremely grateful to you. How much longer must he remain here, do you think?'

For dinner Madame Verney had changed into an exquisite frock that could only have been made by one of the master couturiers of Paris. Evidently she was not pining for her husband, Ernestine thought – she looked much too contented and well-loved to have been virtuous during his long absence. Ernestine repeated what she had told Maurice Brissard – that Monsieur Verney's health was improving satisfactorily, but that he seemed to have lost the will to resume a normal life. Jeanne Verney nodded – Maurice had told her that much.

'Be frank with me, Mademoiselle,' she said, 'could this occur again? This physical breakdown, I mean.'

'It is possible, Madame, I regret to inform you. From little remarks Monsieur Verney has made to me I have formed the impression that he might well return to his former habits, unless some restraint is exercised.'

'Self-restraint, you mean?'

'That is out of the question, I fear. Restraint by others may be necessary.'

Jeanne wrinkled her pretty nose.

'Understand me, Mademoiselle,' she said in evident disgust, 'his tastes are his own affair, even if they prove catastrophic to him. But there is the possibility of scandal when a man's tastes lead him in a certain direction. Any scandal of that kind is utterly unacceptable, to me and to my family.'

'I understand, Madame.'

'You can't stay here with him forever. So what is to be done?'

'But Madame – I can stay with him for as long as you like – for as long as it is necessary.'

'What – you would be willing to sacrifice your life to take care of him?'

'I am devoted to my work,' said Ernestine, 'Monsieur Verney gives me no trouble – I can manage him very well.'

'I see,' said Jeanne thoughtfully, 'have a little glass of this cognac, Mademoiselle, it is excellent.'

'Thank you. The sacrifice, if I may say so, is yours rather than mine,' said Ernestine, pursuing her unexpected advantage, 'I shall be performing my chosen duty. It is you who will be deprived of the company of your husband. A sad circumstance, Madame – almost like being a widow. Could you bear it?'

'For my husband's sake I must be brave,' said Jeanne, smiling warmly at the ungainly woman sitting opposite her in a chair which her bulk made seem small, 'I am pleased that you reminded me of the call of duty. I must carry out my duties as a wife by ensuring that my husband is properly cared for, even though it means that I shall be parted from him.'

'I am certain that your courage will be equal to the burden,' Ernestine said guilelessly, returning the smile – two women in silent agreement for their own different reasons.

'What you have said must be thought about carefully,'

207

said Jeanne, 'I must discuss it with other members of my family – so large a step cannot be taken lightly.'

'Nor in haste,' Ernestine pointed out, 'Perhaps if you and Monsieur Brissard can come here again in another month, the situation can be reviewed then. Monsieur Verney's own wishes can be ascertained and taken into account.'

'Yes,' said Jeanne, 'We must consult his wishes, that goes without saying. Have you any idea of what they are?'

'No positive idea, Madame. We have not yet talked of the future. But when you visit him again, he will be ready to make his wishes known.'

'Can you be sure of that?'

'Yes, Madame.'

'And sure that he will make the right decision?'

'Leave that to me, Madame. I am an expert in caring for difficult patients. Monsieur Verney will make the right decision of his own free will.'

'Then I shall be greatly in your debt and shall be generous in every way.'

After she had left Madame Verney and was going down the hotel stairs – the servants' stairs – Ernestine passed a handsome young man in evening clothes, very much out of place. She said 'Good evening' to him and he returned her greeting. Then, struck by a thought, she waited until he had disappeared and followed him back up noiselessly. She peered round the corner of a corridor and saw that he was standing at the door to Madame Verney's suite, tapping lightly with one knuckle.

It would seem, thought Ernestine, that Madame did not come unaccompanied to Deauville. Well, that's life – a woman like her isn't going to let her youth and beauty go to waste simply because her husband is useless. Good luck to her – and what an opportunity she has given me, if I can make use of it.

In the days that followed, Guy's regime underwent a certain transformation. Instead of massaging him to exhaustion with her hands – which no doubt was good for his muscles and internal organs, Ernestine began to bring her big naked body into contact with his – informing him that this was an advanced form of therapy. With him face-down on the bed, she sat her wide bottom on his back and grasped his ankles to bend his legs rapidly up and down – to strengthen his calves and thighs, of course. When his legs ached from the fatigue of this, she released them and spanked his bottom lightly and quickly with both palms – to make the blood circulate, she explained.

That accomplished, she turned him over and reversed her position to sit on his belly, her massive thighs gripping him like a vice, while she massaged his neck and shoulders forcefully with those strong fingers of hers. Placed as she was, her legs spread to encompass him, she afforded Guy an unhindered view of her fleshy mound and its covering of dark hair – and the long pouting fissure in it. Her big round breasts bobbed and rolled above his face to the movements of her arms and hands.

Guy was enchanted – by the spectacle and by his own position. He was helpless in the grip of a strong woman – just as he had been in Nantes! But Ernestine inflicted no pain on him, as Yvette Bégard had done. Far from it – Ernestine's domination of him was curative! Guy's eyes closed in bliss. Her hands moved down to his chest and her palms rubbed briskly over his nipples, where the marks of former ill-usage now hardly showed. He sighed and she moved her broad bottom down his body until she was across his thighs. His male part stood quite stiffly and trembled against the fur between her legs as she kneaded his belly.

'One day, Monsieur Guy,' she told him, 'you may ask me to put it inside me.'

'No,' he replied, 'that would be to exhausting.'

'Not for you – I would do all the work.'

But Guy shook his head, unwilling to venture into that territory because of his memories of how he had been abused in Nantes and the lack of pleasure he had derived from having his stiff part pushed into a female receptacle. Ernestine took the hint. Her fingers kneaded down his belly until she reached his upstanding part. She took it between her two palms and rolled it firmly.

After a long time Guy uttered a gasping sigh and shook beneath her. Ernestine felt a small warm splash between her palms.

'There!' she said, smiling at him, 'that has relaxed you, hasn't it?'

'That was marvellous, Ernestine,' he murmured, 'you are very kind to me.'

In another week she encouraged Guy to try out his restored strength in a mild bout of wrestling with her. To begin with they knelt naked on the bed, facing each other, their hands interlocked. On her command, Guy exerted himself to force her onto her back and claim the victory. In truth, not even a normally strong man could have beaten her at this game and Guy, still not even averagely strong, had not the slightest chance of winning. But Ernestine allowed him to twist her down sideways after a time. They rolled around together, bellies and thighs rubbing and gradually, for she was keeping a close eye on progress, Guy's limp adjunct grew longer and thicker until it was of a respectable size. Since she did not wish to fatigue him too much, she used her strength to roll on top of him and clamp her legs round his hips, her breasts squashed against his face, and in this position she rocked back and forth until she was rewarded by a warm squirt along the inside of her thigh.

'You did well,' she said, mopping the perspiration from his face with a handkerchief, 'when you can beat me, then we shall know that you are fully well again.'

'I feel very well now,' said Guy contentedly.

'The exercise is very good for you. Now it is time for you to sleep. Tomorrow we will walk five kilometres before lunch.'

By August Guy had been at the sea-side for more than three months. Ernestine judged that the moment was auspicious to write to Maurice Brissard and inform him that her patient had recovered to the point where decisions could be made in regard to his future. Two days

210

later, Maurice arrived. Jeanne came with him – and also in the party were Dr Moulin and someone Ernestine had not met before, a lawyer named Bernard Gaillard. Evidently matters of great importance were to be discussed.

They dined in the hotel restaurant and this was the first time that Guy had done so. Ernestine was not present, of course, but she helped Guy into his evening clothes and talked to him sensibly, telling him that there was no reason to be nervous. She also told him not to drink more than one glass of wine and to eat sparingly. In the event Guy acquitted himself reasonably well, even though he was aware that he was under scrutiny throughout the entire meal. He spoke little, except to answer questions addressed to him about his general health and his impressions of Deauville.

After dinner, for the serious discussion, the whole part moved into the sitting-room of Guy's suite. Ernestine was requested to be present and she sat on a hard-backed chair by the wall, outside the circle of Brissards, Verneys, and their professional advisers. She wore a new grey frock with long sleeves and starched white cuffs and looked for all the world like a hefty sentinel, who said nothing but heard everything and thought her own thoughts.

'Well, my dear Guy,' Maurice began, when they were comfortably settled, 'a few weeks here has done marvels for you. I am sure that Dr Moulin agrees.'

'Without doubt,' Moulin nodded, 'a great improvement.'

'That being so,' Maurice continued, 'we must talk about what is best for you now.'

'What do you have in mind?' Guy asked suspiciously.

'In my opinion,' said the doctor, 'you have derived as much benefit as you ever will from your stay here. It is perhaps time to consider returning to your home and family.'

'Is that your idea?' Guy asked Jeanne.

'I want what is best for you,' she answered.

'You see,' said the lawyer, 'there are various complicated matters arising from your business interests and

211

your investments. Decisions have been postponed during your illness, but they are becoming urgent. A return to Paris is most advisable, Monsieur Verney.'

Guy looked unhappy at that.

'Maurice,' he said, 'what do you think?'

'I think you should do what you want to do, Guy. The duty of professional advisers is to give advice. It is your privilege whether to take their advice or not.'

'Monsieur Brissard!' said the lawyer. 'My advice is given in the best interests of my client.'

'And I protest,' said the doctor, 'my advice is in the best interests of my patient.'

'I believe you,' said Maurice, 'but a man's life is still his own. What do you want to do, Guy?'

'I want to stay here.'

'Certainly a few more weeks here can only be for the good,' said Dr Moulin judiciously.

'I regret to say that I do not think matters can be delayed for a few more weeks,' Gaillard objected.

'I don't mean for a few weeks,' said Guy with more determination than he had displayed for a long time, 'I mean forever.'

'Guy – you cannot seriously expect me to move here with the children!' Jeanne exclaimed, her expression one of dismay.

Guy shook his head.

'I want to be left here in peace, with just Ernestine to look after me You and the children must stay in Paris. That's what I want.'

'Is this merely an expression of boredom with this discussion,' Maurice asked, 'or have you thought about this with due care?'

'I've thought about it a lot in the last week or two. My mind is made up.'

'But your business affairs,' Gaillard protested, 'millions of francs are at stake, Monsieur Verney.'

'I don't care. Draw up a document for me to sign – something to say that my brother-in-law and my wife can have joint control of my financial affairs in return for keeping me here with Ernestine to look after me. That's all I want – they can concern themselves with the rest.'

'Are you certain that this is what you want to do?' the lawyer persisted.

'I am certain.'

'Then that is what will be arranged,' said Maurice, 'there is no more to be said.'

After they had gone, Ernestine helped Guy to undress for bed.

'Did I do well?' he asked as she knelt to take off his evening shoes.

'You expressed your decision very clearly, Monsieur Guy. I was proud of you.'

'They all wanted me to go back to Paris, didn't they?'

'You should be grateful to Monsieur Brissard,' she replied, unbuttoning the front of his trousers, 'he protected your right to live as you choose.'

'Strange,' said Guy as she pulled off his trousers, 'I didn't think he had any regard for me at all. But you're right, he defended me from the others.'

'You are trembling slightly – has all that talk upset you?'

'A little,' Guy admitted, 'we have been so tranquil here, you and I. Then these people force their way in to bully me and disturb me. You won't let them near me in the morning, will you?'

Ernestine helped him into his pale green silk pyjamas.

'You may rely on me,' she said, 'you will not be disturbed again. If there are papers to be signed, I will take them and help you deal with them after everyone has gone.'

'What would I do without you!' said Guy, 'no one has ever cared for me and loved me as you do.'

When he was in bed, Ernestine lay on her side facing him. Her new grey frock had buttons to the waist – it was more convenient like that, she found. In a moment she had the buttons undone and one of her big breasts out for Guy to suckle gently to soothe him to sleep. She watched his face as the lines of tension caused by the meeting with

213

his family slowly faded and left his expression peaceful again. Her hand crept down under the bedcovers and into his pyjamas to find his limp part and caress it lightly.

'The problems have all gone away,' she told him, 'there's only you and me here together. When you wake up tomorrow your family will have departed and you never have to see them again unless you want to.'

'Mm,' Guy murmured, her nipple in his mouth.

Ernestine's fingers detected a slight stiffening of what they held.

'That's better,' she said, 'I know you're not upset any more when this dear little thing raises his head. Shall I stroke him?'

'Oh, yes!' Guy whispered against her breast.

The process was a lengthy one, Ernestine knew, but eventually Guy would attain his climactic moment and enjoy his little spasms – the result very unimpressive to her but deeply satisfying to him. After that he would fall asleep quickly and she could leave him until eight the next morning. She would put on her hat and go out into the town to seek adventures of her own, happy in the knowledge that her employment was secure and that her savings were growing satisfactorily.

Towards midnight Bernard Gaillard tapped gently at the door of Jeanne Verney's suite. She opened it herself – evidently her maid had been dismissed for the night. To his delight Bernard saw that Jeanne had changed out of her evening frock into an ankle-length négligée of soft rose velvet trimmed with kolinsky fur round the neck and down the front where it closed. What was she wearing beneath that – his imagination ran riot with the charming thought!

'A thousand pardons for disturbing you so late,' said Bernard pleasantly, 'but I felt it important to assure myself that everything is arranged to your satisfaction. It was not easy in the presence of Maurice and the doctor to be certain that your interests were fully considered.'

Jeanne smiled and invited him into the sitting-room of her suite.

'That's very kind of you,' she said, 'will you take a little glass of something while we talk?'

Bernard seated himself and accepted a glass of cognac. Jeanne Verney was extremely beautiful, he thought as he looked at her – the delicately slender arms that were bare earlier that evening at dinner were now hidden inside the long sleeves of her négligée, but the wrists and hands that emerged from the fur-trimmed cuffs were so graceful that Bernard could hardly restrain himself from pushing up her sleeve so that he could kiss the soft skin of her inner arm from wrist to elbow. Her face – ah, the flawless complexion of her cheeks and the vivacious sparkle in her eyes! Bernard was wholly enchanted.

Jeanne sat on a pale turquoise sofa opposite him and crossed her legs inside her all-concealing négligée. Bernard caught a glimps of her feet in high-heeled and backless slippers and the gleam of her bare ankle. To touch that slim ankle – to run a hand up that satin-skinned leg to a rounded little knee – even further to a warm and soft thigh! Bernard's head was dizzy with the thought.

Jeanne smiled at him as if she had read his thoughts.

'We must be businesslike,' she said, 'you are the lawyer – tell me if my interests have been protected, Bernard.'

'I am of the opinion that they have,' he replied, 'you and your brother will have complete control. But it is important that you believe yourself that your interests have been protected, not merely accept my word for it. I would like you to regard me as a friend as well as a legal adviser.'

'But I do,' she said, her expression one of innocence, 'I am certain that it is as a friend that you have come here to make sure that I am satisfied.'

'Precisely. I would be desolated if you suffered a sleepless night because of any omission on my part,' Bernard said, equally innocently.

'Good! There is another matter I would like you to make clear to me. Come and sit by my side so that our discussion can be conducted in a confidential and friendly manner.'

215

Bernard accepted the suggestion with alacrity. When he was sitting beside her he became aware of her perfume – a sensuous fragrance that seemed to emanate from her hair and from her skin as she gestured and talked.

'Your reputation inspires a certain confidence,' she said.

'I am entirely at your service,' he said, daring at last to take her hand in his to imprint a kiss upon it.

'It is comforting to hear that,' said Jeanne, raising her hand when he freed it so that she could trace the line of his cheek and lips with her finger-tips.

Bernard at once took her into his arms and kissed her. He could sense the warmth of her soft body through her flimsy attire.

'You are adorable, Jeanne,' he murmured when the long kiss ended.

Her thin velvet négligée seemed to have fallen open at the top, as all well-designed garments do in moments of intimacy, to reveal Jeanne's low-cut nightdress almost to the waist. It was of apricot-coloured silk and lace, so fine that he could see her pretty breasts and their rosebuds through it. It was the most natural thing in the world for his hand to move from her back to stroke those delicious playthings.

'We were speaking of your reputation,' she sighed.

'Were we? What of it?'

'Perhaps it is false, after all.'

'What do you mean?'

'I was told by a friend that you have a reputation for being more than usually endowed in a certain respect.'

'It is true,' said Bernard proudly, 'there are ladies who esteem me highly.'

Jeanne's hands were in his lap, undoing his trouser buttons.

'Perhaps, but there are women whose experience is so limited that their judgment may not be reliable,' she pointed out.

'Then see for yourself!'

'I intend to,' and she tugged his upstanding part out of his evening trousers so that she could look at it.

216

'Yes,' she said, squeezing it with affection, 'at first sight there is a certain impressivemess.'

He knew that she was teasing him. In the matter of the size and strength of his virile part he feared comparison with no one. He sighed under the caress of her hand along his pride.

'But first impressions can be deceptive,' said Jeanne softly, 'as with the fruit on a market-stall – it looks attractive but one needs to handle it to be sure it is sound.'

'Handle this fruit as much as you like,' said Bernard, trembling with pleasure at what she was doing to him.

'Even that test is not infallible,' said Jeanne, 'the feel may be right, but in performance there may be disappointment.'

Bernard's hands had succeeded in unfastening her négligée all the way down – a very simple trick – so that he could reach under her nightdress and run his palms along the satin skin of her thighs. Her legs parted without demur and between them he touched petals of tender flesh.

'As to performance,' he murmured, 'I can guarantee that you will not be disappointed.'

'Promises are easy to make,' she sighed, her legs moving further apart to let him explore more deeply.

'I made no promise – I offered a guarantee. We lawyers know the difference.'

'Guarantees are not always what they seem, Bernard, particularly in the mouths of those with wares to dispose of. Suppose I permitted this piece of furniture to be installed in my private boudoir, only to discover that it collapsed at the first use? That would be embarrassing for both of us – particularly to one who had issued a guarantee.'

'There is no fear of that,' said Bernard, his voice trembling with passion, 'It is exceptionally strong in construction and will endure any wear you require of it.'

'You have convinced me,' Jeanne sighed, her hand clasping his upright part as if she would never let go, 'carry me into the bed-room, Bernard.'

CHRISTOPHE AND THE VIRGIN

The suggestion that Christophe should move into a spacious apartment on the Rue La Fayette, not far from its conjunction with the Boulevard Haussman, came from Monsieur Robineau the moment that Christophe mentioned that he was thinking of leaving his tiny bachelor apartment. Robineau had extensive dealings with Christophe's uncle and employer, and it was in this connection that Christophe had made his acquaintance. The move was occasioned, on Christophe's side, by his increasing affluence and his desire to establish himself as a person of some consequence as early in life as possible. On the part of Robineau there were perhaps also motives of ambition, but these were not immediately apparent.

As soon as he was comfortably established on the second floor with Robineau as his neighbour, Christophe was invited to dinner and made the acquaintance of Madame Robineau and Danielle, the nineteen year old daughter of the family. The food and the wine were excellent, Madame Robineau was a kindly woman approaching fifty who made a fuss of her handsome young guest, Robineau himself proved to be an admirable raconteur and host. Danielle was one of the prettiest girls Christophe had ever met, and charming in every way. She was slender, had light brown hair that shone with good health, an oval face and delicate little ears. Christophe, an ardent young man, was immensely captivated by her and she clearly found him to be interesting.

In the week or so that followed Christophe went to some pains to cultivate this promising beginning. With all his heart he wanted to make love to Danielle. The thought of what it would be like to undress her and kiss the little breasts he could discern under her clothes, this enchanting thought – and further speculation on her other charms – gave him a restless night or two. With the permission of

218

her parents he took her to the theatre a couple of times, took her dancing and to dinner – the understanding being that she was to be home punctually at eleven in the evening and not one minute later. He was allowed to accompany the entire Robineau family to Mass on Sunday, but that was not much to his taste, even though he was invited to lunch with them afterwards. When they were alone together, Danielle gave him certain signs of affection which encouraged his hopes – she permitted him to kiss her warmly when they said goodnight before he rang the door-bell for her. She even went as far as to let him put his arm round her in a taxi on the way home from the theatre. But – with parents as watchful as hers – was there any chance of accomplishing his heart's desire, he asked himself more than once.

In these circumstances, his delight may easily be imagined when, one rainy Saturday afternoon, he answered a tap on his door and found Danielle standing in the hall! He took her hand and kissed it tenderly.

'May I come in?' she asked.

'I shall be honoured. Your parents – are they at home?'

'They're out until dinner time. I've never seen your apartment – I thought that this would be an ideal opportunity. Unless you have guests, of course.'

'I am quite alone.'

'Then you must show me round. I want to see everything.'

Danielle was dressed casually, as if for an afternoon at home by herself, in a long-sleeved geometrically-patterned jumper down to her hips and a finely pleated skirt to the knee. She wore neither hat nor gloves, having come only across the hall from her own apartment. The effect was ravishing, Christophe's heart was beating rapidly and his mind was racing. After his patience, this was the moment of his reward!

He showed her the sitting-room, furnished in the modern style, which she professed to find delightful. In particular she admired the zigzag patterned rug, which he himself liked, if only because it had cost him far more than

219

he intended. She praised the effect of the pastel-tinted walls, free of pictures.

'You hardly wish to see the kitchen,' said Christophe, 'kitchens are just kitchens, after all.'

'But who cooks your meals and cleans for you?' Danielle asked. 'Where are your servants – you answered the door yourself.'

'I have only one – a woman who comes in daily. Usually I eat out, so there is little cooking to do.'

'I think I may have seen her then, coming up the stairs one morning. A thinnish woman in a navy-blue coat. Hair dyed yellow, pale-faced. Is that her?'

'That sounds like her.'

'But she's hardly older than I am. Where on earth did you find her?'

'She's the niece of the concierge at the building where I used to live. She cooked and cleaned for me there, so I asked her to continue here.'

What Christophe did not tell his pretty visitor was that Mireille also slept with him when he had no other arrangements, so that she was in his apartment overnight two or three times a week. It was a private arrangement between him and her which suited them both well.

'Show me your bedroom,' Danielle suggested.

She liked that too when she saw it. He had equipped it with a very modern divan bed, low and broad, a fine wardrobe of pale oak and a dressing-table to match. On the parquet, by way of rug, lay a tiger-skin, complete with head, which he had acquired after much hard bargaining, in the Flea Market. It was only natural that, once in the bedroom, Christophe should put his arms about Danielle and kiss her warmly. She had no objection to that – on the contrary, she put her arms around him and held him closely against her to prolong the kiss. Inevitably Christope's little friend inside his trousers raised his head during the embrace and pressed himself insistently against Danielle's thigh.

Just as it was natural to kiss her, it was equally natural to lead her gently towards the divan bed and press her

220

tenderly on to it. Danielle smiled and sighed and let him lie beside her, their kisses becoming warmer and warmer until they were candidly passionate.

Christophe slipped a hand under the hem of the brightly-striped jumper until he touched and then caressed a bare little breast. She was wearing nothing under her jumper! His heart raced at the discovery, and he asked himself if she had thus deliberately prepared herself for this delicious encounter with him. What was she wearing under her skirt, he wondered – what fantastic discoveries lay ahead!

'I would not want you to stretch my jumper out of shape,' Danielle whispered, 'Let me take it off.'

He released her and propped himself on one elbow to watch as she sat up to pull the jumper over her head and then shook her glossy hair to rearrange it in place. She was an enchanting sight, sitting there on his bed, naked from the waist upwards, her round young breasts a miracle of symmetry and grace. Christophe got her to remain sitting, her back against the satin-quilted head-board of the divan, so that he could kiss those little breasts a hundred times each and, with the tip of his tongue, feel their little rose-buds grow firm.

'You are adorable!' he sighed, a phrase he used with almost every woman he became intimate with – words that meant nothing in particular except that his emotions were aroused.

In due course his hand slid affectionately down her satin-smooth belly to the waist-band of her pleated skirt and would have proceeded further, but Danielle took hold of his wrist and stopped him.

'No,' she said, 'you must not touch me there.'

Christophe was astonished, to say the least of it. After so many tender preliminaries – well-received by her – to be denied any subsequent advances was incredible! The logic of her visit, of her presence in his bedroom – and on his bed itself – the logic dictated that matters should continue to their natural conclusion. Not only logic – sentiment too insisted that his hand should secure control

221

of her little secret. If logic and sentiment joined together were not sufficient, then the condition of his hard-standing male appendage fully demanded that Danielle should permit this intimate encounter to follow the usual path, withholding no part of her exquisite person. Why else was she here now, naked from the waist upwards, on Christophe's bed?

Evidently she was slow to arouse and not quite ready for the next step, he concluded. He shrugged his shoulders in resignation and applied his warm lips to the rose-pink tips of her breasts again. To his complete surprise Danielle pushed his head gently away from her and covered those delectable playthings with her hands.

'There is something I have not told you,' she said.

'And what is that?'

'Sit up and listen to me properly. No more kissing while I explain – agreed?'

'Agreed. What do you want to tell me?'

Her hands were clasping her breasts in an affectionate rather than a defensive manner, Christophe noted. It was certain that she enjoyed the feel of them in her hands, as much as the sensation of their being touched. That promised well, he considered.

'Look at me while I speak to you,' she said, making him raise his eyes from her delicate bosom to her pretty face, 'what I have to say to you is this – I am a virgin. Do you understand?'

Christophe's eyebrows rose slightly at the statement. It required an effort to imagine how she had achieved the age of nineteen, being so ravishingly pretty, while remaining untouched. Yet so much the better – his would be the inestimable privilege of introducing her to the full delights of love. The prospect was appealing, particularly as he had never before in his life been afforded such an opportunity.

'Have no fear,' he said, 'I am not a brute. I shall be kind and tender – there will be no pain, I promise you, only the most marvellous pleasure.'

'It is obvious that you do *not* understand! In a few

222

months I shall be twenty years old. Surely you do not flatter yourself that you are the first man who has found me desirable? The truth is that I am virgin by choice.'

She had removed her hands from her breasts and Christophe stared at them with longing as he strove to make sense of what she was saying.

'I am sure that you have had admirers ever since you grew up, Danielle. But you are here with me, you have removed your jumper and let me kiss your pretty breasts. Now you defend yourself with this talk of wanting to be a virgin.'

'Men have been pursuing me since I was fourteen,' she answered, a certain note of pride in her voice.

'Fourteen? That seems very young.'

She nodded and smiled at him.

'So you see, for the last five years or more men have been sighing for me – wanting to kiss me and touch my breasts and stroke my thighs. They all hoped that I would let them love me, as you hope. After all, I *am* pretty, don't you think?'

'Ah, yes,' Christophe breathed.

She smiled again at the effect she was having on him and the open way in which he showed his emotions.

'I shall remain a virgin until I marry,' she announced, dashing his hopes.

'But why?' he exclaimed in grief.

'Because I intend to marry well. My husband will be a man of wealth and distinction, someone very important. In return for sharing in his position I shall offer myself to him intact. He will be the first.'

'Do you have any particular person in mind?'

'There are three possible candidates at present. My parents are busy with the matter.'

'I believe it,' Christophe said sourly, 'but consider what you are saying! You propose to surrender the pleasure and beauty of love for status. The treasures of your young body will never be offered freely to a lover, but sold to the highest bidder – and he will most probably be twenty years older than you. How is it possible

223

for one so young and charming to make such a suggestion?'

'You are very severe,' she said, unperturbed by his outbreak.

'With good reason. You will lower yourself in this to the level of the women who stand all night in the rue Quincampoix to sell themselves for a few francs to any passer-by.'

'I see that you know where to go to find love, dear Christophe. But what right have you to play the stern moralist with me? I have been told that when you first came to live in Paris a year or two ago and be a clerk in your uncle's business you made his wife your mistress! Have you forgotten that? Now you are the director of his company, second only to your uncle. Was your rapid promotion the result of pleasing Monsieur Verney in matters of business – or was there some small connection with pleasing Madame Verney in bed?'

Christophe was taken aback by this onslaught. He was dismayed that the girl knew so much of his personal affairs – and he was angry that she had so misunderstood the situation.

'It wasn't like that at all!' he said with some heat. 'How can you speak so casually of events of which you know nothing!'

'I know what everyone else knows – that you and your aunt were lovers.'

'Who told you that?'

'My mother, or course. She is a friend of your aunt's.'

'Good God!' Christophe exclaimed, 'How women gossip about the most intimate concerns!'

'You do not deny it then?'

Danielle's finger-tips were tracing slow circles on her belly above the waist-band which just concealed the dimpled little belly-button which Christophe wanted to probe with his tongue.

'It was a long time ago,' he said, 'I was very young.'

'How old are you now – seventy?' she mocked him.

'Twenty-five.'

'Are you still in love with your aunt?'

'Madame Verney is not my aunt – not in any real sense. To answer your question, she and I ceased to be lovers two years ago.'

'I am pleased to hear it,' said Danielle, smiling amiably at him. 'Aunt or not, such a liaison is too much like incest, a most unfortunate event.'

'Unfortunate?' said Christophe, surprised by her choice of word, 'surely you mean immoral?'

'No, I meant what I said.'

'But what can you know of the matter?'

'Not as much as you do, I am sure – you've been your aunt's lover. I told you that I was fourteen when a man first approached me. That was my uncle Armand, my favourite uncle – a marvellous man. Do you know him? He's tremendously handsome and his manner is so suave and self-assured that every woman falls in love with him on sight.'

'Armand Budin?'

'I see that you have met him.'

'He tried to make love to you when you were a child?'

'In a playful sort of way. We were all out in the country to celebrate Grandmama's sixtieth birthday and I went for a stroll with him one afternoon. It was a hot day and we sat on the grass under a big tree, to be in the shade. Armand kissed me – that was the first time a man had ever kissed my lips. He put his arms round me and held me.'

Danielle's hands had crept back to her bare breasts. She fondled them almost imperceptibly as she spoke, evidently enjoying the memory of that distant afternoon.

'I'd been in love with him since I was six,' she said. 'Ah, it was incredibly exciting when Armand unbuttoned my blouse and touched my breasts. They were small then, hardly half-grown. His moustache tickled my nipples when he kissed them! The sensation was so delicious that I thought I was about to faint from sheer pleasure.'

Christophe could picture the scene vividly in his mind. A young girl with a white blouse open to the waist, half-lying on the cool grass on a hot summer afternoon.

225

Armand Budin using all his charm and experience of women to arouse the girl for his own amusement!

'Did he touch you elsewhere?' Christophe asked awkwardly.

Danielle laughed at his question.

'But of course he did! He put his hand up my skirt and stroked me between the legs.'

'Did that frighten you – as you were so young?'

'Not in the least. It felt absolutely marvellous. Besides, I trusted him completely.'

'More than you trust me,' said Christophe, 'for you pushed my hand away.'

'I had the advantage of knowing him far better than I know you.'

'Yes, I understand the importance of that. What happened next?'

'My little story interests you, does it?' she asked, her thumbs circling her nipples lazily.'

'I find it fascinating!'

'Then since you are such an attentive audience, I will continue. What happened next was that my beloved Armand opened his trouser front and pulled out his long pink baton for me to see. He told me to observe it closely so that I would know what men possessed that they wanted to put into women.'

'You were not shocked at the sight?'

'I thought that it was very interesting, even though it was bigger than I had supposed. He let me hold it and that was very nice – it was warm and it kept trembling in my hand.'

'My God!' said Christophe, his face pink with suppressed emotion, 'if only you trusted me that much, Danielle! How delightful these moments could be for us! What else did he do – surely he wanted to go further?'

'He played with me for a long time with his hand inside my knickers. I got hot and shaky and more and more excited. And then – well, you can guess what happened to me when I could bear no more sensation.'

Christophe ran his finger round the inside of his collar.

His imagination was ablaze with the thought of the young girl brought to the point of squirming ecstasy by Armand's fingers fluttering between her legs.

'And then?' he gasped.

'He said that I had found out how a woman feels when a man makes love to her. He asked me if I had enjoyed it and I kissed him in gratitude. He put his hand over my hand that was holding his trembling part, jerked it a few times and – *voilà*! I saw everything as it occurred – his pink column was suddenly turned into a fountain! Afterwards he had to use his handkerchief to wipe my skirt where he had splashed it.'

'This early experience – it did not make you averse to love?'

'Certainly not! That afternoon with Armand was a thoroughly enjoyable introduction to the possibilities of what men and women do together. To be frank with you, he and I played together many times after that day – nearly always at my suggestion.'

'So that is not the reason why you have never given yourself fully to a man?'

'No, I have already told you my reasons for that.'

'I find it impossible to believe that you are so mercenary, Danielle.'

'No more than you. Afer all, your business career is founded on love-making with Madame Verney – isn't that so?'

Christophe found the accusation unjust.

'You are acquainted with Madame Verney,' he said, 'therefore you know how beautiful and elegant she is. I was honoured to be her lover for a time. I wish I still were!'

'Then you did really love her, besides sleeping with her?'

'I loved her to distraction. I can say with complete sincerity that my motive for loving her was in no way connected with Monsieur Verney's patronage.'

'Very commendable,' said Danielle, 'I am almost convinced.'

'I doesn't matter to me in the least whether you believe me or not. You have made your own attitude clear enough – you deny yourself the pleasures of love in the expectation of material gain.'

'Who says that I deny myself the pleasure of love?' she asked, 'why do you think I am here with you, only half-dressed?'

'But you insisted that you intend to remain a virgin!'

'That is true, dear Christophe. But a virgin is one who has not been penetrated by a man, in my understanding. Short of that, there are many ways to enjoy pleasure.'

'With other women, you mean?'

'Oh no, I have no inclination towards that. It is of men's bodies that I dream – hard masculine bodies with that fascinating extra limb between their thighs.'

'And when you dream these dreams – what then?'

'I pleasure myself,' she said softly.

'Ah,' Christophe sighed, his hand moving of its own accord to press itself lightly against the aching bulge inside his trousers.

Danielle smiled at the gesture.

'If I could trust you as I trusted Armand when I was a girl!' she said.

'You can! I am ready to swear the most solemn oath you can devise!' he exclaimed in his feverish excitement, 'you may trust me absolutely not to take the least advantage of your trust.'

'The fact is,' she said, squeezing her soft breasts a little, 'that in telling you of that marvellous afternoon under the tree I have become aroused to some extent. If I could believe in your sincerity of purpose, I would let you stay with me while I relieve myself of this delicious passion. But prudence suggests that I should return to my own home and deal with the matter in the safety of my own bedroom.'

'Danielle – stay here! I promise that I will not touch you.'

'You want me to stay here so that you can watch?'

'More than anything else in the world at this moment!'

'I am too trusting,' she sighed, 'but my need is very great.'

She was sitting propped against the padded headboard of the bed, one elbow in the pillows, one knee half-raised. She unfastened the waistband of her skirt slowly, amused by the greedy way in which Christophe's eyes followed the movement of her hands.

'Men are all voyeurs,' she observed in a friendly fashion, 'pull my skirt down for me, Christophe.'

He took the hem and eased it down her legs, from under her bottom, and cast it carelessly aside. As he had imagined, the delightful truth was revealed to him – Danielle had come to pay her visit wearing no underwear at all. Above her stockings and her plain pink garters, her slender thighs were bare, leading the eye up to the patch of curly brown hair where they joined.

Christophe moved from beside her to further down the bed, so that he could sit facing her. He sighed tremulously as she moved her bent knees outwards to give him an unrestrained view of her furry little mound. His sigh became a moan of pleasure as Danielle put a finger in her mouth to wet it and then used it to trace slowly upwards the tender lips half-hidden by her fleece.

'What do you think?' she asked, not too seriously, 'do I have a pretty one?'

'More than pretty – it is exquisite,' he breathed.

On its second stroke upwards the finger-tip pressed inwards to part the lips – then again, going deeper and opening them a little wider. Her other hand was busily employed in massaging a breast. Christophe caught a glimpse of the pink inner petals as she found, within the heart of her flower, a tiny rosebud and caressed it.

'Ah!' she sighed, 'that does feel good! With you staring into me like that it is as if . . .'

'As if what, chérie?'

'You know what I mean,' she whispered, 'as if the impossible were happening.'

Her sighs grew more profound as her fingers continued their pleasurable exercise. Christophe sat in sensual fasci-

229

nation at the spectacle of this very pretty young woman performing so intimate an act for his delection – or more precisely – for her own. He enjoyed every tiny tremor of passion that rippled through her firm-pointed breasts and belly, so much so that his breath was rasping in his throat.

'Show me your toy, Christophe,' she said softly.

Her plea was utterly irresistible – no man honoured by Danielle's open display of eroticism could have denied her what she asked – certainly not Christophe, who was dizzy with excitement. He tore open his trousers and presented to her view, not without pride, the strong appendage she had requested to see.

'Marvellous!' was her verdict, 'so straight and smooth!'

'And on the point of bursting with frustration!' Christophe sighed, all the while watching her little hand caress herself.

'Poor thing,' she soothed him, 'stroke it a little, then, to console it.'

Christophe, susceptible as ever, took hold of his proud part and rubbed it tenderly to ease its ache. The rhythmic action had a great and immediate effect on Danielle. Her other hand crept between her thighs to spread the petals of her pink flower wide open and in this glistening moist niche her fingers moved at a very rapid pace.

'Christophe!' she wailed suddenly, 'faster!'

He saw her bottom jerk off the bed as she dissolved in spasms of delight, and he saw this and understood its significance even through the pink haze of emotion that enveloped him. The sight was too much – the fleshy stem he held leaped and splashed his tribute onto the bed-cover between her trembling thighs.

'Danielle!' he groaned. 'Oh, Danielle!'

These little games were amusing enough at the time, but needless to say, much more was required to appease Christophe's appetite. Less than an hour after Danielle has left his apartment, imprinting a chaste kiss on his cheek as salutation, he made his way to an establishment

230

he had frequented often enough in the past – the Maison Suzy on the rue Grégoire-de-Tours, a little off the Boulevard St-Germain. Paris is the most civilised of cities, of course, and has an abundance of such establishments in every district. Christophe had sampled a number of them, including some of the most expensive to be found round the Opera. Maison Suzy was not very far from the tiny apartment he had rented when he first came to Paris from Lyon, and he had never lost his fondness for it. It had, he thought, a cosy atmosphere of its own, not found in the grander establishments.

Viewed from the street, Maison Suzy might almost have been a small shop. There was a large stained glass window through which nothing could be seen, and a door, a very ordinary door on which there was no inscription at all. The window, discreet as it was, hinted at the pleasures to be bought within by its row of vignettes at eye-level amongst the coloured scrollwork, for they portrayed in miniature a series of women posing only half-dressed. Although, it must be admitted, the style of the women and of their négligées indicated clearly enough that they had been painted before the War. Fortunately for the client, the women of the establishment were considerably younger than a casual passer-by might have guessed from the pictures.

There was a little bell on the door, just like an old-fashioned shop, that tinkled as Christophe entered. Madame met him at once in the small entrance hall, smiling her professional smile. She was a thickset woman of at least fifty, dressed in an ankle-length evening frock of black satin – her regular working uniform from two in the afternoon until two the next morning. Her arms were bare and resembled those of a wrestler, she had a multiplicity of chins and her hair was dyed jet-black. Nevertheless, though the years – and the strains of her profession had not dealt kindly with her – she had a pleasant, almost motherly manner.

'Good evening, Monsieur Larousse,' she greeted him, 'we haven't seen you for some time. Welcome back.'

'I've moved across the river to live,' Christophe explained.

'Ah, but old friends and old haunts are the best,' said Madame.

She clapped her hands together and from an inner room five of the house's girls – the ones disengaged at that moment – came into the hall to greet him and await his choice. The custom of the establishment was that they wore only their shoes. They arranged themselves around him in the tiny hall for his inspection, hands on bare hips, smiles on their faces.

Christophe stared for a moment or two at the array of naked femininity lined up for his approval. He knew all five of the girls and had been with each of them more than once.

'Can't make your mind up?' Madame prompted him, 'they're all lovely, aren't they?'

'Enchanting,' said Christophe, as was expected of him.

He chose the tallest of them, a small-breasted and wide-hipped young woman named Gaby. Madame collected his money and he was on his way upstairs. The room Gaby led him to was small and had hideous wallpaper with a geometric pattern, a bed, a chair, a wardrobe and a bidet. Christophe had often wondered what was the purpose of the wardrobe to be found in every room in the house, for he was sure that all the men who came here did what he did – draped their clothes over the chair.

Gaby, he remembered when they were on the bed together and he was making use of her charms, was from the North of France somewhere – one of the innumerable girls who had left their homes to seek their fortunes in Paris and had come to realise all too soon that there was only one type of work in which they could earn a reasonable income and save a little. She was cheerful and willing and, lying naked on top of her long body, he was able to quench the fire which Danielle had lit with her little games.

'Thank you, Gaby,' he said when he rolled off her at last, and he meant it, to her surprise, for she was unaccustomed to being thanked for her services.

It was entirely by chance, some time later, that

Christophe made the acquaintance of Claire Diard, a friend of Danielle. He was passing a cafe not far from his apartment when he heard his name called and turned to see, at a table on the pavement, Danielle with a pretty young companion. Christophe was in no hurry – he paused at the table, raised his hat and was introduced to Mademoiselle Diard. He took a seat, ordered drinks for the young ladies and for himself and joined in the conversation. Danielle's friend, of about the same age as herself, had a lively manner and shining eyes. She smiled and laughed often in her conversation and gave every indication of being a most interesting person – or so Christophe thought.

Perhaps half an hour elapsed before Danielle asked Christophe the time and said that she was expected home shortly for lunch. She suggested that he might escort her home, but he apologised profusely and informed her that he was on his way to lunch with a friend.

Mademoiselle Claire stared for a moment or two after Danielle as she left them.

'You've annoyed her, you know,' she said in a familiar manner.

'Really? How is that possible?'

'We were talking about you earlier on. The impression Danielle gave me was that to some extent she owns you. Now why would she believe that, Christophe?' said Claire, smiling at him.

'Surely you are mistaken, Mademoiselle.'

'Oh, call me Claire. I feel that I know you very well.'

'Do you feel that you know me well enough to have lunch with me in a little restaurant not ten minutes stroll from here?'

'But what about your friend waiting for you?'

Christophe shrugged and smiled.

'I see,' said Claire, 'it was an excuse for Danielle. Then I accept.'

Over the meal and a bottle of good wine Claire became increasingly amiable towards Christophe. At first she was content to answer his questions about herself – she and

233

Danielle had been to school together, like Danielle she lived with her parents, her father was a lawyer of importance, she adored wild strawberries – and so on, all the meaningless little things which people like to know about each other. After that it became evident that she already knew a lot about Christophe, from her friend Danielle.

'You and she are very close friends, I believe,' she said with her bubbling little laugh.

'I wouldn't say that,' Christophe demurred.

'What would you say then?'

'Danielle is a charming person, the daughter of a neighbour whom I know through business. I met her only a week or two ago when I was invited to dinner. We've been to the theatre once or twice together, that's all.'

'And the rest!' Claire said mockingly.

'What do you mean?'

'You've left out the most interesting part – the little episodes in your apartment. Are you shy?'

'Good God!' Christophe exclaimed, 'She told you that?'

'She tells me everything. I am her closest friend.'

'And do you tell *her* everything?'

'Perhaps,' Claire replied, her face displaying a teasing expression.

'Since you know so much about her, you must be aware that Mademoiselle Danielle is a virgin,' Christophe said in self-defence.

'Still?'

'To the best of my knowledge.'

That made her laugh again.

'You have not been able to educate her, Christophe?'

'I fear not.'

'It's all that silly business with Armand years ago,' she said. 'Poor Danielle had a tremendous passion for him when she was a girl – did she tell you that? He played with her a little and she has never recovered from it. She wants every man she likes to be Armand and cuddle her as if she were still fourteen. Isn't that ridiculous?'

'I find it sad.'

'Do you? I'm sure your sympathy didn't stop you from

234

giving her a little thrill. Did you enjoy the experience, Christophe?'

'You ask very intimate questions.'

'Why not? This is the twentieth century. We are modern people, you and I. These matters can be discussed freely, don't you think? Or am I embarrassing you?'

'Not in the least,' he assured her, even though he knew his face was flushed.

'Good. Danielle has a well-shaped body and pretty breasts. I should think that you find it extremely pleasant to fondle her all over, even if she makes you get off the tram before it reaches the terminus. Do you do it often?'

'I am sure you know that already,' he said, smiling at her expression.

Claire nodded and laughed again.

'Would you believe,' she said, 'we are such close friends that Danielle tells me all about it every time you and she are together. In every detail – imagine that! According to my information, you have progressed to the point where she encourages you to put your fingers into her while she holds your plaything – is that so?'

'Claire – you have just made me realise that the situation is impossible,' said Christophe seriously, 'it can lead nowhere.'

'But it can – and it will, unless you take action.'

'You think that she will change her mind?'

'Not that – there is no hope in that direction.'

'What then?'

'The scheme is that you will become so determined to relieve her of this unnecessary burden of virginity that you will marry her.'

'What?' he exclaimed in dismay. 'Is that what she thinks?'

'Originally it was her father's scheme. Monsiuer Robineau believes that you will make a most suitable son-in-law because he has high hopes of your prospects in business. Naturally, he doesn't know – nor does her mother – anything of Danielle's little games in the bedroom. They fully expect you to fall in love with her in the

235

old-fashioned way, inspired by no more than a few furtive kisses. But Danielle herself has come to like you very much and she too thinks that you will make her a good husband. Then you will reap the reward for your patience.'

'My God! I must get myself out of this predicament immediately.'

'Are you sure that you want to?'

Christophe stared at her in amazement, his eyebrows climbing up his forehead.

'How can you ask? I have no intention of marrying Danielle – I do not love her. It is impossible!'

'But you play with her,' Claire reminded him, with a little laugh.

This time Christophe laughed with her.

'Claire, you have opened my eyes and I am extremely grateful. But tell me why?'

'To be truthful, when I heard from Danielle at the beginning how she was leading you on, I thought you were a complete idiot. Not the first, of course – there have been several before you who were enticed into her make-believe world. Whatever their capacity to amuse her, not one of them was suitable as a husband. Then you came onto the scene and the scheme looked to be working out at last. Then I met you this morning – and I thought that you deserved better.'

'I am eternally in your debt,' said Christophe, 'but suppose that I had escorted Danielle home, as she wished – this conversation would never have taken place, would it?'

'No, but instead you would have had the pleasure of playing your little games with Danielle this afternoon. See what you've missed!'

'That may be,' he answered, giving her his most charming smile, 'but as we have been speaking so freely to each other, I know that you will not be offended if I tell you that I would infinitely prefer to play a more adult little game with you, dear Claire.'

She shrugged prettily and laughed.

Christophe was a most ardent young man, a born admirer of women – so much so that he was never able to resist any opportunity that offered itself. This susceptibility to women's charms had in the past led him more than once into unfortunate situations, which gave him cause for regret. At twenty-five he had vowed again and again to put all that foolishness firmly behind him. Yet so fragile are even the best of intentions in matters of the heart – he had once more allowed himself to be manoeuvred into an awkward corner! Danielle, pretty and charming – and only nineteen – had succeeded in enmeshing him in her plot merely by letting him touch her! It was too much!

In such circumstances, to take Claire back to his apartment was more than the prelude to an entertaining hour – it was a gesture of determination, he told himself – a way to rid himself of the unwelcome hold which Danielle had established over him by showing him her body. The gesture of determination would also be an act of liberation! Christophe was proud of himself at that moment.

Mademoiselle Claire exhibited no inconvenient modesty – her actions were as frank as her conversation. Once safely inside Christophe's bedroom, she threw aside her hat and white gloves and stripped off her green-striped frock with an endearing giggle. She draped her hand-embroidered knickers of magnolia-coloured silk over the bedside lamp with another giggle and in moments she and Christophe were naked together on the bed, kissing and caressing. When his lips moved down to her throat and she could speak, she said:

'It is here, on this bed, that you cuddle Danielle and sigh over her virginal charms, is it?'

'Do not remind me,' Christophe breathed.

'Ah, what little comedies of frustrated love have been enacted here,' she said with a broad smile.

Christophe's hand was already between her legs.

'There is no reason to hurry,' she told him, 'I am not like her. I do not intend to close the door when you reach the threshold.'

237

'Forgive my clumsiness,' he murmured, 'let me look at you.'

Claire was well worth looking at. She was not as slender as Danielle and her body was somewhat shorter. But her breasts were fuller and more rewarding to fondle, their dark-pink buds more prominent. Her little round navel was deep-set into the smooth flesh of her deliciously curved belly and, below, between silk-skinned thighs, she had an enchanting nest of dark-brown and curly hair. What a plump little partridge she was, Christophe thought.

'But you are exquisite,' he said.

She laughed and took hold of his upright fixture and pretended to assess its weight and stiffness.

'I think you're gorgeous too,' she said, 'why haven't I met you before?'

Matters progressed in mutual enjoyment, with much kissing and touching, stroking and squeezing, until the divine moment could be delayed no longer. Claire settled herself comfortably on her back, knees raised and well parted – an invitation Christophe accepted at once. Poised above her on his hands, arms straight to take his weight, he encouraged her to insert the crimson head of his most treasured part between the tender lips exposed in the furrow of her dark-brown fleece. They both watched in delight, Claire smiling all the while, as he pushed slowly forward into her velvet depths.

'Ah!' she sighed, her smile broadening, 'that feels marvellous! Poor Danielle doesn't know what she's missing!'

Christophe lay forward over her warm body, enraptured by the thrilling sensations he was experiencing. He rocked slowly and easily, his wish to give this dear girl pleasure of a sort she had not known before – and which she would therefore want to experience again. For this he was well qualified. His education in love-making had not been confined to encounters with untried young girls and the women of establishments like Maison Suzy – far from it! His real education in the tender arts had been during

238

his long and memorable liaison with Madame Verney, his uncle's wife, than whom there was no greater expert in the whole of Paris, according to Christophe's opinion.

In giving this superb pleasure to Claire, he also enjoyed it himself, as is the usual way. Ah, those delirious minutes when a man and a woman are united in the intimacy of love! No poet has ever found words that can begin to describe the delights and the magnificence of the fusion of male body with female body! No painter has ever depicted the ecstatic triumph of those moments – only the physical posture without the radiant emotions. Some few – Albert Marquet and Monique Chabrol, for example – have caught a small part of the astonishing ecstasy of love in drawings, but these are not intended for public showing and are known only to connoisseurs of the erotic.

Christophe reaped the reward of his skill and patience when, at the climactic thrust that released his passionate outburst, Claire shuddered violently and cried out in her frantic delight, her body arching off the bed to support him.

'I adore you!' she moaned over and over again.

The sound of the bedroom door being opened caused them to turn their heads to look, both still bemused by the emotions now gently subsiding within them. Framed in the doorway stood Danielle, her mouth wide open, her eyes staring in dismay at what she saw. She gulped loudly, turned and ran away and they heard the apartment door slam behind her.

Claire looked up into Christophe's face and laughed.

'You forgot to lock the outside door,' she said.

'That was very careless of me, chérie – I hope that you are not embarrassed.'

'Of course not. But you've really upset Danielle now.'

'What a pity,' he said, smiling back at her.

Claire laughed and her velvet sheath of flesh squeezed his embedded part like a hand.

'I've just realised,' she said, 'you left the door unlocked deliberately!'

239

THE ARRANGEMENTS OF FRANÇOISE DUMOUTIER

After Picard had dressed himself and taken his leave with a thousand protestations of eternal devotion, Françoise lay comfortably in her bed and composed herself to sleep for a while. She was hot from Picard's strenuous lovemaking – she could feel the trickle of perspiration under her arms and between her breasts – yet she had the prudence to pull a corner of the satin sheet over her naked belly to prevent any possible chill to the stomach while she dozed.

She was lying easily and almost ungracefully now that she was alone, her hands under her head to expose her armpits to the soft breath of air from the open long windows that gave onto the stone balcony, her legs apart to feel the cooling touch between her thighs. In truth it was a warm summer afternoon and through the floor-length frilly curtains over the open windows came not only the gentle breeze but the muted and familiar noise of the traffic on the Boulevard, only one street away.

Françoise was certain that her hair was tousled from romping with Picard. And as for her make-up, that surely was ruined. None of that was of the least importance at that moment. While the afterglow of passion faded in her body, her beautiful face smoothed into tranquillity and she slept lightly.

Her maid returned to the apartment shortly before six in the evening, entering with silence of long practice. It was not until she tapped at the bedroom door that Françoise awoke and her eyelids opened to reveal her velvet brown eyes – those eyes which had ensnared many a man.

'I've made you iced coffee as it's so hot,' said Louise, 'is that all right?'

'Perfect.'

Françoise pushed herself up on one elbow to a near-sitting position to take the glass gratefully.'

'Have you had time for a proper rest, Madame?'

'Yes, he left well before five. I feel fine.'

'That's good,' said Louise, 'two gentlemen in one day is excessive. What a pity that your new acquaintance's first visit has to be on the same day as Monsieur Picard's regular Thursday call.'

'Highly inconvenient,' Françoise agreed, sipping her iced coffee, 'but what can one do? Picard is necessary at present to help defray the costs of living here and so his Tuesdays and Thursdays are sacred. I have put off Monsieur Fromont twice already – he may take offence and not ask me out with him again if I refuse this evening.'

Louise seated herself on the bed facing Françoise, an act of familiarity which would have indicated to any stranger who chanced to observe it that there was a friendship and understanding between mistress and maid not normally found.

'And he is very rich, this Monsieur Fromont?'

'Incredibly rich, everyone says.'

'A man to be taken seriously, then?'

'Extremely seriously, particularly now that the stupid Radicals have ruined the country and everything costs twice what it cost two years ago. How is one supposed to live – like the peasants?'

'You were only a girl when the War started,' said Louise, 'but I remember what things cost then. A hundred francs then would buy what costs you five hundred francs today. Still, those days won't come back. We have to do what we can – and with your looks you'll never go hungry.'

'Life is more than a full stomach, Louise.'

'Perhaps, but believe me, you wouldn't like it on an empty one. I'll run your bath in a minute. I'd better look you over first to see if Monsieur Picard marked you this time. I would never do for the millionaire Fromont to find another man's traces.'

Françoise put her glass on the bedside table and ar-

241

ranged herself face-down on the bed. Louise began a minute inspection of her body, sweeping Françoise's chestnut brown hair up with one hand to examine the nape of her neck and then her soft-skinned shoulders.

'Three faint marks of fingers here,' she said, touching Françoise's left shoulder, 'but they are fading already.'

'I want to wear the backless frock tonight. Will the marks show? My shoulders are very attractive and we must give Monsieur Fromont every encouragement.'

'They won't show after I've powdered you, I promise.'

Louise ran her fingers down Françoise long and slender back, inspecting every centimetre of skin, down to the neat, rounded cheeks of her bottom.

'Ah!' she exclaimed, 'teeth-marks on your behind.'

'Where?' Françoise asked curiously.

'Here,' said the maid, pressing the warm flesh lightly, 'how did that happen?'

'How can I say? Picard is such a vigorous man in bed. He rolls me about and twirls me this way and that way like a doll. If I close my eyes I swear it seems to me at times that he has eight hands and four tongues all doing things to me at the same time.'

'And two shafts?' Louise asked, chuckling.

'That wouldn't surprise me either, though I've never noticed more than one when he takes his clothes off.'

'What a Cossack the man is,' said Louise, her hands kneading Françoise's bottom lightly, 'I'll have to put a cold compress on to make the marks fade. At least the skin isn't broken. Didn't it hurt when he bit you there?'

'Hurt? When he gets going everything is such a turmoil of movement and sensation that I've no time to wonder whether he's giving me pleasure or pain.'

'My God, what a lover he must be! Well, if your evening with Monsieur Fromont goes as far as entertaining him in bed, stay on your back and don't let him see your backside. Now turn over and let's see if there's any more damage.'

Obediently Françoise turned onto her back. Louise leaned close to inspect the flawless skin of her neck, then

242

squeezed her small breasts critically and ran her thumbs over their crimson points.

'Your nipples are darker than they should be,' she observed, 'did the brute try to bite them off? They're usually a pretty shade of pink but now they're dark red.'

'He used his mouth on them to bring me to the verge of ecstasy and then finished me off instantly by pushing two fingers up me like a knife into butter.'

'Was that before he got down to the serious business?'

'Yes, that was just the overture.'

'Heavens, the man still believes that he comes here to pleasure *you*! I don't know how you've managed to keep him thinking that after nearly two years.'

Françoise raised her head to look at her own nipples.

'They feel a little tender when you touch them,' she acknowledged, 'I hope that Monsieur Fromont will not take too prolonged an interest in them tonight.'

'What a shame,' said Louise, 'those beautiful little breasts have delighted so many charming men. To think of them being mauled by a brute!'

'Not all that many men,' Françoise said sharply, 'I'm not a streetwalker!'

'Forgive me, Madame, I did not mean it to sound like that. Truthfully, there have been no more than six or seven regular companions since your husband died so tragically in the influenza epidemic. And that's at least six years ago.'

'If only I had married his brother instead of poor Jean-Jacques! I would be much better provided for now – and not a widow so young! I could have had Edmond, but I chose the younger brother because he was more handsome. What idiots young girls are!'

'You couldn't have guessed what would happen,' Louise soothed her.

'I should have known that Edmond was the better bet. Even then he was cleverer and more vital than Jean-Jacques. Fool that I was! Then Edmond married that ginger-haired creature with the fat bosom. How utterly stupid life can be!'

'Oh Madame, should you speak of a sister-in-law like that? She is always most friendly when she visits you.'

'No, you are mistaken, Louise. She comes here to gloat over the fact that I married Jean-Jacques and left the way clear for her to ensnare Edmond. But the feeling is not all on one side, you know – Edmond still desires me. More than once he has made certain proposals to me. But I say to myself that with a wife and family to maintain he would not provide for me in any great style. So I kiss him on the cheek and say *No*, but with regret, and I let him touch me for a moment just to keep his interest alive.'

'Life can be tragic,' said Louise, who had heard the story many times before, 'but the good Lord made you beautiful and there has never been a lack of wealthy men to amuse you since you became a widow.'

Her hands were stroking Françoise's delicate and narrow belly to ease her out of the melancholy which easily overtook her when she recalled her fateful choice between the Dumoutier brothers and what it had cost her.

'There, there,' she murmured, 'not a mark and a skin like satin.'

Her fingers smoothed Françoise's pliant thighs, fortunately undamaged by the vigour of Picard's passion. Then as Françoise trembled slightly, the fingers stroked upwards into the join of her legs and brushed over the neat little triangle of dark-brown hair.

'Louise . . . you are beginning to arouse me. I have been ravaged all afternoon and I shall need my strength to cope with Fromont tonight.'

'Of course,' the maid replied, 'I'm only checking you for marks. Did that savage bite you here?'

Her finger-tips were playing over the soft lips beneath the crinkly hair, teasing them expertly.

'He may have done,' Françoise sighed, her eyes half-closed, 'he did so many things to me.'

'We must be sure. Open your legs wide. That's it, now we can make certain that all is well when you entertain Monsieur Millionaire.'

Her examination of this attractive and valuable area of

244

Françoise's body was conducted with great care and thoroughness. Under the scrutiny of her sharp black eyes Louise's fingers probed her mistress' smooth groins, traced over her shapely mount of Venus and along the tender lips half-hidden under dark-brown fur.

'No scratches or bites there,' she reported with evident pleasure, 'has he harmed you inside by his rough ways, the brute?'

'I hope not,' Françoise murmured, her small breasts rising and falling in time with her faster breathing.

'We shall soon know,' the maid declared, parting the soft folds of flesh to lay bare the moistly pink interior, 'does it feel all right, Madame?'

'It feels very warm.'

Louise bent over her to blow gently into her secret place to cool it and Françoise gasped.

'Louise . . . you must stop now.'

'Be patient for one moment longer while I make sure that no damage has been caused by that brutal man. Otherwise you could suffer torments tonight with Monsieur Fromont, and that would never do. What would he think if you cried out with pain when he made his entrance?'

'Be careful then, I beg you!'

'Have no fear, I've inspected your body enough times in the past to know what I'm doing.'

Her finger sank by millimetres into the yielding channel which had been used so forcefully not two hours before by the energetic Picard. Françoise uttered little sighs until the finger was in to the third knuckle.

'Does that hurt at all?' Louise enquired.

'No!'

'Squeeze hard on it. And again. Anything hurt?'

'No!'

'Good.'

Slowly, very slowly indeed, Louise withdrew her finger from its warm place of concealment. She performed this simple action in such a manner that the entire inner surface of her finger as it emerged slid over the tiny bud she had exposed. The soft friction sent involuntary quivers of pleasure through Françoise's belly.

'Keep squeezing on my finger,' Louise instructed.

'Ah no, no . . .' Françoise gasped brokenly.

When at last the finger-tip arrived at the small swollen rose-bud and flicked over it, Françoise's legs jerked on the bed and a light climax released her tensions. Louise nodded in satisfaction – it was so simple to rid Madame Dumoutier of her regrets and memories and make sure that she would be lively and cheerful for her meeting with her new acquaintance.

'You devil,' said Françoise, opening her eyes, 'you did that on purpose. I shall be as limp as a rag tonight with Monsieur Fromont – good for nothing. He'll never invite me to dinner again and I'll be stuck with Picard for the rest of my days.'

But there was a vivacity in her tone that belied her words.

'What nonsense,' said Louise, 'all you have to do is put your mind to it and you'll give him a night he'll never forget. Men are easy enough to please in bed, God knows. Once they've had a bit of a feel, all they want is to get on top of you and pound away.'

'That's what you think!' said Françoise. 'You make it sound like a village wrestling match. I can assure you that to fascinate and retain the interest of men like Picard and Fromont requires a good deal of skill and art.'

Louise shrugged. To her mind physical pleasure was a very straightforward affair. She was convinced that if she had been born with Madame's looks she would have no problems at all in getting herself kept in style.

'I'll run the bath for you,' she said, 'otherwise you'll never be ready in time.'

After the warm scented bath there began the long and elaborate process of preparing Françoise to enravish every man who saw her, and in particular Monsieur Fromont. She sat on the side of the bed, wrapped in a charming little peignoir of Chantilly lace while Louise removed the vermilion varnish from her finger-nails and toe-nails and applied a fresh coat. After that she sat at her toilet-table for Louise to brush out her chestnut brown hair until it shone and arrange it to perfection. She attended to her own face – embellishing her complexion with a little rouge and powder and painting herself a vivid rosebud mouth. When she was satisfied with her work she opened the front of her peignoir to apply her perfume. It was in a large and ruinously expensive crystal bottle – a present from Picard, of course – a heady and sensuous fragrance that clung to her skin and was almost guaranteed to make a man's senses reel.

Françoise was generous in her application of this olfactory aphrodisiac bought in the Place Vendôme. She dabbed it behind her small ears, in the hollow of her throat, on the pulses of her slender wrists, as women do – even wives. But then she opened her flimsy lace garment and smoothed a touch of perfume beneath each small breast, then into her fine-skinned groins and finally behind her knees, since it was probable that these areas of her delightful body would be explored most intimately before the evening was over.

She stood up and slipped out of her peignoir, dropping it on the dressing-table stool for Louise to put away later.

'The mark on my bottom – has it faded yet? Tell me.'

Louise knelt behind her mistress to peer closely at the smooth cheeks.

'It's much better, but it's still there if you know where to look for it. Take my advice and stay on your back tonight.'

'Powder it when you do my shoulders, that should help.'

With a large fluffy powder-puff Louise applied a fine layer of fragrant powder of the most delicate shade of apricot to Françoise's slender arms and shoulders, down to between her breasts and then all the way down her back to her rounded bottom, for it was Madame Dumoutier's intention tonight to wear her most audacious evening frock. The powder-puff dabbed carefully against those deliciously supple cheeks, concealing the offending mark as well as was possible.

247

'Does it still show?'

'He'll never notice, trust me.'

The undergarment selected to grace the marvellous lower half of Françoise's body was a confection of damask-pink silk, with bands of hand-embroidered appliqué round the legs. Louise held it while Françoise stepped into it and slid it up her legs and fastened the tiny button that held it over her hips. This triumph of the lingerie-maker's art covered her from just below her tiny navel to half-way down her thighs, its colour contrasting piquantly with the beautiful pale skin of her legs and body. She smoothed the almost transparent silk against herself while she studied the effect in her long mirror.

'What do you think, Louise?'

'Very pretty. When Monsieur Fromont sees you in those knickers he'll go raving mad with passion and rip them off you.'

'Then I'll make him buy me half a dozen new pairs.'

She seated herself again to allow Louise to smooth sheer silk stockings up her legs.

'Which garters, Madame?'

'The pink ones, of course, to match the knickers.'

'The plain pink ones or the pink ones with the rosebuds?'

'The ones with the rosebuds. Monsieur Fromont is worth an extra effort.'

'I hope it won't be too much for him,' said Louise, 'how old is he?'

'Not yet fifty – or so I have been told.'

'Everybody lies about their age. If he says that, you can be sure he's over fifty. Don't let him over-excite himself – it would be a tragedy if he collapsed with a stroke as soon as he got his hand up your skirt.'

'Peasant!'

'No offence, Madame, but let's see the colour of his money before he dies of pleasure.'

The evening frock was a mere nothing in poppy-red, but from the hand of a master couturier. When it was on, the hem was no more than a centimetre or so below Françoise's pretty knees, the decolletage swept down in a vee, its point somewhere between her breasts, leaving the viewer to imagine the tender delights just barely hidden from sight. The shoulder-straps were as narrow as a finger and the back – there simply was no back to it! The whole expanse of Françoise's own delectable back was fully exposed right down to a fraction above her slender bottom – an expanse of voluptuous skin, shoulder-blades and elegant spine to dazzle a man!

Louise stood back with her arms folded to survey the effect.

'Well, how do I look?'

'Enchanting! I don't know how you dare show yourself in public half-naked like that, but Monsieur Fromont will be bowled over. If you were going to dinner with a younger man I'd say you were running a big risk of being raped on the restaurant table, but with an over-fifty he ought to be able to hold on till he gets you back here to bed.'

'Don't be coarse,' said Françoise, smoothing her hands over her flanks where the frock outlined her figure closely. 'Are you sure that the line of my underwear doesn't show through? If it does, I'll go without.'

'Go out to dinner bare-bottomed? What a suggestion! Twirl round as if you were dancing and let me see.'

Françoise did a graceful step or two.

'No, nothing shows. You can stay decent. Sit down while I give your hair a last touch. Are you going to wear the pearls or the jade?'

Françoise glanced down at her deep decolletage.

'The pearls will look well against my skin tonight, I think.'

'The jade would look nice against the red frock.'

This was an argument they had embarked upon many times before. Sometimes Louise won and sometimes Françoise had her way.

'The pearls,' she said firmly.

'Very well. Of course, if you give Monsieur Millionaire the thrill of his life tonight it could be diamonds from now on. They look good with everything.'

249

'Diamonds,' said Françoise dreamily, 'large diamonds, yes. Bracelets, necklaces, ear-pendants, rings, diamonds to twine in my hair . . . do you think it would suit me?'

'Diamonds suit everybody, believe me.'

'I believe you're right. I must have diamonds – all over me – diamonds for day wear and diamonds for evening wear. Perhaps even something special to wear in bed.'

'A soldier I used to go with told me he'd seen a dancing-girl in Algeria who had a diamond in her belly-button. That would go well in bed.'

'You're making fun of me! If she was a dancing-girl it couldn't be a real diamond.'

'Maybe not, but it's not a bad idea. Try and get Monsieur Fromont thinking along those lines.'

'These things have to be accomplished with great tact. Only women of a certain type ask men for money.'

'All women ask men for money. Some get it and some don't.'

'Louise, you say the most terrible things!'

'I'm a realist. There, your hair's perfect. I'll put a bottle of champagne on ice in the salon and a bottle of cognac, just in case Monsieur needs any refreshment when he brings you home.'

'Don't put it out before midnight or the ice will melt and I loathe tepid champagne.'

'I'll do it on the stroke of midnight and then vanish. After that, it's all up to you.'

Louise did not disturb her mistress until the salon timepiece showed twelve o'clock the next day, that being the established routine in Madame Dumoutier's household. Then with a tray of café au lait and fresh croissants fetched from the baker she entered the darkened bedroom with a discreet 'Good day, Madame.'

Françoise was alone in the broad bed, as was to be expected, for gentlemen of good manners take their leave before daybreak so as not to be seen departing and thereby perhaps compromising the lady who has been gracious enough to permit them to express their ardour in so intimate a fashion.

It was warm in the bedroom and she lay face-down, sleeping gently, the ivory-coloured silk sheet thrown aside and only her feet covered. Naturally, in the circumstances, she was naked, her long back and pretty bottom fully on show. The sunlight woke her when Louise drew back the heavy curtains, she turned over slowly and yawned like a kitten stirring. Louise helped her to sit up and tucked down-filled pillows behind her.

Say what you like, thought Louise, she's got a marvellous body – why couldn't I have grown up like that? Still, she makes the money and we both of us live well on her looks.

She pulled the sheet up to Françoise's middle and poured a big cup of coffee for her.

'Drink that, Madame. I've got a surprise for you outside.'

'Flowers? Very well, bring them in.'

Louise carried into the bedroom a huge display of red roses that had been delivered by a florist's errand-boy an hour ago.

'Now this cost a packet,' she said, setting it on the floor, 'at least Monsieur Fromont knows his manners.'

'What does the note say?'

The maid opened the small envelope attached to the display and read the message aloud.

'It says *I adore you, H-E*. What does H-E stand for, Madame?'

'Henri-Eugène.'

'That's a fancy name. Wait, there's something else here tucked into the flower basket – a little packet.'

'Let me see.'

Françoise tore open the wrapping of the packet to reveal a small jeweller's box. She opened it with an expression of surprise on her face, to discover a bracelet set with diamonds.

'My God!' Louise exclaimed, 'you really did it! Your fortune's made.'

251

Breakfast forgotten, Françoise clasped the glittering bracelet round her wrist and stretched out her arm to observe the effect from a distance, turning it this way and that to catch the sunlight on the stones.

'Well, he's not mean, at least,' she pronounced at last.

'A man sends you a bracelet like that and you're not even smiling!' said Louise, 'What's wrong?'

'You must understand, Louise, that there are certain vexations with Monsieur Fromont.'

'Vexations – whatever can you mean? Ah, I know – he's too old to do it. But you can't deny that he's properly grateful for a cuddle.'

'He's not so old, only forty-eight, and he can do it very well.'

Louise had never seen Madame Dumoutier in this mood before.

'Tell me what the problem is,' she suggested, 'I'm sure I can think of something. He's married, of course.'

'For over twenty years and has two grown-up sons. That I expected.'

'But?'

'He has unusual tastes.'

'Lots of men have. What's unusual about this one?'

'He likes to make love in his partner's mouth,' Françoise said primly.

'That's not unusual. Most men like a bit of that before they get down to the real thing.'

'But he wants only that, never the real thing.'

'Never?'

'That's what he said.'

'Obviously he has no interest in pleasing a woman, only in pleasing himself. Some men are selfish, no doubt about it. On the other hand, you managed to please him because there's the proof on your wrist.'

'Even so . . .'

'Don't tell me its the first time you've ever done that to a man. I'm not that simple.'

'You don't understand,' said Françoise in a tone of annoyance. 'How could I contemplate for one moment a

252

liaison with a man like that? All he wants is to visit me a few times a week and have me do that to him. I find the prospect both depressing and degrading. I would be no more than a common prostitute.'

'Prostitutes don't get paid at those rates,' said Louise, tapping the bracelet with one finger.

'You are impossible!' Françoise said sharply, 'I wonder why I put up with your insolence!'

'You'll never find anyone to look after you as well as I do, Madame. I've been with you ever since your husband died and besides serving you I've given you the best possible advice.'

'I don't need your advice!'

'In that case. Madame, I see that I've stayed in your service too long. I shall leave today.'

'Louise – don't go!' and Françoise burst into tears.

The maid sat on the bed and took Françoise in her arms to comfort her. When the tears were exhausted, she dried Françoise's face with her handkerchief and smoothed the hair back from her forehead.

'I won't leave you, Madame, you know that. Now let's consider what's to be done about Monsieur Fromont. Shall we send his trinket back and get rid of him?'

'I think that would be best.'

'And stay with Monsieur Picard until something better comes along?'

'I really don't want him anymore either. He's too fierce. I want to be loved, not raped.'

'Of course you do. But we must be practical, Madame. Without either of them we shall be hard put to it to live in our normal style on the income from your inheritance, what with the cost of everything today.'

'Oh Louise, what am I to do?'

'Eat your croissants and I'll pour you a fresh cup of coffee and we'll look at things from both sides. First things first – do you suppose that Monsieur Fromont sends a bracelet like that to every woman he ever sleeps with?'

'How should I know? He may scatter them around like ten franc notes. He's very rich.'

'The very rich don't give much away,' said Louise tartly, 'otherwise they'd soon be the very poor. Mark my words, that expensive present is a clear sign that he's fallen for you.'

'How can you say that? All he wanted was – you know.'

'There is a word for it, Madame.'

'I forbid you to be vulgar.'

'Very well, let's continue – where did he take you?'

'First to Maxims and afterwards to dance at Les Acacias. Molyneux was there and complimented me on my dress – imagine that!'

'Even though it wasn't made by him. He must know Monsieur Fromont and thinks you may soon be a client.'

'That's a very mercenary suggestion, Louise. I'm sure that wasn't in his mind at all. He's very handsome and his appearance is incredibly distinguished.'

'Never mind about the dressmaker – did Monsieur Millionaire enjoy himself?'

'Without question. He talked and laughed and danced without stop. It was I who suggested that we should leave – that was about one in the morning. I kept thinking about the ice melting in the champagne bucket.'

'Had it?'

'I don't know. He didn't want it – only a small glass of cognac before retiring.'

'Yes, well we know what he wanted after that, even though I mustn't say the word. Was it to his liking?'

'Louise – such a question!'

'I'm trying to understand this Monsieur Fromont. There's no point in being modest with me, Madame, you should know that by now.'

'If you must have an answer, he expressed great satisfaction.'

'There you are then, it's all obvious.'

'Not to me.'

'Monsieur is looking for a companion who is beautiful, intelligent, witty and well-dressed – someone he can take everywhere and who will make him the envy of his friends.'

254

'Paris is full of such women,' said Françoise, 'he can take his pick.'

'At the same time he wants one who will be complaisant towards his little desires in the bedroom and not make him feel the object of scorn, as these high-class women would.'

'What follows then?'

'He believes that he has found in you the ideal combination of his two requirements. This present means that he wishes to continue.'

'I guessed that hours ago. But what of me? He is not my ideal combination of anything.'

'Only consider, Madame, if he is prepared to pay out on a big scale to entertain you and buy your clothes and give you jewellery and take care of the household expenses – that is a proposition to take seriously.'

'But I shall not be loved!'

'As to that, once you are assured of the luxuries Monsieur can provide, there is no reason why you can't choose a lover of your own, with no regard for his bank balance.'

'Deceive Monsieur Fromont, you mean?'

'You wouldn't be deceiving him, Madame, surely you can see that?'

'I don't understand you.'

'Monsieur Fromont lays no claim to your heart, nor to that important part of your body between your legs. For him neither signifies in the least. Therefore there is no deception if you bestow either or both elsewhere. Isn't that so?'

'This requires thought,' said Françoise.

'More than thought – what you have to do is find out how far Monsieur Diamonds will go with the cash. When are you seeing him again?'

'He has invited me to dine with him tomorrow evening.'

'Good. Now what you have to remember is that you have the upper hand in this arrangement. He wants you more than you want him. Right?'

Two months later Françoise moved into a very grand apartment between the Arc de Triomphe and the Bois de

255

Boulogne. Not that there was anything wrong with her old home, of course – Monsieur Fromont thought that it was in excellent taste, like everything about Françoise. He said so repeatedly, and added that, for a person as marvellous in every way, nothing was too good. She must live in the best district, in a house decorated in the most superior style, and with more than a single servant.

He found much pleasure in accompanying her in his chauffeur-driven limousine on the unending shopping expeditions necessary to find the best and most tasteful furniture and carpets and curtains and glassware and wines – and all the myriad things essential for her new setting. Together they looked and discussed, she chose and he paid. And paying was a pleasure for him, a pleasure repeated again and again and again. And amid all this foraging and looting and avid acquisition to prepare her superior home, there was for him the incredible experience of lying naked on her bed while her pretty mouth brought him to the climactic bliss which he had pursued all his life and found in the past only in establishments of a certain type. To have a woman as young and beautiful and of such good breeding as Françoise willingly give him this joy was for Monsieur Fromont a continuing miracle of good fortune.

And it was his for the price of what he regarded as a few sticks of furniture and the lease of an apartment. Of all the money he had amassed over the years it needed only an inconsiderable fraction to bring his happiness into being – something he had never quite realised before. And besides that, it gratified him enormously to observe the reactions of his friends and acquaintances when they saw Françoise with him in fashionable restaurants, or at the theatre, or at the Opera or the races. There was a fierce joy in his heart to watch their eyes turn yellow with envy and their complexions go green with jealousy. For it must be acknowledged that their own women vanished into obscurity beside Françoise – there could be no question about that. No one in the entire world, in Fromont's view, could wear a sable coat as sumptuously as she did. No one could achieve so striking an effect as she did by means of a simple strand of emeralds twisted into her glossy hair. No one but she had the complexion to display so perfectly a diamond collar round her pretty neck. And all with such style, such elegance!

In the way of things, Françoise learned that Monsieur Fromont's extensive business interests put heavy pressures on his time. His attendance was required at frequent meetings of directors and bankers and financiers, often in the evenings as well as the day. Regularly each Sunday he dined at home with his wife and children – he regarded that as a sacred family duty. By reason of all this, there was little room in his life for manoeuvre – almost everything had to be arranged neatly and conveniently into a fixed timetable, even his affairs of the heart.

His timetable allowed him to call for Françoise three times a week to take her to dinner and to dance, or some other entertainment, and to stay the night with her afterwards. But there were times when some urgent business manifested itself unexpectedly and his evening would not be free. On those occasions he would arrive at her apartment at five for a short but pleasant chat over an aperitif and he brought her some expensive trinket by way of apology for the cancelled evening – silk stockings, perfume, even underwear. In due course, the aperitif finished, a brief glance at his watch was the signal for Françoise to seat herself on a cushion before his chair, unbutton him and employ her exquisite mouth to relieve him of the tensions that oppress businessmen. By six o'clock he was on his way to his appointment, giving her an affectionate kiss on the cheek as he departed to make more money.

There came the afternoon when Louise announced Monsieur Dumoutier.

'My dear Edmond,' said Françoise, 'I am very pleased that you could come to see me.'

She looked quite ravishing in a simple afternoon frock of white silk with a scalloped hemline and neckline. Her only jewellery was a single emerald the size of an egg, worn round her neck on a heavy gold chain, drawing attention to the tender division of her breasts by nestling there.

'It was kind of you to ask me,' said Edmond, kissing her hand, 'so this is your new home. What a magnificent drawing-room!'

'Do you like it? Please sit down. Louise – a drink for Monsieur Dumoutier.'

When the drinks were served and the maid gone, they talked of family and friends for a time, as people do when they meet after an interval. With great tact, or so he thought, Edmond steered well clear of the topic of his most devouring curiosity – Henri-Eugène Fromont – and that person's role in the new-found prosperity of his sister-in-law. Eventually it was Françoise herself who introduced Fromont into the conversation by asking Edmond if he happened by any chance to know him.

'I've met him casually once or twice in the course of business dealings,' said Edmond cautiously, 'but no more than that. I know nothing about him really.'

'I have no doubt that your wife has told you that I have become his mistress.' said Françoise tartly.

'As to that,' Edmond answered, glancing round the room with an appraising eye, 'certain friendships are never discussed, as you well know.'

'But we can speak openly, you and I, Edmond. The truth is that Monsieur Fromont has been very generous to me.'

'*Very* generous,' Edmond agreed, impressed by the summary valuation he had worked out in his head for the contents of the drawing-room alone, 'I am happy for you, my dear. You are too beautiful to live in depressed circumstances.'

'Do not misunderstand the reason for this generosity – it is not for the reason which the world thinks. I am not his mistress.'

'There is no reason why you should feel it necessary to tell me of your arrangements,' Edmond replied, wondering where this conversation would lead.

258

'But you are wrong there – there is a very good reason.'

'What then?'

'The best of all reasons, Edmond,' she said boldly, 'I have loved you for a good many years – and you have given me cause to think that you love me too.'

'But . . .' exclaimed Edmond in astonishment, then words failed him.

'There is no question of *but*,' she continued, 'what I have said is the truth.'

'Françoise – the fact is that you married my poor brother, not me, though I was in love with you then and told you so many times. I wanted you to marry me.'

'I was foolish. We are all foolish when we are young, especially girls. It is also a fact that after I married your brother you went off and married Adrienne. Tell me truthfully now – if we could go back over the years and start again, would you not marry me instead of her?'

'Without doubt,' said Edmond, 'but we cannot change the past.'

'No, but perhaps sometimes we are given a second chance,' she said, her beautiful eyes shining with emotion.

'Françoise – tell me what you mean?'

'Must I spell it out for you? Do not compel me to do that, Edmond – I have already gone far beyond the bounds of what is proper in laying my heart open to you in this way.'

He stood up, pulled her to her feet and embraced her, covering her face with passionate kisses.

'You do love me,' she sighed, 'I knew it.'

'I adore you, Françoise!'

'Then I am yours. I cannot be your wife but I can be your mistress, if that pleases you.'

'But what of Fromont?'

'I swear to you that he has never touched me,' she answered.

'I find that hard to believe, though God knows I want to believe it.'

Françoise took him by the hand and together they sat down on the elegant sofa.

259

'Listen to me,' she said seriously, 'what I have told you is the truth. There are men who wish to give the world the impression that they are strong and virile, but in private their power to please a woman has already disappeared forever. You must have heard of such circumstances.'

'Yes, I once knew a man like that – a friend of my father's – old Auguste Lemaitre the banker,' said Edmond thoughtfully. 'He set up an eighteen year old girl in great style when he was over eighty. Everyone marvelled at his apparent eternal youth and his contemporaries envied him. But after a year or so the young lady let slip that it was all for show.'

'He did nothing with her at all?'

'Twice a week he dined at her apartment and afterwards dismiss the servants so that she could take off her clothes and wait on him herself in the drawing-room with coffee and cognac. He sat there fully dressed, a glass of cognac in one hand and a cigar in the other, like a prince, admiring her naked body as she paraded round the room for him. It was on one of these occasions that his heart finally failed and he died in her arms.'

'How tragic!'

'Not in the least. He died happily, his head cradled to her bare bosom. And she received a large sum of money in his will, so she too was happy. She eventually married a Portugese count and went to live in his palace in Lisbon.'

'That is an enchanting story!' Françoise exclaimed, her pretty face aglow with pleasure, 'then you can understand the delicacy of my friendship with Fromont.'

Thus reassured, Edmond picked her up in his arms and carried her to the door. In moments they were in her bedroom, the white silk frock was off and she lay waiting for him on the bed, clad in only her stockings and the huge emerald round her neck, while he tugged at collar and tie and the rest of his clothes. At last they were naked in each other's arms, kissing and caressing.

This was Edmond's first view of her delightful body – that body created purely for the delight of love, one might well say. He wanted to feast his eyes on it and kiss it, from

260

the rosy tips of her impertinent little breasts to the delicately pouting little lips between her tender thighs! But there was an impatience in him to consolidate his unimagined success by possessing her wholly and quickly. Françoise herself, deprived of the pleasures of love for so long by Fromont's little foibles, was equally eager to consummate her new liaison with Edmond. She urged him not to linger but to content her with all speed.

'Edmond, Edmond!' she gasped as she lay on her back with her knees up and well apart and he pressed her body beneath him and obliged her gladly.

After the first frenetic explosion of pleasure there was time for tenderness. There was time for Edmond to explore her charms in the minutest detail with hands and mouth, murmuring his admiration of the delights of her fascinating body, from top to toe. He held her in a thrilling haze of voluptuous sensation for what seemed an eternity and, when she could bear no more, he remounted and gave her a second proof of his devotion, making her radiant with happiness.

'Tell me that you love me,' she murmured, her fingers twining in the dark hair of his chest.

'I love you with all my heart,' he said.

'You will be my lover and visit me here very often?'

'Very often, I promise you.'

'Will you always love me, Edmond?'

That, of course, would depend upon the continuing generosity of Fromont, but Edmond had no intention of saying anything so banal to the enchanting woman in his arms. He kissed the pink tips of her breasts and said,

'I shall love you for as long as you wish me to love you.'

Françoise too knew quite well on what depended the duration of their love. The difference was that she had the power to ensure that Fromont's generosity lasted for a long time and she intended to exercise that power to the utmost.